VOYEUR

A LESBIAN ANTHOLOGY

VICTORIA RUSH

COPYRIGHT

For the uninhibited...

VOLUME ONE

THE DINNER PARTY

1

HUNGER

It started innocently enough. After my passionless marriage dissolved, I resolved to push the boundaries of my boring love life. I'd jumped into wedlock with my college sweetheart at a young age, and neither of us had much prior sexual experience. Unless you count fully-clothed heavy petting with high school boys, which I think hardly qualifies.

Maybe it was my strict Pentecostal upbringing, which frowned upon any kind of sexual exploration before marriage. Or maybe it was my parents' frequent admonitions against all forms of sexual 'deviancy', including masturbation. Apparently, my husband had been equally repressed, because he never seemed to have much interest beyond quickies in the missionary position.

But I'd read enough steamy romance novels to realize there was a whole other world of sexual expression beyond boring monogamy. In spite of my frequent suggestions and gentle guidance, my husband never became adept at pleasing me. I was left to my own devices, alone with my romance novels, to find release.

When my husband eventually left me for another woman, I welcomed my newfound freedom. I dated with relish, jumping from one lover to another, even trying a few one-night stands. But no man seemed to have the spark that ignited my passion and imagination like my hunky literary heroes. So began my tentative and rapidly escalating online explorations to find sexual fulfillment.

I started with mainstream dating sites like Match.com then 'hook-up' sites like PlentyofFish and Craigslist—even AshleyMadison.com. Each forum presented more exciting prospects and more adventurous partners. I enjoyed getting in touch with my newfound sensuality and experimenting with new sexual practices.

But something was still missing. All the men I met ultimately just wanted the same thing—to get me into bed as quickly as possible and initiate contact in the typical manner, with the usual predictable ending. It was satisfying but somehow unfulfilling. I longed to find that truly transcendent experience that shattered my erotic expectations and left me completely spent, yet still wanting more.

One night, while trolling the usual online suspects, I tried typing something new into the search box: "transcendent erotic encounters". Amidst the usual litany of porn sites and massage parlors, I saw a listing near the bottom of the page that simply read *Fantasy Feast: Satisfy All Your Senses*.

Intrigued, I clicked on the link. A glowing website opened with a picture of beautiful men and women seated around a large dinner table wearing nothing but masquerade masks. Undeniable expressions of excitement and ecstasy adorned their faces.

Now *this* is something different, I thought. I clicked on the site's *About* tab and held my breath as I read with increasing excitement about the club's service.

Fantasy Feast is a members-only club where patrons meet over a sumptuous five-star meal to explore and excite ALL their senses in an intimate and safe environment.

We are very discriminating about who is accepted into our club, with only the most alluring and uninhibited invited to join. Upon qualification, you'll schedule an intimate dinner feast at our luxurious private villa.

We prepare you for the meal with a full spa treatment, including sensuous bath, massage, and esthetic grooming. You'll be given a silk robe and slippers to don in preparation for the main event. We ask you to bring your own masquerade mask to wear at all times to protect your privacy and anonymity.

You'll join a small group of pre-selected patrons at our elegant dining table in the main hall, where you'll be feted and serviced by our highly trained sensualists over four courses that will stimulate and excite all your senses: taste, sight, smell, sound—and touch.

We guarantee you will not be disappointed. You can choose from a broad selection of a la carte services and waive any 'dishes' that are not to your liking. Upon completion of the feast, your senses will be excited beyond anything you've ever experienced and you will be satiated in every sense of the word.

Call the private line below to begin your journey of discovery and fulfillment. We look forward to exciting your senses like they've never been before!

The more I read, the more I could feel the heat build up between my legs. By the time I finished, I'd completely soaked my panties imagining myself seated at the Fantasy Feast table watching my fellow dinner guests being 'serviced'—and being watched myself.

But there were so many questions. Exactly what kind of 'services' were offered? Who exactly did the servicing? Did the dinner guests engage each other directly, or did we remain passive in our chairs? Was everybody naked around the table, or wearing robes? And who were these 'sensualists'?

I was intrigued and excited in a way I'd never been before. I knew this was something I had to explore further. I reached for the phone and dialed the number.

2

———

HAUTE CUISINE

A woman with a sultry Scarlett Johansson voice answered on the second ring.

"Fantasy Feast. How may we satisfy you?"

Now *that* was a proposal I'd never heard phrased so perfectly before.

"I...was looking at your ad," I stammered. "I mean your *website*. I was wondering if I could talk with someone about your services. I've never tried anything like this before..."

Gawd, I thought. I sound like such a lightweight. They'll probably disqualify me even before I get through the front door.

"Not to worry," the Scarlett voice replied. "I completely understand. Our goal is your complete fulfillment. Was there something specific you wanted to ask about?"

She's not going to make this easy. Maybe that's all part of the game. I had to admit, the mystery and intrigue definitely added to the excitement.

"I was wondering about your 'a la carte' menu items. Can you clarify what this includes?"

"Of course," Scarlett replied. "Do you have our website open?

Click on the Menu tab and you'll see our chef's selections for each course."

I clicked on the tab and scanned a mouth-watering list of dishes.

Chef's Menu:

First course: tomato gazpacho soup
Second course: arugula salad with baby beets
Third course: Chilean sea bass or filet mignon
Fourth course: chocolate mousse or crème brûlée

It certainly *looked* like a Michelin Star-worthy meal. But I was more interested in the *non-culinary* items on the menu. Had I somehow missed their intent?

"I sensed there were some—*other*—items on the menu," I probed. "Besides...*food*. Although the dishes do look delicious. I was looking for something *more*."

There was a momentary pause on the other end of the line.

"We wish to leave some of the *special* menu items to your imagination," Scarlett said. "We wouldn't want to shape your expectations or spoil the surprise. We engage *all* of your senses. I guarantee you will not be disappointed. We've never had a client ask for a refund."

I fully understood her reluctance to provide more specifics. This *was* after all a commercial enterprise that was operating on a precarious legal boundary. Promising sexual favors for money could get anyone in trouble with the law, and the woman couldn't be sure I wasn't the police fishing for ammunition to raid their premises.

But I was still a bit concerned about the line of *consent*. I wanted to be certain I'd be safe and able to say no if things got outside my comfort zone.

I paused, as I struggled to delicately express my concern.

"Will I have...*control* over the services at all times? I mean, will I be able to stop the activities, *the menu delivery*, if it's not to my tastes?"

"At all times," the woman assured. "Every patron will have a signaling device at their personal place setting that can be used to stop or return any menu item at any time."

Patron. I kind of liked the sound of that word. It sounded like I'd be the focus of their attention and that I'd be getting some very *special* attention.

That got me thinking about the *company* I'd have at the dinner table, and how far exactly our mutual 'engagement' might go.

"How many people attend each dinner event?" I asked. "What is the typical makeup in terms of age and gender?"

"Each dinner serves eight guests plus one hostess who orchestrates the service and facilitates engagement. This keeps the gathering suitably intimate and gives everyone a chance to get to know one another in a safe and comfortable environment. We ask each member to let us know their preferences in advance, then we carefully align the patrons and services for each event to ensure a stimulating mix of guests and activities. I think you'll find your dinner guests suitably arouse your interests."

I was already getting aroused just thinking of the possibilities. There was something appealing about the idea of pre-qualifying the people I'd be sharing intimate moments with and still having them be complete strangers. But I was still a little unclear with whom, and how, the erotic engagement would occur.

"What kind of engagement normally occurs between the guests?"

"During the actual dinner, it's limited to discussion only. And *watching*, of course. All of your senses will be engaged entirely from the privacy of your own seat at the table. After the final course is served, if you'd like to engage one or more patrons directly, you'll have the use of one of our private boudoirs for the remainder of the evening. This is included with our twenty-four-hour service."

"And we keep our masks on at all times to maintain our anonymity?"

"Yes. We ask every patron to wear a mask throughout the entire event. Just enough to veil your identity, but not so much to hide your facial expressions and beauty. I think you'll find most of the fun is in watching the expressions of our guests as they savor every stimulating course."

Wow. A five-star culinary experience at an intimate and upscale villa, with an exotic sampling of beautiful strangers. And complete anonymity. *I'm in.*

"I'm interested in attending one of your events," I said without hesitation. "What's the first step?"

"At the bottom of our home page you'll see a button labeled 'Profile,'" Scarlett said. "Just click on this to set up your personal profile, fill in your preferences, then select one of the available dates. We'll notify you when you've been accepted. Then pay the required deposit and arrive at our villa with a hungry appetite at the appointed time."

Everything about this operation screamed first-class professionalism. From the woman's voice on the phone, to the soft music playing on their website, to the vetting process of their customers. This was no cheesy escort service or massage parlor. I couldn't wait to get started.

"Thank you so much for your time and help," I said to Scarlett. "I'm looking forward to attending your feast!"

I hung up the phone and immediately clicked the Profile button.

3

———

TASTING MENU

The first field on the Profile page asked what anonymous profile name I'd like to use. I chose the exotic and sensuous-sounding name 'Jade'. I'd always loved that name, and now I had a chance to fulfill my fantasy of role-playing a mysterious Asian beauty. With my dark hair and high cheekbones, I might even be able to pull it off partially camouflaged under a masquerade mask.

The next field asked for my gender and gender-preferences. Men? *Check.* Women? I'd long-fantasized about having a tryst with a woman, and here was my chance. *Check.* Transgender? Maybe another day—this was already stretching my boundaries pretty far.

Next up was my age and age preferences. This is supposed to be a *fantasy*, right? As an attractive thirty-six-year-old woman with a well-exercised, nicely-toned body, I had nothing to be ashamed of. Nevertheless, I lied just enough to make me feel all the more desirable. I clicked the Age 25-35 box for myself and the 18-24 plus 25-35 boxes for my preferences.

Ethnicity? That might be tough to conceal, even under a half-face-mask. But that wouldn't stop me from imagining myself any way I chose, once I got there. After some hesitation, I clicked the Caucasian box. Preferences? Asian—*check*. African-American—*check*. My dream husband had been a biracial African-Asian man with coffee-colored skin. I always thought they produced the most beautiful children. Curly brown hair with honey skin and doe eyes—absolutely adorable. Caucasian? Fine—*check*. I suppose one or two in the mix won't completely ruin it.

I scrolled down to the required payment fields where there was a short note:

A deposit of five hundred dollars is required to schedule a face-to-face interview. Upon final acceptance, a second payment of five hundred dollars will secure your private membership. We accept PayPal only, to ensure your full anonymity.

Five hundred bucks was substantial, but a five-star meal and one night at a luxury hotel would easily cost that much. This promised so much *more*.

I smiled as I clicked the 'Submit' button. *Submission*, indeed. I was taking a giant leap into an unknown realm. I felt a mix of nervous tension and release imagining myself joining a mix of exotic strangers around the mysterious fantasy table. Now it was just a matter of getting final approval and scheduling the date.

My hand wandered unconsciously from the keyboard to my inner thighs as I began to think about what erotic adventures lay in wait for me.

4
———

HORS D'OEUVRES

The next day, my heart skipped a beat when I logged onto the Fantasy Feast website and saw a notification in my inbox. I clicked on the message and read it with bated breath.

Congratulations on pre-qualification for membership to the Fantasy Feast club. The next step is to schedule a date to attend one of our dinner parties.

We'll complete the final qualification with a personal interview on the approved date. Please arrive three hours before the scheduled dinner time to complete the process and receive your personal spa preparation.

I clicked on the Schedule tab. It displayed a calendar for the current month with the first two weeks blacked out. I took this to be a good sign that they were popular enough to be booked up. I clicked on the first available Saturday, which pulled up a new window. An agenda displayed on the screen:

6:00 p.m. — Personal Interview
7:00 p.m. — Spa Treatment
8:00 p.m. — Final Preparation

9:00 p.m. — Dinner Party
11:00 p.m. — Guest Room Rendezvous (optional)

Submit

I loved the double meaning with the 'Submit' imagery, and I had to admit I found it a turn-on to click that button again. Those weren't the *only* buttons that were being pushed!

I was also a little intrigued by the cryptic agenda items 'Final Preparation' and 'Guest Room Rendezvous'. It was all so mysterious and exciting. My mind began to wander again imagining the surprises that awaited me as my legs parted and my erect nipples pressed against my silk blouse.

On the scheduled date, I could barely contain my excitement as I prepared for the mysterious event. I visited three costume shops before I found a masquerade mask that suited my style. I settled on a black lace eye mask that concealed enough of my face to disguise my identity, but still permitted my skin to breathe with comfortable facial movement. I didn't want any rough edges getting in the way of my—or anyone else's—pleasure. Thinking about all the things I could do in the guise of my fantasy Asian beauty was beginning to drive me wild with desire.

As dusk approached, I drove out to the address of the country estate and pulled up to a wrought iron gate at the end of a long driveway. A call box sat on the driver's side of the entrance. I pressed the button and an unfamiliar woman's voice answered.

"Good evening. May I help you?"

"Yes, I have an appointment for this evening's Fantasy Feast."

"May I ask your profile name?"

I liked how they protected my privacy at every stage of the affair. I hadn't had to provide any revealing personal identification information, not even my credit card. Apparently, my profile name would be my pseudonym for the rest of the evening.

"It's Jade," I said. It was such a thrill to vocalize my new name. I could feel myself already getting into character.

"Please come in. A hostess will meet you at the front door."

The gates swung open, and I drove slowly up the long tree-lined driveway toward an enormous floodlit villa. It was a magnificent chateau in the French Renaissance style, clad in pale yellow lime-stone with tall Palladian windows rising three stories above mani-cured gardens. It had to be five times the size of a normal home. To my provincial eyes, it looked like the Palace of Versailles.

I parked my car in the designated area and walked toward the large double entrance door. Soft incandescent light shone through the glass sidelights and an overhead crescent window into the gath-ering dusk. I tapped gently with the brass door knocker and heard the sound of high heels on a tile floor coming toward me from behind the door.

A gorgeous young woman wearing a cat mask opened the door and motioned me inside. She was completely nude except for her skimpy mask and tall stilettos. Her slender, toned legs rose to the perfectly bald 'V' of her pubis, framed by hourglass-shaped hips. Her breasts were full and firm and swayed gently as she moved toward me. I couldn't help but glance downward to take in her breathtaking beauty.

"You must be Jade," she said softly. "Please come in. May I take your coat?"

"Thank you," I practically choked, my mind still swimming in shock.

The young woman stepped behind me and helped me remove my coat, then hung it in the large closet in the entrance foyer. Even just the soft touch of her hands on my fully clothed shoulders put a charge of electricity through me.

"Please follow me," she said. "Our hostess is expecting you."

I followed the nude woman across the expansive open foyer as her heels clicked on the marble floor tiles. My eyes were locked on the perfectly shaped globes of her ass as they flexed and bounced with each forward step. I could barely keep myself erect as my knees weakened beneath me.

The woman escorted me into a large private study with mahogany paneling and leather armchairs.

"May I get you a coffee or glass of wine?"

"A coffee would be fine, thank you," I said, trying my best to sound sophisticated. "Black, with just a bit of sugar."

"A hostess will be with you shortly. Please make yourself comfortable."

The woman exited through a side door, and two minutes later a slightly older woman in her thirties entered carrying a cup of coffee on a platter. She too was completely naked, other than the feathered Mardi Gras mask partially covering her eyes. She placed the platter on a table beside my chair and extended her hand to me.

"It's a pleasure to meet you, Jade."

I recognized the sultry voice immediately. It was the Scarlett Johansson voice from my earlier phone conversation.

She took a seat in the leather chair directly opposite me and crossed her legs, barely concealing her bare vulva resting on the edge of the chair.

"My name's Blair. I just wanted to take a few minutes to ask you a few brief questions before you begin the festivities. Just to clarify expectations and ensure you're comfortable moving forward."

I liked how she didn't call it an interview, though I knew this was part of my final qualification to participate in the event. I was actually glad they didn't take just anyone who walked in off the street and were careful to set expectations before jumping right in.

Blair was a contemporary, roughly my age. We both took care of ourselves and were equally attractive. We might even have passed for sisters, especially cloaked under our masquerade masks. The main difference between us was our hair color—mine was a shimmering brown and hers a silky blond.

Of course, she had the benefit of a superior position by virtue of her role as interviewer. But this didn't stop me from imagining myself entwined with her in lots of less *formal* positions.

Her plump breasts pointed toward me, with dark nipples peering like amber eyes, daring me to make contact. A little lower, the shadow at the apex of her legs just under her thighs beckoned even stronger. It took every ounce of my power to keep my eyes leveled with hers.

Two can play this game, I thought. I decided to have some fun and begin role-playing.

"Ask away," I teased, "I'm an open vessel."

Blair paused briefly to appraise my figure and comportment. I was wearing a tight taupe-colored gabardine skirt, hemmed just above the knee, and a cream-colored silk blouse opened to the third button, revealing ample cleavage and my flawless alabaster skin. I'd intentionally gone braless, partly to put myself in an erotic mood—and partly to display my best assets.

I straightened my back and crossed my right leg over the other slowly. I could feel my nipples swelling as they protruded teasingly in the outline of my flimsy blouse. I was pretty sure I'd pass this part of the test.

Blair cleared her throat.

"That's good to hear," she said. "Actually, that was one of my first questions. How open are you to engaging with others this evening?"

"You mean besides enjoying the *food* and *conversation*?" I let a slight smile cross my lips.

"If the opportunity presents."

"Well, as you suggested on the phone, I'm looking forward to exploring *all* of my senses."

"Wonderful. We wouldn't want you to miss out on the potential to fulfill all of your desires." Blair paused for a moment. "And if some of the contact is—*unexpected*—will you be comfortable engaging?"

The more Blair spoke, the more turned on I got by her sexy voice and subtle nuances of meaning. She was seriously hot, and her sophisticated manner was getting me all the more worked up. I knew exactly what she meant, but I wanted to extend the foreplay a little longer.

"I suppose that depends on what you mean by 'contact', and 'engaging'."

Blair looked me directly in the eyes as her lips curled in a faint smile.

"You understand that the Fantasy Feast experience will engage all your senses, including *touch*? Are you open to being touched, gently and with your full permission of course, at one or more times during the course of the dinner engagement?"

I was pretty clear on the terms of engagement coming in, but I still wanted to confirm a few details.

"On the phone, you said everyone would remain seated at the table until the meal is finished. Only then would we have an opportunity to approach other patrons directly?"

"That's true. But there may be opportunities over the course of the meal for our *own* sensualists to engage you in various pleasurable ways. Are you open to that?"

I paused for a moment. The idea of being 'serviced' while others watched was in fact one of the main attractions for my wanting to come.

"Will I have the ability to control or stop the activities at any time?"

I was backsliding a little in my confident role-playing, but this was not a matter to be ambiguous about. This was my only hard and fast rule when it came to sex. "No" always means no.

"Yes. You'll have a signaling device directly at your place setting and will be able to stop—or start—any of the activities at any time."

Blair paused to ensure I was comfortable with what she'd said.

"Did you have any *other* questions or concerns before you begin your spa preparation?"

There was only one other concern that had crossed my mind. I wasn't quite sure how to put it delicately.

"What precautions have you taken to ensure the...*cleanliness* of the participants and the utensils"? I wasn't sure who, or *what* exactly, would be touching me, but I wanted to be sure everything would at least be sterile and disease-free.

Blair nodded, understanding my meaning.

"That's an excellent question. All of our servers and sensualists receive a weekly medical checkup and blood test for any communicable diseases. Our dinnerware and other paraphernalia is steam-cleaned with organic detergents at 220 degrees-plus water temperatures to ensure absolute sterility."

I could see that Blair was impressed by the type of questions I was asking.

"Of course," she nodded, "we expect *reciprocal* disclosure from our guests. You've already verified your health when you submitted your online profile, but if you have any concerns regarding this matter, now is the time to share."

I breathed a sigh of relief to get this awkward subject out of the way.

"I'm fine, thank you, Blair. I too have received a full check-up and clean bill of health recently."

Blair stood up and smiled.

"In that case, if you're ready to begin the process, I'll take you to our spa where you'll meet with our esthetician, who'll prepare you for the main event. Please follow me as I escort you to your private room."

I followed Blair out of the study and up a long winding staircase. From my vantage point three steps below her, I could see her thighs opening slightly as she lifted each leg, revealing the tantalizing cleft between her cheeks. It might have been my over-active imagination, but I could have sworn I saw her lips glistening in the bright light of the chandelier hanging above the foyer.

I wondered if I would see her again before the evening was over.

5

───────

FINGER FOOD

When we got to the top of the stairs, Blair led me into a beautifully appointed private boudoir with ensuite bathroom.

But this was no *ordinary* bathroom. It was a luxury spa with heated white marble floors and countertops. In the middle of the expansive floor rested a linen-covered massage table with a plump pillow at the head. Next to a large window covered with soft sheers sat a large soaking tub filled with steaming water and floating rose petals. A subtle aroma of lemongrass permeated the room as soft music played from the overhead speakers.

"This will be your private suite to use as you please for the next twenty-four hours," Blair said.

"If you'd like to relax with a warm bath or a stimulating shower, please make yourself comfortable. In thirty minutes, your masseuse will arrive to complete your preparation for the main event. If you need anything at all, please feel free to call us on the courtesy phone."

I was amazed how relaxed and utterly nonchalant a naked woman could be in the company of strangers. Before the evening was over, I hoped to achieve a similar state of intrepidness. I wanted to strip off my clothes right there and ask Blair to join me in the tub, but I knew that was against the rules. Instead, I simply smiled and made love to her with my eyes.

"Thank you, Blair. I think a stimulating bath is *just* what my body could use right now. How will I find my way to the dining room?"

"Your attendant will escort you to the dining hall at the appointed hour. I look forward to seeing you then."

So this wasn't to be the last of her *after* all. My heart raced and my pussy pulsed at the thought of seeing her again. Blair turned and left the room, closing the main bedroom door softly behind her.

I took a few minutes to walk about the bedroom and washroom to appraise my surroundings. Everything about the accommodations was first-class. From the high thread count Egyptian cotton sheets on the king-size bed to the cherry-wood furnishings, it felt like a five-star hotel. They even had a large bottle of Evian water and a collection of dark chocolates on the nightstand beside the bed.

I swung open the doors to the large armoire to hang my clothes. A beautiful floral kimono hung on a padded silk hanger. I reached out and caressed the softness of the fabric. Forget one *day*—I'd like to book an entire *week* at this spa!

I disrobed and hung my blouse and skirt in the armoire, then laid my panties on the paper-lined shelf of the top drawer. Normally, I'd be reluctant to place my intimate clothes in a public area, but the paper smelled fresh and looked newly laid.

Now completely naked, I appraised myself in the full-length wardrobe mirror. I looked pretty damn good for a nearly middle-aged woman. My yoga-toned body was tight and curvy in all the right places. My full and natural breasts still sat high and firm on my chest with large brown nipples. Long shapely legs cascaded down from my heart-shaped ass, a small wedge of light showing between my slightly parted thighs.

I'd booked an appointment with my stylist the day before, and my shoulder-length hair rested perfectly straight just above my shoulders. The only thing that needed a slight trim was my pubic bush, which I'd intentionally let grow over the last week in anticipation of the esthetic grooming I knew was yet to come.

I unhooked the kimono from the armoire hanger and carried it to the edge of the bath, where I hung it on a hook next to the window. The water had been pre-heated to the perfect temperature—warm enough to relax my muscles, but not so hot to feel uncomfortable or scalding. I slowly lowered myself onto the oil-covered surface and parted the rose petals as my body submerged into the heavenly ocean.

I immediately felt the tension begin to ebb from my body as I lost myself in the sublime sensation enveloping me. The only sound I could hear was the soft music playing from the surround speakers and the gentle lapping of water against the sides of the tub. I lay my head back against the pillow placed at the top edge of the tub and soon nodded off.

Sometime later, I heard a soft tap on my bedroom door. Not wanting to remove myself just yet from my cocoon of luxury, I called out to answer.

"Yes?"

"It's time for your massage," a woman's voice replied.

"Just one minute please."

I reluctantly stepped out of the bath and quickly toweled myself dry. I wrapped a large bath sheet around me, re-donned my mask, then opened the bedroom door.

A petite young Asian girl greeted me, wearing a kimono similar to mine and a crimson masquerade mask.

Apparently not *everybody* who works here always walks around stark naked.

The girl was utterly breathtaking. Long jet-black hair cascaded over high cheekbones past her pouty lips with delicate collarbones peeking from the top of her kimono. I could see her breasts and hips outlined by the tightly wrapped kimono and suddenly wished that she too had come to my boudoir naked.

"My name is Jasmine," she said. "I'm your personal masseuse and esthetician. Are you ready for your final preparation?"

Just the thought of this beauty laying her tender hands on me sent a shiver down my spine.

"Definitely," I said. "Please come in. How would you like me to prepare?"

"Come with me, please."

Jasmine led me into the bathroom, where she nonchalantly removed her kimono and hung it behind the bathroom door.

Oh my God.

I didn't think anyone in this place could get more beautiful or sensuous. Jasmine had perfectly shaped B-cup breasts with a thin indentation running down the center of her toned stomach. Like everyone else in this place, her pubis was utterly bald and flawless. She barely looked eighteen and I was just about to ask her age, but she spoke first.

"If you'd like to remove your towel and lay face down on the table, we can get started. May I call you Jade?"

There was something about her confident manner and tone that belied her youthful appearance. I had no inhibitions whatsoever about displaying myself unclothed to this stranger.

"Yes, thank you, Jasmine." I unhooked my bath sheet and threw it against the side of the tub.

"Would you like me to drape your backside?" Jasmine asked.

"That won't be necessary," I quickly answered.

Jasmine walked over to the vanity counter and picked up two small bottles of oil resting under an orange radiant lamp. She brought them back to the massage table, opened one, and poured the oil into one cupped hand then rubbed her hands together. The scent of lavender wafted toward my nose.

I closed my eyes in anticipation of her touch. I'd had massages before, but nothing as sensuous and stimulating as this. When her hands touched the small of my back, I flinched reflexively from the sexual tension. My heart was beating a hundred miles an hour as I felt the blood coursing through my veins.

Jasmine must have sensed my nervous tension and began pressing her fingers more firmly into my back as she moved them slowly up each side of my spine. The warm oil allowed her hands to glide effortlessly across my skin. She used every surface of her hands to massage my muscles, expertly kneading my skin with her fingers and palm.

I began to relax as my muscles softened and surrendered to her touch. She sensuously massaged every part of my back, shoulders, and neck, applying just the right amount of pressure. Periodically, she would pour more warm oil on my lower back, dipping her hands in it to replenish the silky lubrication against my pliant skin.

Just as the sexual tension began to subside from the utter relaxation of the massage, Jasmine moved her hands down to my buttocks and began to caress them in soft circular motions. My glutes contracted involuntarily and I unconsciously pressed my mound into the firm padding of the table. Suddenly I was quickly reminded that a gorgeous young woman was caressing my naked body. She cupped each buttock between her hands as she massaged my ass tantalizingly, her little finger sliding slowly into the cleft just above my anus.

Periodically, I'd partially open one of my eyes with my head turned in her direction to look at her gorgeous body. My head was at the same level as her midsection, and my mouth watered as I watched her stomach muscles flex and her hips undulate with each movement of her hands. At times her pussy was almost right beside me and I wanted to reach out and run my own fingers up her soft legs.

I was in total heaven, and getting wetter by the moment. Just when I thought I couldn't stand it anymore, she suddenly moved her hands down to my feet and began massaging her thumbs into my soles.

I'd always loved having my feet massaged, but nobody did it like Jasmine. She cradled my foot and used every part of her hands to massage and knead every surface from my heel to my toes. I didn't want her to stop, but there were *other* parts of my body that were screaming for attention.

As if reading my thoughts, she began moving her hands up toward my calf, using her thumbs to spread the muscle apart. She lingered almost as long on my calf as she had on my foot, rolling the ball of my calf between both of her hands, sliding her slick hands up and down erotically. I couldn't help imagining how she might use those same hands to massage a man's erect cock in a similar manner. My mind wandered again to what pleasures lay in wait for me over dinner.

After shifting her hands to my right leg and giving my other foot and calf similar attention, she placed each hand just behind my knees and began to slowly move them up towards my buttocks. Her thumbs pressed against my inner thighs as she glided tantalizingly close to my apex.

I rolled my legs outward in an invitation to move closer. My legs were parted enough that I was sure she could see my vulva from her vantage point behind me. In my highly aroused state, my lips were engorged and spread apart, revealing my moist and quivering opening.

But as much as I desperately wanted her to, Jasmine never touched me there. She repeatedly slid her hands right up to the edge of my slit, pressing and rotating her thumbs on the fleshy meat of my upper thighs just below my aching pussy. I suppose this was part of her master plan—to tease me mercilessly and inflame my passions so I'd be ready for just about anything at the main event.

It was certainly working. After thirty minutes of Jasmine's ministrations, I was grinding my pussy into the table trying desperately to give my clit some needed direct stimulation.

Just when I thought I couldn't be teased any more tantalizingly, Jasmine opened one of the bottles of warm oil and poured it directly into the crack of my ass. She paused as the fluid flowed down and directly over my parted lips. I almost came from the gentle movement of the warm liquid as it trickled across the folds of my labia, channeled toward the junction where they joined together at my clit. I shuddered in pleasure at the feeling, even if it was only the subtlest of touch.

Jasmine suddenly interrupted my thoughts.

"Would you like to turn over now?"

It was the first time she'd spoken directly to me since the massage started, and it surprised me in my catatonic, pre-orgasmic state. I practically flipped over like a fish out of water, spreading my legs expectantly. Finally, I'd get some relief. Surely, she couldn't leave me hanging like this.

"It's time for your final grooming," she said. "I'll need you to part your legs a bit further to provide full access."

Grooming? I knew this was part of the process, but somehow it didn't seem fair to transition at this precise moment. At least I'd be able to stay on the comfortable massage table instead of the clinical vinyl chairs used by my regular esthetician.

Jasmine walked over to another cabinet by the makeup table and withdrew a leather bag from one of the drawers, then brought it back to the table. She reached into the bag and pulled out a cordless hair trimmer.

"Do you have a preference regarding your appearance?" she asked. "Do you prefer natural, neatly trimmed, or bare?"

I knew she was referring to my pubic hair, which I generally kept neatly trimmed. I'd always thought going fully bald was unnatural and unseemly, catering to men's prurient fantasies of fucking young schoolgirls. But in this situation, it seemed entirely appropriate, like I was stripping away all my camouflage and armor.

If tonight was all about being *watched*, I might as well bare myself in every sense of the word and truly let my inhibitions go. I began to fantasize about rubbing my bare pussy against Jasmine's while she poured warm oil between us. The more work she had to do on me, the more chance I'd have to make this last and hopefully get off.

I didn't hesitate. "Bare, thank you."

"As you wish," she said. "I'll remove the long hairs first with the trimmer, then shave you smooth with a razor."

No *waxing*? This was different. I was relieved to not have to bear the painful and violent trial of having my hairs ripped out en masse. Although shaving down there was always a scary proposition, I felt safe in the capable and practiced hands of this beautiful esthetician.

Jasmine nodded, then flipped a switch on the trimmer. The

device buzzed softly as she placed it gently on my mound. I had only a light dusting of fur and it didn't take long for her to remove it with a few short strokes over my pubis. I shuddered as the vibrations penetrated deep into my core. If she had placed the flat head on my clitoris, I would have popped off in a millisecond. Instead, she turned the trimmer face-down and gently swiped the vibrating teeth against the sides of my vulva, sensuously separating my labia with her hands as she moved the device between my legs to trim the hairs on the inside and outside of my labia.

It was an insanely titillating feeling, but just clinical enough to bring me down from my plateau and shift my focus. My mind wandered to the upcoming feast, and I contemplated what surprises lay in wait at the main event. The hostess had suggested there would be 'contact' of some sort during the meal, and I was intrigued as to who and how it would be administered. The idea of being fully bald, cleansed, and thoroughly stimulated going into the event was an incredible rush.

Jasmine continued with the trimmer all the way down my perineum to my anus, barely touching me with the trimmer so as not to pinch any delicate tissues. Apparently, there were no parts of my erogenous zone that would remain untouched, now—and perhaps later.

She turned off the trimmer and placed it at the foot of the table. Then she took a bottle of gel from the bag and spread the gel on her hands. Using both hands, she spread it gently between my legs, starting on my mound all the way down to my rosebud.

My body almost levitated above the table as Jasmine finally laid her hands directly on my clitoris. The gel had a mild stinging quality that added to the stimulating sensation. If this was meant to excite my follicles in preparation for the shave, it wasn't the *only* feature of my anatomy that it made erect. I could feel the hood of my clitoris retract as my button filled with blood and began to push outward. Suddenly, I was fully stimulated again and lusting for Jasmine's touch. I fantasized about her bending down and taking my swollen nub between her puffy lips and letting me come in her mouth.

Unfortunately, my satisfaction would have to wait a little longer. Instead, Jasmine reached into her bag and pulled out a straight-edge razor. In anyone else's hands, it might look threatening, especially in my prostrated and vulnerable position. But something about the way she delicately and sensuously opened the jackknifed tool instantly evaporated my fears. I could see how this type of razor would in fact give her better control safely cutting my stubs instead of the usual ladies' plastic razor.

With her right hand, Jasmine gently laid the razor on its flat edge at the top of my mound, while she gently pulled my skin upwards with her other hand. Then she slowly turned the sharp edge perpendicular to my skin and began softly scraping the razor downwards. I could hear the bristling sound as the razor edge removed my nubs right down to the follicles. She repeated the pattern in one-inch-wide swipes on one side then the other of my pubis, being ever-so-careful to stop just where my clitoris lay quivering in a mixture of fear and excitement. There was something about the utter vulnerability of the procedure that made it the most erotic experience I'd ever had.

Jasmine used the same deft touch as she moved down my vulva and perineum, scraping the vestiges of stray hairs away with gentle swipes of the long blade, while sensuously separating my folds and flesh with her other hand. She took extra time and care around my anus and clit, using the gentlest and slowest motion I've ever felt someone apply to my body. The combination of fright and titillation as she probed my most sensitive body parts created a river of sensuous fluids running down my vulva. By this time, no shaving gel was necessary to provide a smooth gliding surface for the knife.

When she was finished, Jasmine retrieved a fresh wash towel from beside the sink and held it under the warm water faucet then twisted the excess water into the basin. She returned to the table and placed it over my splayed legs then gently cleansed the excess moisture and remaining shaving gel with gentle massaging movements of her hands. The warm, moist towel felt exquisite against my newly shaved skin. Jasmine's hands now felt comforting between my legs rather than erotic.

She had taken me on an incredibly sensuous erotic arc, right to the edge of ecstasy and back, to a quiet relaxed place. I exhaled fully and completely for the first time in almost an hour.

Jasmine removed the towel from between my legs and held up a large hand mirror at a forty-five-degree angle toward me.

"What do you think?" she asked.

I tilted my head up and studied her masterpiece. Far from the usual red and swollen vulva that I typically experienced after the violent waxing with my regular esthetician, I'd never seen my pussy look so beautiful. Utterly bereft of any hair, my entire perineum from my pubic mound to my anus was totally bald, pink—and gorgeous. I just stared at my beautiful pussy, utterly transfixed by the transformation.

"You have to *feel* it to really appreciate how beautiful you are," Jasmine purred.

I moved my right hand down, running my fingers along the edges of my pussy. I gasped from a feeling I'd never felt before. It felt smooth as silk: no bumps or blemishes or cuts or bruises. It was almost as if I was feeling somebody *else*—somebody I'd never felt before. I couldn't stop my left hand joining the other in rubbing and caressing my sensitive organs.

Jasmine lowered the mirror and smiled at me as I felt the moisture begin to accumulate between my legs again.

"It's almost time for your dinner appointment," she said. "Why don't you save the best for last? I think you'll find plenty of ways to satisfy your appetite over the next couple of hours."

She lifted my kimono from the hook at the edge of the bathtub and held it open for me.

"I'll escort you downstairs now if you're ready. All you need to bring is your kimono and slippers—and your mask of course."

I sat up slowly and stepped off the massage table. Turning around, I held my arms out as Jasmine lifted one arm of the silk robe onto me then the other. Then she turned around to face me, wrapped the silk tie around me, and tied a single bow over my belly button. She retrieved my matching silk slippers and knelt down on one knee to gently lift my feet one at a time and place them softly inside. It took every ounce of my power not to grab her head and pull it into my pulsating pussy.

Jasmine stood up gracefully and smiled into my eyes.

"If you'll follow me, I'll escort you now to the fantasy feast."

She didn't even bother putting her own robe on. Her tight little ass barely jiggled as she stepped smartly ahead of me. I wasn't sure if I'd have a chance to feel Jasmine's touch again before the evening was over, but for now I was in total bliss ogling her petite, curvaceous figure from behind.

6

MAIN COURSE

I followed Jasmine down the circular stairs, across the marble-tiled foyer, past an open kitchen where a group of chefs wearing white hats were busy cooking, to a closed set of French doors. Jasmine paused, opened the doors and motioned me inside. I walked into a palatial dining room with a large table seating eight people, all wearing robes and masquerade masks.

The table was covered in a large white linen cloth extending down to the floor. The place settings were beautifully decorated with crystal wine goblets, polished silverware, and gold-embossed dinner plates. At the head of every place setting was a folded tent card with each person's first name and a little silver bell.

The entire scene was surreal. As I followed Jasmine toward the one remaining unoccupied seat at the table, everyone watched me. There was an even mix of men and women appearing to be in their twenties and thirties and of mixed ethnicity, just as my profile preferences had requested. And all of them were beautiful. Some smiled at me as I approached the table.

Jasmine pulled out the empty chair and motioned for me to have a seat. I noticed the chair had a hollow opening in the middle and front section of the seat cushion, shaped almost like a toilet seat. On the back of the chair was a small wooden hook. Otherwise, the chairs were tastefully detailed in full upholstery with high backs and armrests. I sat tentatively down onto the chair and found it surprisingly comfortable. Jasmine exited the room and closed the French doors quietly behind her.

"It looks like we're all here," the woman sitting at the head of the table announced. It was Blair from my interview. She had replaced her feathered mask with a Venetian-style mask and was wearing a robe, but I recognized her unmistakable voice immediately.

"My name is Blair," she said. "I'll be your hostess for the evening. If there's anything you desire at any time, please don't hesitate to ask. We want you to feel comfortable, stimulated, and uplifted throughout the course of our fantasy feast. To that end, may I suggest we begin by disrobing, as a way of releasing our inhibitions and opening ourselves to a fully liberating experience? I'll be the first. If you'd rather keep your robe on for now, that's fine too."

Blair stood up and slowly removed her robe, then hung it on the hook on the back of her chair. She paused for a moment before she sat down to allow everyone to take in her breathtaking beauty. Her plump natural breasts swayed delicately as she turned to face the guests on each side of the table. She was an exquisite specimen of feminine beauty and everyone around the table, men and women alike, were staring just as I was. I was disappointed when she sat down. I could have soaked up her beauty all night long.

"Who else would like to reveal their full beauty for the rest of us to enjoy?" she said.

Blair turned and looked suggestively at the male guest to her immediate right. His place card read Isiah. He paused, momentarily taken aback. But after a few seconds, he also stood and confidently removed his robe then turned and placed it on the hook behind his chair. As he twisted his torso, his tight muscular buttocks flexed to balance his weight. When he turned around, he paused briefly in full frontal view before sitting down. Not everybody was quite as comfortable as Blair getting naked in front of a room full of strangers.

Nonetheless, I saw enough to gain an appreciation of Isiah's toned physique. An African-American with light brown skin, chiseled pecs and six-pack abs descending to a neatly trimmed pubic area, his half-erect circumcised member betrayed his obvious excitement. Already at least six inches long in a semi-flaccid state, I could only imagine how large he might be fully aroused and erect. As he lowered himself onto his chair holding the armrests, his well-toned arm muscles flexed in a light sheen of perspiration.

He wasn't the *only* one already beginning to lubricate this evening.

Everyone around the table looked towards Blair. You could hear a pin drop from the nervous and excited tension in the room. Blair peered at the pretty redheaded woman seated next to Isiah and smiled. The redhead's place card read Venus. Where do these people come up with their profile names?

Perhaps she was trying to overcompensate for her shyness. Her eyes widened in a mix of fear and nervousness. She paused, looking at Blair uncertainly. Then she took a deep breath, quickly stood up and removed her robe, and hung it behind her chair. She sat back down immediately, her back arched a few inches away from the back-rest with a ramrod straight spine. Her perky breasts rested firmly on her chest with pinched nipples betraying her excitement.

Her face was expressionless as she stared straight ahead, afraid to make eye contact with anyone in her fully exposed state. It was obvious this was the first time she'd done anything like this, probably coming from an upper-class repressive home, like myself. It was kind of comforting to know that I wasn't the only relatively inexperienced one among the group.

One by one, everyone around the table removed their robes, sitting stark naked except for their masks. The men seemed more comfortable disrobing than the women. The next woman awkwardly removed her robe while still seated, apparently not ready to reveal her most intimate parts to the group just yet. The last woman simply parted the top portion of her robe, revealing half of her bare bosom. I was glad that Blair didn't make anyone feel uncomfortable or set any expectations as the disrobing ritual continued around the table. She simply smiled and acknowledged each person as they revealed as much as they wanted.

The four women and four men were evenly spaced around the oversize table in alternating sexes. Just as I had specified, everyone was young, beautiful, and of mixed heritage. Besides Isiah, there was a Latino man who looked like a young Benicio Del Toro, a dark-haired Patrick Dempsey lookalike, and a thick blond-haired hunk who reminded me of his McSteamy counterpart on the TV show Grey's Anatomy. All the men were tall, fit—and gorgeous. It was like my own *Chippendale* show, and I stared shamelessly at the strong toned torsos of the men sitting majestically around the table.

In addition to the shy redhead Venus, the women were represented by a pretty young Asian woman who reminded me a bit of Jasmine, a dark exotic black woman who looked like Naomi Campbell, myself—and of course, Blair. As with the men, all the women were young, attractive, and perfectly toned. It was obvious that this was a discriminating club that catered to the most beautiful and uninhibited.

When it became *my* turn to disrobe, I hesitated briefly, feeling slightly inadequate amongst this stunning group of Adonises and Lorelei. Blair simply smiled at me and nodded. I paused for a second, then stood confidently, pulling my kimono away in a flourish. My plump breasts bounced firmly as I bent over and hooked my robe behind my chair. The idea of displaying my newly sculpted nude body to a group of strangers was a huge turn-on, and I hesitated for a few seconds before sitting down to let everyone have a good look.

I could feel the electricity in the room as everyone looked around the table and took in the sights and sounds and scents. A distinct womanly perfume permeated the room as an obvious state of arousal began to build among the dinner patrons. My vulva twitched as I felt the cool movement of air against my genitals in the opening of my seat cushion.

Knowing everyone else was feeling the same thing and was equally exposed under the tablecloth was incredibly stimulating. My pussy throbbed and moistened as I imagined the men growing hard and the women getting wet looking at me and the others. I wasn't sure what was going to happen next, but this was definitely the most titillating experience I had so far, and the evening had barely started.

Blair was the first to break the tension as a door swung open and two pretty waitresses began filling our champagne glasses with bubbly.

"I'm glad everyone has made themselves comfortable," she said. "We will begin serving our first courses shortly. Please enjoy our services and allow all your senses to be stimulated. Don't be alarmed if you experience something new at one or more times during the dinner service. The only rule we ask you to honor is that you keep your hands in plain sight at all times. And remember, all you have to do is ring this little bell at your place setting if you feel uncomfortable and wish to stop the services at any time."

Blair picked up the silver bell at the head of her place setting and tinkled it teasingly. Then she lifted her champagne glass in a toast and everyone followed her lead.

"To unleashing inhibitions, and experiencing transcendence!"

Everyone took a deep swig of their champagne and smiled. They knew the main event was about to begin. The pretty waitresses returned carrying silver platters and placed bowls of gazpacho in front of each dinner guest. Over the next hour or so, Blair facilitated polite chit-chat around the table, referring to everyone by their first name only. Occasionally, one or more guests engaged each other directly in conversation, but always over safe subjects. Whether it was the awkward feeling of being utterly naked or trepidation over what was coming next, everybody seemed on edge.

I was almost disappointed when I picked up my dessert spoon and cut into my crème brulée. So far, it had been a fairly uneventful dinner, except for the obvious staring among the dinner patrons at each other's nude torsos.

Then, for the first time over the course of the dinner event, Blair became conspicuously quiet. Everyone ate their dessert silently, glancing nervously at each other around the table. None of us were still entirely comfortable engaging each other in direct conversation without Blair's facilitation.

Suddenly, the redheaded girl gasped and jerked in her chair. Her right hand reflexively reached out to the bell and she considered shaking it as she glanced uncertainly in Blair's direction. Blair simply smiled and nodded at her. Whatever was going on at Venus's seat, Blair was apparently fully aware and giving her silent encouragement to continue.

Venus's breathing became more labored and she set her fork down beside her chocolate torte to steady herself. She moved her hands to her chair armrests and closed her eyes. It was obvious that something was going on below our line of sight as she began squirming seductively in her chair. Her lips parted and she moaned softly. She sank lower in her chair as it was apparent her legs were spreading apart.

Who, or what, was ministering to her under the table obviously was having the desired effect. My pussy began dripping down the crack of my ass as I watched Venus enjoying herself, imagining what was being done to her under the table. Her hands stayed above the table, so she apparently didn't need any help getting satisfaction.

Suddenly, Venus gasped, locking eyes on me. She was moving rhythmically now in her seat, thrusting her hips in a violent motion as her passion progressively rose. By now, *everyone* around the table had placed their utensils down and was watching the beautiful redhead enjoy her erotic encounter.

I wanted desperately to reach down and touch myself as Venus looked at me through glistening eyes with lust and abandon. I began to move in synchronicity with her, rotating my hips to her rhythm, trying to find the edge of my seat to rub against my twitching clit. Venus's cheeks flushed and the pale skin on her upper chest reddened as her breasts heaved with the movement of her hips. Whatever was happening to her under the table, I wanted some of that.

By this point, Venus's inhibitions had completely evaporated as she was lost in the moment. As her passion rose and she moved closer to climax, she moaned louder and more lustfully. Whimpering in ecstasy, her release came like a volcano as she screamed and grunted like a wild animal with a long and powerful orgasm. Her chest heaved in rhythmic spasms as each wave of passion rolled over her. When she was finally spent, she slumped in her chair and closed her eyes in utter satiation.

Everyone looked at one another around the table in total shock and excitement. Nobody said a word, but we were all thinking the same thing. This had been the most erotic experience any of us had ever witnessed, and each of us was dripping and throbbing in anticipation of receiving similar treatment.

Unsure exactly how to respond, I simply picked up my fork and resumed eating my dessert. Others around the table followed suit. Blair smiled at Venus when she finally regained her composure and sat back up in her chair.

"Did you enjoy your *dessert*, Venus?"

"It was exquisite," Venus panted.

Everyone around the table smiled. For another minute or so, all I could hear was the sound of silverware tinkling against dessert dishes and Venus's contented sighs.

But it didn't take long before *Isiah* started squirming in his seat also. Suddenly, he slammed his palms on the table and jerked his body. It was obviously his turn to be serviced under the table. There was something incredibly erotic about not being able to use your own hands and simply abandon yourself to the ministrations of some unknown stranger or strangers. The long skirt of the linen tablecloth obscured any direct sightlines—even *he* couldn't know if it was a man or woman massaging his erogenous zones.

Whoever, or whatever it was, he was obviously enjoying it. His eyes glazed over and his arm muscles tensed as he held the armrests of his chair to secure himself. The six-pack muscles in his abdomen flexed as he began to thrust his hips rhythmically. My mind was going crazy imagining what was being done to him. I could hear a slapping noise mixed with a wet sound. Whether it was a mouth or a set of hands on his cock, it was difficult to tell. Something told me at this particular moment Isiah didn't care.

His breathing was becoming more ragged and his mouth was fully open now, and I could tell he was nearing the point of no return. Suddenly, his body lurched and he let out a guttural moan that indicated something new was happening. He hadn't come yet though, since his breathing was still rapid and building. What could they be doing to him under the table? I wondered if there might be more than one person servicing him. There certainly was enough room under the large table to accommodate multiple sensualists.

My pussy was throbbing with excitement as I became more conscious of the hole in my chair. My entire vulva was exposed as I felt the movement of air from the activity under the table. Isiah was now bouncing up and down in his chair in complete abandon. I'd read about how some erotic masseuses could stimulate a man's prostate by inserting a finger or dildo in his ass—maybe this is what he was experiencing.

Whatever it was, it didn't take long for the procedure to have its desired effect. Isiah let out a long guttural moan and he thrust his hips upward in one last jerk as he threw his head back. He held the armrests tightly in an epileptic spasm that seemed to last thirty seconds, his head and chest jerking in synchronicity with the orgasmic contractions he was experiencing. All I could think about was how much I wanted that thick cock buried in my aching pussy right now. I was dying for relief, having never been stimulated so intensely for so long. Even Jasmine's erotic massage hadn't gotten me this worked up.

I was desperately hoping it would be my turn next, but it was not to be. In fact, I would have to wait until the very end for my turn. One by one, each guest received personal treatment under the table while everyone watched in wonder and unrequited lust. Some took only a few minutes to reach orgasm while others took a little longer. Nobody held out for more than fifteen minutes or so. The turn-on of having eight strangers watching them as they had their erogenous zones stimulated, together with the mystery of not knowing what to expect under the table, was simply impossible to resist. Everybody eventually experienced a strong and explosive orgasm.

Some remained fairly motionless in their chairs as they were being serviced, while others thrashed and hopped about in their seats. It seemed as if some patrons were receiving oral stimulation, while others were being literally fucked under the table—though it was hard to imagine how that could be accomplished in the tight spaces under each chair.

I particularly enjoyed watching the other *women* being serviced. Within a minute or so after beginning their massages, the once demure ladies had thrown open their robes and flung them on the floor to provide easier viewing—and access—to their entire body. I loved watching as their breasts swayed and their skin progressively flushed as their passion mounted and crested. Beyond their telltale cries of ecstasy, I could always tell when they reached orgasm by how the skin on their chest suddenly darkened, then slowly faded along with the tumescence of their engorged nipples.

This Fantasy Feast was definitely on to something. It was true that being able to focus on every sensation in this way, unencumbered by the needs of an active sexual partner, was far more erotic and liberating than straight sex. In our detached and voyeuristic seating positions, all of our *other* sensations could be super-stimulated.

I could literally *smell* the bodily fluids and scented oils flowing from every person. I could see every nuanced movement and expression in their faces as they enjoyed their erotic journey. And of course, I could *hear* their telltale moans of ecstasy, recognizing whenever something changed under the table. Even my sense of *taste* was stimulated from the mouthwatering flavors and textures of each meal course laid out at my place setting.

Of course, the *best* sensation—touch—would have to wait. Which made it all the more tantalizing and enjoyable when it finally happened.

When the last guest before me had finally come down from her high, the anticipation was almost killing me. I was burning with desire like never before. I hoped that I might be able to make my turn last a little longer; I wanted to savor every pleasurable moment. But I knew it would be almost impossible to make it last very long with so much pent-up tension. I glanced at Blair and she simply gave me a knowing smile as if to say: 'just lose yourself in the moment and let it happen.'

I felt some movement under the table in the vicinity of my chair. I parted my legs to invite whoever was there to do as they pleased. Was it too much to hope for my beautiful masseuse Jasmine to finish what she started? She had left me with a cryptic smile. I never actually saw anyone go under or emerge from under the table the whole time. Maybe there was some kind of trap door in the floor to permit easy access to each guest's open chair? It didn't really matter, of course. The whole mystery of who was under the table administering to me simply added to the excitement and eroticism of the moment.

Then the mystery suddenly became clearer. A pair of petite hands began caressing my thighs. The touch was familiar. The motion of the hands, the subtle pressure of the fingertips, the way they floated upward toward my vulva was undeniable. This had to be Jasmine! I spread my legs far apart, fully exposing my pussy, practically *begging* her to fuck me. Or suck me. Or do whatever she pleased with me. I was totally at her mercy, and she knew it.

But she was in no hurry. As with my previous massage, she teased and caressed my thighs with the lightest touch of her fingertips, stroking them up and down my inner thighs. I wanted to cry out "fuck me, Jasmine!"

I could feel her move closer to me as her torso spread my legs further apart. Her hands shifted to the sides of my hips and I felt something touch my vulva. It was soft and round and firm, and it was rubbing softly up and down against my wet twat.

It was her breast! Her gorgeous, perfect, plump, natural breast. She was tribbing me with her breast! My gushing juices coated her skin with a natural lubricant as she pushed up and slid against me. I swear I could feel her erect nipple penetrate me as she thrust rhythmically against me. The combination of the fucking action with the stimulation of her nipple against my clit could easily have brought me to orgasm in less than a minute, but this was obviously not the way she wanted to finish me.

She backed away slowly and I felt her long hair move down lower on my belly and thighs. She began kissing my bald mound that she had so perfectly groomed earlier. I was in utter heaven as I closed my eyes and lost myself in the reality of being kissed by this beauty.

Her hands slowly moved from my hips and began exploring the inside of my thighs as her kisses moved lower and lower toward my nerve center. She kissed around and above and on top of my clit, coming ever so close, but never quite touching me directly. This wasn't like so many fumbling men I'd had who couldn't find my clit for the life of them. This was an expert sensualist who knew exactly how—and where—to tease and please me.

When her lips finally landed on my clit, I almost leaped out of my chair. She surrounded my swollen nub with her full mouth and pursed her lips. The idea of being sucked off by this gorgeous vixen was too much. I groaned uncontrollably and spasmed a mini-orgasm.

But this was only the beginning. Jasmine was obviously far too experienced and practiced to let me off so quickly and so lightly. With my clit still embedded within her lips, she extended her tongue and began swirling it in slow and sensuous movements along the shaft and underside.

Meanwhile, her lips bobbed softly up and down my swollen shaft. If this is what it's like for a man to get a blowjob, I can see why some of the other guests were being driven crazy earlier. Had they gotten similar treatment from Jasmine, or from someone else?

It didn't matter, because for now at least, Jasmine was all mine. I desperately wanted to move my hands under the table and hold her beautiful head while she licked me. I wanted to let her know how much I was enjoying her caresses and feel her soft brown hair flowing in my hands.

My passion rose inexorably as I tried to hold off coming. I wanted to savor this moment as long as I could. This was the first time I'd been intimate with a woman, and I wanted to savor it as long as I could.

Just when I thought it couldn't get any more intense, I felt Jasmine's right hand move to my opening, and she slowly inserted three fingers deep into my vagina. God, I had desperately needed to be fucked, and now this divine creature was answering my prayers.

She began thrusting firmly as she continued sucking and licking my clitoris in a way no one had ever done before. Then she curled her fingers upward and began stroking my G-spot in a come-hither motion that took me to an entirely new level.

I was writhing and thrusting in my chair now, taking everything Jasmine was giving me. I pushed down in my chair wanting more. I wanted my pussy filled up and fucked while I fucked her beautiful mouth with my burning pussy. As if sensing my need, Jasmine inserted her fourth finger inside me and pushed her hand further up inside. I was bucking wildly now and pushing harder and harder against her hand and her mouth. She pressed further until I felt the knuckles of her petite hand slide all the way inside me. She was fucking me with her whole fist!

I threw my head back and grunted like a wild boar. I no longer wanted her gentle touch. I wanted her to ram her fist into me and suck on my swollen button while I flooded her mouth with my erotic juices. I could feel my orgasm building, but I fought it. This was too good. I just wanted another minute in symbiotic union with this beautiful woman.

Jasmine must have sensed what I was up to, because what she did next sent me over the edge. She reached underneath me with her other hand, now thoroughly oiled with my juices running down my legs, and began circling my anus with her middle finger. This was something else I'd never experienced. Far from being dirty or disgusting, it raised my passion to an entirely new level.

I could tell from Jasmine's delicate touching of my rosebud that she wasn't sure if I wanted to be touched there, but I soon answered her question. I pushed my ass down hard in my chair, pushing the tip of her finger into my opening. Sensing my newfound inhibition, Jasmine slowly worked her finger deeper into my rosebud until it was just past the second knuckle.

My Gawd! The feeling of being fucked on two ends, with my clitoris being sucked and flicked was simply too much. My orgasm washed over me like a tidal wave. I screamed Jasmine's name at the top of my lungs while I pushed my entire vulva as hard as I could into her face, fist, and finger. I could feel the gush of my juices exploding all over her pretty face as I squirted one after another jet of cum into her waiting mouth. My orgasm must have lasted a full minute as I had one hard contraction after another. I could actually feel my pussy and anus clamping down on Jasmine with each contraction.

As my contractions finally began to subside and eventually stop, Jasmine remained perfectly still with my clit still twitching in her mouth, her hands in my most private parts. When my breathing returned to normal and I slumped in my chair, she slowly pulled her hand and fingers from within me. It was the most delicate and intimate thing I had ever experienced. I could sense Jasmine's connection to me, as if she were saying how she enjoyed the experience almost as much as I had.

I never felt so cherished and uplifted in my entire life. I wanted to kiss her and taste my juices in her mouth while I reciprocated with my own delicate touch. I was already thinking about how I'd like to use my private boudoir for the rest of the night...

VOLUME TWO

THE DARK ROOM

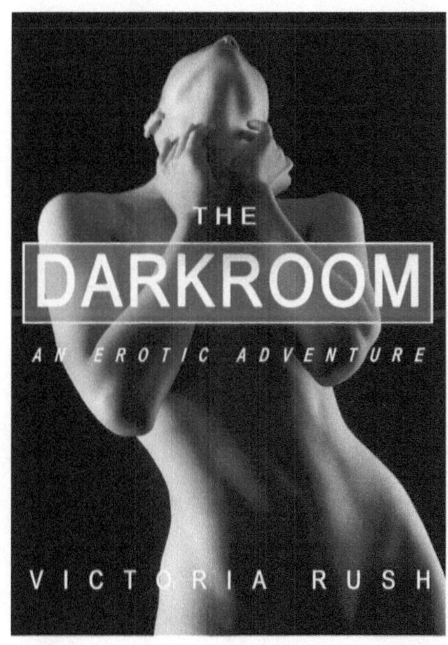

1

IN THE SHADOWS

After my exhilarating experience at The Dinner Party, I was ready for more sexual exploration. The idea of being watched and watching other people releasing our inhibitions in a group setting was incredibly erotic. There was something about being with strangers that took the encounter to an entirely new level.

But it was more than that—it was the *anonymity* that made it especially appealing. With my mask on, I felt empowered to try new things, to do things I would never do in my regular guise. It was like I had superpowers. With my identity hidden, I could try anything, and the results were equally surprising. The sexual feelings were stronger and the climaxes were more powerful than anything I'd experienced before.

I wanted more. But I also wanted something different. I wanted to stretch my boundaries to see how far my new powers of sexual expression could take me. What other exotic destinations might I discover in the erotic underworld?

One day late at night, I sat down in front of my computer and typed in the search words 'anonymous group sex'. Among a litany of listings for gay bathhouses, swingers parties, and wife-swapping groups, I found a cryptic heading on the bottom of the second page, reading *The Dark Room: Explore Your Sensuality*. I clicked on the link and a video opened with a naked dancer undulating under the mesmerizing effect of black and white zebra-like stripes illuminated on her body.

I watched, transfixed, as the light patterns flowed over every sensuous curve of her body. In the background, soft instrumental music added to the trance-like effect. The alternating dark and light patches provided just enough camouflage to mask her identity. But as the light parts moved over different areas of her physique, they briefly revealed her erogenous zones. The curve of her shapely breasts, a fleeting glimpse of her bare nipple, the glorious cleft in her tight round ass. She was completely naked, but I had to look carefully to recognize the naughty parts.

And what a sight it was to behold. As the illuminated stripes curved and stretched around every contour of her body, they accentuated her gorgeous figure. When she moved closer to the screen and briefly revealed her face, it had the same effect. I could see the fullness of her lips and the sensuous curve of her cheekbones. But the light never stayed in one place long enough to betray her identity, even if someone knew who was hidden behind the unusual light effects.

Now this was something completely different, I thought. *Erotic, stimulating, and anonymous.*

But where were her playmates?

As exciting as I imagined it might be to dance naked under the relative obscurity of these light effects, it would be infinitely *more* fun to participate actively with others in such a room. I scanned the webpage and noticed a heading in the menu at the top of the page titled 'Group Packages'. I clicked the link and three more video thumbnails appeared on the page: one labeled 'Men', one titled 'Women', and another marked 'Mixed'. I tapped on the first one, and another video started playing, showing multiple figures gyrating to the music.

This time, the light-projections were in different colors, shifting and bending around the moving figures like a psychedelic kaleido-scope. The bodies were masculine, with broad shoulders, muscled chests, and washboard stomachs. Occasionally, the men would brush up against one another and move their hips in a feigned anal inter-course motion, but the action was too slow and measured to be real. And the camera never strayed far below the subjects' bellybuttons, so it was impossible to tell if they were actually aroused. Even though they occasionally embraced in lip lock, it all seemed staged and dispassionate, like strippers putting on a show in a dance club.

I wasn't much interested in watching gay sex anyway, even with buff Chippendale characters such as these, so I clicked the next video thumbnail labeled 'Women'. This was definitely more my thing, and I could feel the stirring in my pussy as I reflected back on my last lesbian encounter at The Dinner Party. The video began with three slim and shapely women dancing sensuously under a new light effect. Instead of black and white alternating zebra stripes, this time the illuminated light resembled streaking raindrops.

The effect was even more captivating than the previous videos. Like an animated expressionist painting, the streaks danced across every curve and valley of the women's bodies as they swayed their hips and torsos in tantalizingly rhythmic ways. I had to concentrate even harder to catch fleeting glances of their breasts, nipples, and midsections, with the light patches even sparser than before.

At least in the women's videos, the camera panned below their waists to highlight the resplendent shape of their hips and buttocks. I strained to recognize the telltale protrusion of their mound or catch a glimpse of the mysterious slit between their legs. But as my pussy began to moisten imagining what was hidden behind the dancing raindrops splashing across their figures, the models never bent in such a way to reveal anything explicit.

Maybe this was the intention of the producers—to tease our interest just enough so we'd want to click for more information, leading to some kind of sale. This was, after all, the tried and true model for virtually every porn site—to show the viewer just enough to get them worked up until they were horny enough to pay for the real thing. Although in this case, I was still confused as to what the 'real thing' was this website was selling.

Was it just beautiful videos, orchestrated to appear as legitimate art? Were they just trying to sell me a fancy video version of a self-portrait that I could share with my husband or partner? That might be intriguing, but I was looking for more. As I continued watching the video, the three women moved closer to one another, eventually rubbing their hips and torsos together like in the all-male video. But this time, I could see their lower bodies as they caressed one another.

I watched them rub their hips and breasts together as the light streaks raced across their erect nipples. They were kissing one another far more sensuously than the men, like they were really losing themselves in the moment. It was definitely a turn-on and I imagined myself in the mix, caressing their beautiful bodies in the darkness with the streaks of light providing fleeting glimpses of their figures. As I thought about what it would feel like to have a stranger stroking my body in the dark, I slipped my fingers under my panties and began to play with my clit. But just as the action started flowing in the video, the clip suddenly ended.

Fuck! I screamed. *Just as I was getting turned on! Even a normal porno is better than this. At least they go all the way and offer some release.*

I was tempted to divert to my favorite porn site and watch some good lesbian tribbing action to get off when I noticed the last video thumbnail on the screen, labeled 'Mixed'. At least *this* one, if it was real, would be hard to hide the state of arousal that heterosexual men would experience in the presence of sexy naked women—light or no light.

I clicked on the icon, and the last video started to play. This time the light effects were in the form of multi-hued geometric circles, stretching and undulating over the curves of the naked figures like a rolling spirograph. I had to give it to the video producers—they were certainly creative in using unusual light effects that looked beautiful when projected onto shapely naked bodies.

And there was no denying that the bodies were gorgeous. Both the men and the women were firm and well-toned, with curves in all the right places. Every one of them was seriously fuckable. But much to my chagrin, the interaction between the subjects in the video once again seemed practiced and restrained. Even the men hardly seemed into it, rubbing and caressing their partners like in a cheesy black-and-white B-movie. The camera never strayed below their waistlines, but I didn't need to see their flaccid penises to recognize play acting when I saw it.

If this is what happens in these dark rooms, you can count me out, I thought.

It was all too antiseptic and 'soft-porn' for my liking. I wanted some *real* sex—actual *touching* and *penetration*—where I could feel myself and my dark room partners getting aroused and getting off. I didn't just want to be in some kind of frou-frou art production, I wanted to participate in a live orgy! I was about to click out of the website when a chat bubble popped up in the lower right corner. A text message appeared in the bubble.

'Hi!' someone named Sara wrote. 'How can I help you? Did you want to learn more about our products and services?'

Products and services? Maybe it's worth investigating this a little further after all. Let's see what other 'services' they have to offer...

2
———

EYES WIDE SHUT

'How can I participate in these dark rooms?' I typed in the chat window.

'If you come to our studio,' Sara replied, 'you can join any room of your choosing at any time.'

Studio? This was sounding more and more like some kind of photography service to me.

'How many people will be in the rooms with me?' I typed.

'That depends what time of the day and week you come. Friday and Saturday nights are busiest, but we also schedule sessions during the day, between 2:00 and 4:00 p.m. You can book a session by clicking on the tab for Appointments at the top of the page. We normally only have two or three people in the afternoon rooms and up to ten maximum on Friday and Saturday nights.'

The word *sessions* was beginning to sound more intriguing to me. I decided to probe for more information.

'What kind of clothing should I wear in these sessions?' I asked.

'You can wear anything that makes you feel comfortable, but most of our patrons choose to wear a minimum of accoutrements.'

'Including nothing at all?'

'Yes—if that's what makes you feel most comfortable.'

I loved how Sara kept dancing around the obvious question.

'How do the people in these dark room sessions typically *interact*?' I typed.

'That depends on what you're looking for and the kind of people that join you in the room.'

I hesitated for a moment before typing my reply.

'Is *touching* permitted?'

'Absolutely. That's what makes the experience particularly enjoyable. You're encouraged to explore each other's bodies in the privacy and safety of the dark room. Subject to the consent of each partner, of course.'

Now we're talking, I thought. Exploring each other's bodies was exactly what I was looking for. But I still had lots of questions pertaining to the privacy and safety parts.

'What if I don't want somebody to touch my body? How can I ensure my personal space will be respected?'

'We have a simple rule for everybody entering any of our dark rooms. All you have to do is brush someone's body away if you don't wish to be touched. Everyone is issued a safety bracelet before entering each room. If you feel threatened or forced to do anything against your will, all you have to do is press the alert button and an audio intercom will be activated. Any violators will be immediately removed from the room. You can ask for help at any time, but we rarely receive complaints from any of our patrons.'

I paused to let Sara's comments sink in. I liked the safeguards they had set up, but I didn't like the sound of audio recordings or being leered at by a bunch of security guards.

'What kind of privacy will I have? Will any audio or video recordings be made while I'm in any of the rooms?'

'Never,' Sara said. 'What goes on in the security of the dark rooms is between you and your consenting partners.'

I liked the sound of that.

'What about the video clips on your website?' I asked. 'Those were obviously recorded. Were those actual participants?'

'Those were paid actors, using our own models. I assure you, you will never be recorded while in one of our dark rooms.'

'What about your security personnel or anyone outside the room? Can they see what's happening inside?'

'Each dark room is enclosed in one-way glass all around,' Sara replied. 'You can't see out, but outside observers can see in. This allows patrons to observe the action in the room before committing to go inside. We find this adds to the excitement level for both those watching and those being watched. But the light effects in the room are always moderated in such a way to ensure your identity will be masked. The only thing outside observers can see, including our security staff, are the silhouettes of the people inside.'

Oh my god, I thought. *That sounds so hot.*

The idea of being watched, both within the room and from outside the room, while I got down and dirty with my dark room partners sounded incredibly stimulating. I suddenly became aware of how soaked my panties had become as I continued the dialog with Sara.

'What about...*hygiene*?' I asked tentatively. 'What protections do I have against the spread of diseases?'

Sara and I finally seemed to be talking about the same thing. I decided to dispense with any further niceties and cut right to the chase.

'Every dark room participant must provide a recent blood test from an accredited medical lab,' she replied. 'You must report negative for all known sexual or communicable diseases. You'll also need to submit to a brief exam with our accredited medical doctor on staff to ensure you do not have any open sores or infections that could be spread by physical contact. This is for the safety of all participants.'

Holy shit, these guys don't fool around. A gynecological exam is never fun, but if it's performed by a real doctor and it's not too intrusive, it's better to be safe than sorry.

'Will the exam be performed by a gynecologist? Is the doctor male or female? May I ask for his or her credentials before I submit to the examination?'

'It will be with a female gynecologist for female examinations and a male urologist for male examinations. Their credentials will be on display in the examining office, which is also maintained with the utmost hygienic cleanliness. The examination is external only and very brief.'

Okay, I thought. *Now that we know exactly what we're talking about here, let's get down to brass tacks.*

'What are your fees? And is this...you know, *legitimate*? I mean, it sounds like I'm paying for sex.'

Sara paused for a moment before replying.

'This is a private club in a private residence. Whatever consenting adults choose to do with each other on private property is entirely legal. There is a modest subscription fee to join the club. You can see our fees under the tab marked Rates.'

It was all starting to come together. Just like The Dinner Party erotic club I attended a few weeks ago, they had similar terms of service. In fact, their professionalism and attention to detail made me wonder if it might be run by the same operators. I just had a few remaining questions.

'Are there separate rooms for men and women?' I asked. I was definitely ready for some more girl-on-girl action, but I wasn't ready to rule out a little hetero fun too if the mood struck me.

'We have separate rooms for men-only, women-only, and mixed gender. You may enter the single-gender room that matches your sex and also the mixed gender room, if you so wish, during your visit.'

I was definitely getting more interested by the moment and based on how fast the wet patch between my legs was spreading in my tight jeans, so was my aching pussy.

I wondered if there'd be any equipment to recline onto if things got hot and heavy enough.

'Are there places to relax in each of the rooms, or are they standing room only?' I typed.

'There is small upholstered furniture in each of the rooms, as well as Liberator sex cushions to adjust your position. Everything has neon piping around the edges to help you find it in the dark, and the coverings are laundered after each session to ensure cleanliness. Your safety and comfort is our universal goal.'

Wow, I thought. *These guys have thought of everything.*

This obviously wasn't going to be some kind of seedy swingers' party where just anybody could walk in and fuck anything that moves. This sounded like a first-class operation that was sure to titillate and satisfy all my senses.

I paused as I considered any other questions or concerns that I might have before venturing out to their club.

'How long can I remain in each room?' I said. 'And when I wish to leave, where can I go to freshen up and get dressed?'

'We have separate change rooms and showers for both men and women. Strobe lights are used in these and other public rooms of the residence to protect your identity at all times. From the moment you enter any of our dark rooms to the moment you leave the building, no one will be able to identify you. The only person who'll ask for ID is the doctor who examines you. He or she will verify your blood report belongs to you and the physician is sworn by doctor-patient privilege to maintain your privacy.'

I unconsciously exhaled a long deep breath as I began to relax. All my concerns had been addressed and all my expectations were satisfied. This was the perfect outlet I was looking for.

'Thank you for being patient with all my questions,' I typed. 'I'll check your rates and schedules and book a session in the near future.'

'It's been my pleasure,' Sara said. 'I hope our club satisfies all of your desires. Feel free to chat again if you have any more questions. See you soon!'

Satisfy my desires, indeed. I had no doubt that it would. But right now, I needed some satisfaction that no one else could give me.

I tore off my leggings and threw them on the floor as I reached into my nightstand for my favorite rabbit vibrator. Then I turned the rotating beads and rabbit ears on maximum and plunged the dildo into my aching pussy, moaning in delight as I imagined the pleasures that awaited me in the mysterious dark room.

3

———————

FOREPLAY

As I thrust the vibrator deep inside my snatch, I watched the all-girl dark room video on continuous loop. I was absolutely hypnotized by the swirling light effects rolling over their luscious bodies. Whenever the streaks illuminated their bare nipples and mounds, it made the effect all the more electrifying. My pussy made sexy slurping sounds as my juices sopped up the slick dildo sliding in and out of my hole.

I moaned like a dog in heat thinking about what it would be like to watch and touch these women in a *real* dark room. This experience would take my Dinner Party adventure to a whole new level. Instead of just sitting and watching passively while other people did things to me, in these spaces I could participate actively with whomever I pleased. My mind raced with all the things I wanted to do with these women—and maybe even some of the men in the mixed room. I wanted to fuck and be fucked by these mysterious apparitions.

When the women in the video started touching one another and rubbing their nipples together, I lifted my hips off the bed and thrust the vibrator deeper inside me. I angled the shaft so the oscillating tip massaged my G-spot, while I pushed the fluttering rabbit ears hard against my swollen nub. I could feel my orgasm building and I opened my mouth to kiss one of the models in the video as she did the same. When the tide finally swept over me, I clamped down hard over the pulsing vibrator and spasmed a long stream of powerful contractions.

I hadn't cum this hard since Jasmin had jilled me under the dinner table at the Dinner Party retreat. As I lay on the bed rolling my hips in post-orgasmic bliss, I closed my eyes and imagined myself dancing with the geometric light effects projected on my body. For a thirty-six-year-old, I still had a pretty damn fine figure with a tight ass, perky breasts, and a yoga-toned stomach. I wouldn't be the only one in the dark room admiring the physiques of my fellow participants.

I pulled the vibrator out of my pussy and stood up to admire myself in my full-length dressing mirror. I began to sway my hips and caress my breasts like the women in the video. I looked pretty good, but something was missing. I turned off the bedroom light and closed the drapes, then opened the bathroom door just enough to emit a thin sliver of light. I moved back from the mirror until the ray of light projected a narrow beam on my body.

It wasn't nearly as fancy as the light effects shown in the dark room videos, but it was enough to make me imagine I was there. I experimented with different positions as I watched the light illuminate different parts of my body in the darkness of my bedroom. Just as in the videos, it was fascinating to see how I could briefly reveal the naughty parts by moving in and out of the light. It was almost as exciting to watch my own body as it was the models in the video, and I began to caress my curves like a stripper in a dance club.

I'll have to work on my technique, I thought, analyzing my moves.

I had to be as irresistible as the models in the video if I hoped to attract the attention of men and women with similarly toned bodies.

But that can wait for later.

Right now, the only thing I could think about was booking an appointment for a dark room session as soon as possible. My vibrator, as entertaining as it was, would be no match for the real thing. I sat down again in front of my computer and clicked on the tab marked Rates.

Let's see if I have to pay an arm and a leg to touch some of these arms and legs.

It wasn't as bad as I imagined. There was a one-time subscription fee of $300, plus another $200 for each session. *Seems reasonable,* I thought. The gyno exam alone would cost that much or more in a regular doctor's office. Two hundred bucks for two hours or more of safe, titillating sex with multiple partners seemed like a bargain.

"Sign me up!" I thought out loud, clicking the tab for Appointments.

A registration page opened where they asked me to create an account. I paused for a moment as I considered my next move. I could use an alias and a fake email account, but I knew they'd also want a credit card to pay for the subscription.

So much for nobody knowing my identity other than the doctor who'll examine me.

I looked further down the page and saw a disclaimer promising that my email and credit information wouldn't be shared with anyone else, and that I wouldn't be sent any marketing information other than the confirmation of my appointment.

What the fuck, I said to myself. *Anybody running an internet business these days knows the surest way to lose customers is to share someone's online details without consent. Besides, I reveal a lot more personal financial information when I pay bills and do my banking online—this is pretty minor in comparison.*

I filled in the required fields to complete my registration, then scanned the schedule for available sessions. All the Friday and Saturday nights on the booking calendar were grayed out for the next three weeks.

This place is popular, I thought. *I guess that's a good sign.*

I imagined that meant most sessions would be pretty full and that I'd have my pick of partners to choose to engage with. I remembered Sara saying the daytime sessions were not as busy as the night sessions, so I clicked on the first available weekday. A new window opened indicating that I was about to reserve an afternoon session for the indicated date, then it asked me to fill in the credit card information to complete the transaction. I filled in the required details then clicked the Submit button. After about ten seconds of processing time, a window popped up from my email account confirming the payment and appointment.

Well, that's it, I thought. *I'm committed now.*

I could feel the blood flowing back into my pussy as my mind already started going where I'd been fantasizing for the last hour. I stood up and positioned myself again in the sliver of light emanating from the washroom.

Damn girl, I thought, admiring my figure as my fingers strayed down toward my warm cunny. *This is going to be fun...*

4

<hr>

PEOPLE IN GLASS HOUSES

On my appointment day, I could barely contain my excitement. I drove out to the address provided in my email confirmation and was pleasantly surprised when I arrived at the destination. As with my previous experience at the dinner party, the facility was in a large country chateau. Just like the last place, I had to provide my registration username and password to be permitted access through the security gate. I drove up the long tree-lined driveway to an even larger mansion than before.

If this was any indication of the step up in the level of services that awaited me, I was all-in. I parked my car alongside five or six other cars in the guest parking section and walked over a cobblestone path up to the front door. I tapped on the large brass door knocker and was greeted a few seconds later by an attractive young woman in a smart business suit.

I guess there'll be no naked attendants in masquerade masks this time around, I frowned. *Maybe this place is run by a different operator, after all.*

Nevertheless, the interior appointments and finishings were on a par with the previous home, and I was eager to explore its special rooms.

"You must be Jade," the woman said, taking my coat and hanging it in the closet. "My name's Ali, and I'll be your host for the evening. Can I get you something to drink? Coffee, tea, a glass of wine?"

I was pretty charged up already and thought a bit of alcohol would help relax some of the inhibitions I was beginning to feel about getting naked with a group of strangers.

"I'd love a glass of white wine if you have it, thank you."

Ali motioned to an adjoining room with large French doors.

"Feel free to relax in our waiting room," she said, handing me a piece of paper and a pen. "If you can take a few moments to review and sign this waiver, this will help ensure our expectations are aligned. I'll be back in a few minutes."

I walked into a beautiful room with tall Palladian windows and sat down on the large leather sofa. I quickly reviewed the document, which was mostly concerned with the rules of engagement in the dark rooms. Only women were permitted in the women's dark room it said, and only men were permitted in the men's dark room, but they could commingle in the mixed room. It reiterated the 'golden rule' about touching others only with consent. A simple brush of the hand or step back from an advancing partner indicated that you did not wish to be touched. Any violators would be immediately removed from the room and banned from using the facility in future. I signed the document with my alias Jade and placed it face-up on the coffee table.

I noticed some picture books lying on the table with familiar photos of naked people illuminated with similar light effects to the videos I'd watched earlier. I opened one of the books and flipped through the pages as I admired the beautiful figures of the models and the different light effects displayed in each image.

I hope the people in my dark room will be as pretty as these, I thought, feeling my panties start to dampen again.

A minute later, Ali returned with a large glass of wine, setting it down on the coffee table.

"I see you've been familiarizing yourself with our light productions," she said, noticing the open book laid out in front of me. "Did you have any questions before I take you to the viewing room?"

Viewing room? The voyeur in me liked the sound of that.

"So I'll have a chance to watch some of the dark rooms before I choose to enter one?" I asked.

"Of course," Ali said. "That's part of the fun. All of our dark rooms can be observed from the outside through one-way glass. You'll be able to watch the participants but they won't be able to see you. Most of our patrons find this to be a stimulating experience that helps put them in the mood. If you like what you see, you can then proceed to the doctor's office for a brief exam, after which you're welcome to enter your appointed rooms. Did you bring your lab test report with you?"

"Yes—of course," I said, fishing in my purse for the blood test.

Ali held up her hand to save me the trouble.

"Bring it with you and show it to the doctor when she examines you. Are you ready to head downstairs?"

"Absolutely," I said, pleased that just as Sara had promised earlier, no one had yet asked for anything that could reveal my identity.

"Allow me to escort you, then. Would you like to leave your wine glass here or bring it with you?"

"I think it's better that I leave it here. Something tells me that I'm going to need my hands free for other things."

Ali simply smiled and nodded. I followed her out of the sitting room and across a marbled foyer, where we paused at the top of a declining circular stairway.

"Our dark rooms are in the lower level, where we can control the light more effectively. There are three exits, including a direct exit to the guest parking area. You may leave at any time, or return to the main floor if you need further help."

Ali reached into one of her pockets and handed me a black wristband.

"This is your security bracelet. Please wear it at all times until you leave the building. If you feel uncomfortable at any time, all you have to do is press this button on the side of your bracelet and a security agent will come to your assistance immediately. But I think you'll find it will be quite unnecessary. Our patrons are very respectful of the stipulated rules. I believe you'll find the experience very safe and satisfying."

I nodded my head as I fastened the bracelet buckle behind my wrist.

Ali escorted me down the stairs and opened a door at the base of the steps. A white strobe light and soft instrumental music emanated through the open portal.

"It may take you a few moments to get comfortable with the flashing light, but this will protect your identity while you stay on the lower level. The light is sequenced in such a way to allow you to find your way around while also maintaining your anonymity. Each of the exits are clearly marked, as is the entrance to the doctor's office and the change rooms."

She motioned to three large glass cubes in the center of the cavern.

"Each of the dark rooms is marked according to gender. Which room would you like to see first?"

"Um..." I said, hesitating for only a moment. "I think I'd like to see the women-only room first."

Ali gently grasped my hand and escorted me to the first glass-enclosed cube. It was much larger than it appeared from the other side of the room, measuring roughly twenty feet square on each side and ten feet tall. Inside the floor-to-ceiling glass panels, I could see the familiar movement of furtive figures illuminated under the kaleidoscopic light. The rest of the room was pitch black so the only things illuminated by the projected light were the moving bodies.

I unconsciously moved closer to the glass, captivated by the swirling light effects and soft music. This wasn't some cheesy strip club with pounding music and bright lights illuminating a gaudy stage. The soft instrumental music combined with the pretty light effects projected a feeling of real class. My eyes widened as I watched the naked participants move around inside the room.

Just as in the video, they were swaying their bodies and caressing each other. But there was something different this time. Their hands and bodies were no longer touching each other with fleeting, artificial gestures. This time, they *lingered* and *probed* one another. Their action looked *purposeful*, not like the play acting in the video. Near the front of the glass, two women were locked in a tight embrace, passionately kissing and grinding their hips together in familiar motion. I could see their buttock muscles flexing as they rubbed their mounds together under the swirling light.

My eyes raced around the inside of the enclosure as I took it all in. In the far corner of the cube, I noticed some neon piping tracing the outline of a large sofa. I squinted my eyes to decipher a commingled figure twisting together as the geometric lights swept over a mass of tangled arms and legs. At first, it looked like a single person doing some kind of yoga movement, with her leg stretched over her shoulder. But as I looked more closely, I could see that the raised leg belonged to a woman lying on the sofa with her legs splayed apart. Another woman was resting on her knees, squatting between the prone woman's legs, rubbing their vulvas together, fucking her with rapid swings of her hips while she clasped the prone woman's elevated leg tightly against her breasts.

I gasped audibly and slumped over, unconsciously mimicking the movement of the woman on top.

"Shall I leave you now to enjoy the show?' Ali said, somewhere to my side.

I'd completely forgotten she was still there. I turned and saw her familiar outline flashing beside me under the white strobe light.

"Yes, I'll be fine now," I said, catching my breath and trying to sound composed.

"Wonderful," she said. "You're welcome to remain outside the rooms and watch as long as your session is booked, or enter your allotted rooms at your leisure. The entrance to the dark rooms is via the doctor's office, who'll validate your blood report and conduct a brief external exam before you move on. Remember that if you need help at any time, all you have to do is press the button on the side of your bracelet. I hope you enjoy your stay and that we'll see you again soon. Bye for now."

It was strange watching her talk as the white light flashed over her face. I could see her lips open and close in delayed jerky movements that didn't synchronize with her speech. It was a bit disconcerting and nothing like the flowing movement of the light projected inside the dark room, but it was sexy and mysterious in its own way. Just as she and Sara had promised, it was impossible to recognize her face through the intermittent flashes.

"Thank you, Ali," I said. "I'll let you know if I need anything."

I was glad to see her leave, because my pussy was pounding and my crotch was soaked from watching the action in the cube. As soon as she closed the door leading to the stairs behind her, I unclasped the top button of my jeans and thrust my hand under my panties. My fingers immediately found my opening and I inserted three fingers as far as they'd go inside me while I rubbed my palm against my aching clit. It couldn't have taken more than ten seconds for me to cum hard in my jeans as I watched the women scissoring on the couch in the dark room.

It was difficult to see the expressions on their faces under the shifting light, but I noticed the mouth of the woman on top widen as her movements became increasingly frenetic. Then she suddenly stopped and arched her back as she pulled her partner's elevated leg against her torso and spasmed her body in obvious climax. I longed to be there with them, feeling what they were feeling and listening to their moans of ecstasy as their love juices washed over one another.

After I came down from my orgasm, I suddenly became aware that I wasn't the only one standing outside the cube watching what was going on inside. I noticed another figure standing about five feet to my side, and I glanced in her direction. The flashing light showed just enough to reveal a pretty woman with long hair and high cheekbones. Although I'd never recognize her in the plain light of day, her full lips and gently sloping jawline betrayed her beauty. I glanced down at her body and noticed the bulge of her full breasts in her blouse and the curvature of her hips and ass in her tight jeans.

I blushed in the dark thinking that she might have noticed me rubbing myself in the dark like some kind of creepy flasher. But she just peered at me and smiled.

"Pretty hot, huh?" she said, in a soft, sexy voice.

"Yeah," was all I could manage to pant.

"Are you going in?" she asked, matter-of-factly.

"Definitely," I said.

"Perhaps I'll see you in a few minutes then. I'm going to watch for a little longer to get my nerve up."

"Enjoy," I said, imagining her getting just as turned on as I did watching the action in the cube. Sara was right—it was almost as much fun *watching* the action as participating in it. But I was eager to feel the touch of another woman and experience the hypnotic light effects first-hand.

But those aren't the only body parts I'll be using, I thought as I headed toward the examining room.

5
____

INTO THE LIGHT

The gyno exam wasn't as bad as I anticipated, though it was pretty embarrassing walking into the examining room with a big wet patch in the crotch of my jeans. The doctor didn't bat an eyelash and simply asked me to disrobe and lie down on the examining table. The whole thing was over in a couple of minutes.

She examined me for any sign of open sores then reviewed my lab test and checked my driver's license to verify the report. Fortunately, I'd made a recent visit to my aesthetician to clean things up down below. My smooth pussy was bald and spotless, which made the examination all the faster and easier.

When she was done, she handed me a note with a number and a key code then directed me through a door leading into the women's change room. As with the other public sections of the lower level, a soft strobe light permeated the change room. In between the flashes, I could see a few women in various stages of undress going about their business in the locker room, but I paid them no attention. Part of me wanted to search for the pretty woman who I'd chatted with briefly outside the women's dark room, but I decided it was best to respect everyone's privacy. There'd be plenty of opportunity to engage more directly once I got inside the actual dark rooms.

I located a bank of lockers with combination locks and pulled out the slip of paper the doctor had handed me. I matched the number on the slip with the corresponding locker and entered the code on the tumblers to undo the lock. Inside the locker, there was a freshly-laundered terrycloth robe and towel. I removed my clothes and placed my belongings inside the locker, then put the robe on and carried the towel to one of the shower stalls. I could still feel the vestiges of dried-up lubrication coating my inner thighs, and I wanted to be as clean and fresh as I could be going in to the dark rooms.

As I turned on the shower and stepped under its gentle spray, I reflected back to the video with the rain drop effect. I imagined myself dancing in the dark room as the light streaks flowed over my body, turning and bending my figure to reveal every sensuous curve. I opened a fresh bar of soap and rubbed the silky pod across my breasts, under my arms, and between my legs. My body felt electrified, and for a moment I was tempted to rub another one out, but I decided to save myself for the real thing. I didn't want anything tempering the pleasure that awaited me. I finished the shower, then dried myself off and returned my towel to my locker. I hesitated for a moment, deciding whether to hang my robe in my locker too, or wear it out into the open spaces of the lower level.

Screw it, I said, placing it on the hook. *This whole experience is about letting myself go and losing myself in the moment. Besides, between the strobe lights outside the dark rooms and the light show inside the rooms, no one will be able to recognize me anyhow.*

I closed the locker and scrambled the tumblers, making a mental note of my locker number and combination code. Then I walked out of change room into the open space of the lower level and looked around. It felt liberating to be stark naked in the cool air of the basement under the pulsating strobe lights.

Each of the three dark rooms were bathed with different colored and patterned light effects. On each side of the cubes, illuminated gender symbols clearly indicated who was inside. The glass cubes looked from a distance like a holographic dance show, with three different 'theaters' to choose from. I walked toward the cube displaying two familiar circle-and-cross symbols, knowing the all-girl show was what had initially attracted me to the program.

When I got closer to the cube, I noticed the light patterns inside had changed from when I viewed it earlier. This time, the patterns were in the form of orange and black spots, making the figures inside the room look like human-shaped leopards. I could make out four distinct figures inside the enclosure. Two of the women were quite slim, with tight ballerina figures. The other two were more voluptuous, with full breasts and wide, curving hips. But they all looked mouth-watering gorgeous, bathed in pretty feline leopard spots.

I was transfixed watching the women circle one another like prowling cats in the dark. It didn't take long for the figures to blend together and begin rubbing against one another. I stood spellbound as they huddled their bodies together like a group of leopards feasting over prey.

I want to be their prey, I thought, swaying my body in synchronization with the women.

I looked around the enclosure and didn't see anyone else standing in the flashing light, so I decided it was time to join the action inside the room. A sign on one side of the cube read Open. I ran my hand over the glass near the sign and felt a handle, pulling the glass door toward me. For a moment, the outside strobe light intermixed with the flowing orange spots inside the room, and I was conscious of how chaotic it suddenly appeared. I immediately closed the door and the one-way glass blocked out the outside light, returning the room to its flowing orange and black leopard motif.

By now, the four women in the room had paired off and seemed preoccupied with their partners, so I stood to the side and swayed my hips to the music as I watched the hypnotic movement of their bodies. The women circled around one another as if stalking each other. It was exciting to watch them play-act to the theme of the light show. But the acting soon turned more serious as the couples moved closer together and began rubbing their bodies together. Soon, their lips locked together and I could see them kissing passionately as the light and dark spots flowed over their faces.

I was dying to get in on the action, but I didn't want to interrupt their connection. As I watched their hands slide down each other's bodies, my hands mimicked their movement. When their hips briefly separated and their hands moved between each other's legs, so did mine. I was the odd woman out, but somehow I didn't mind. I could feel the juices flowing down my thighs as my pussy watered in sympathy with the gyrating couples.

I began circling my button and was just about to push my fingers into my slit when suddenly the light in the room was interrupted once again by someone opening the door. The shape of the body in the flashing light looked familiar, and I recognized the shoulder-length hair of the woman who'd stood beside me earlier. She closed the door, then paused for a moment as she looked around the room. Before long, she began walking in my direction then stopped about two feet in front of me. She smiled as the leopard spots flowed over her face and I suddenly felt weak at the knees once again.

Her body was even more beautiful in the buff than in her tight blouse and jeans. Her breasts were a full and firm, with a gentle ski-jump slope on the top. These were no fake balloon-shaped artificial tits—these were the real thing. I glanced further down and watched the leopard spots flowing over her hips as my mouth began to water. There was just enough light flowing over her pubic area to show that she was shaved bald like me. As she danced sensuously in front of me in the dark, her bare mound swayed slowly from side to side.

"My name's Emma," she said in a soft voice.

"Jade," was all I could reply, hypnotized by her beauty.

"Beautiful, isn't it?" she said, turning her face toward one of the couples locked in a passionate embrace.

"Stunning," I said, happy the music was playing softly enough to engage in quiet conversation.

"You look like quite a tasty feline yourself," Emma said.

"You too," I replied lamely.

Emma inched closer toward me, until we were about six inches apart. I could see her looking directly into my eyes as she smiled sexily at me.

"May I?" she asked.

I wasn't sure exactly what she had in mind, but whatever she wanted to do with me, I was game.

"Please," I panted.

She closed the remaining distance and I could feel her breasts push against mine as she locked lips with me. A jolt shot through my body as if I'd been lit on fire. I could feel the heat of her body and the perspiration on our chests as our breasts slid sensuously over one another. She slipped her tongue between my lips and I sucked on hers as we swirled our tongues together. Our hips met and we gently ground our mounds together. When she moaned in my mouth, I practically came from the passion of the moment.

There was something electrifying about being in the dark with a perfect stranger, our bodies pressed together, with these mysterious and beautiful light effects highlighting the curves and shadows of our bodies. I could feel my nipples hardening, and we separated for a moment as we tweaked them together, watching the orange spots highlighting our swollen tips.

I was hypnotized by the sights and sounds and I could feel the juices in my pussy building by the moment as they began to run down the inside of my thighs toward my knees. As if reading my thoughts, Emma's right hand began tracing a line down the side of my waist and curved over my hips toward my love box. I quivered as her hand got closer to my pussy. When she finally slipped her fingers into my cleft and traced them slowly up toward my clit, I gasped out loud.

"Yes," I exhaled onto her bare shoulder as I slumped my body against hers. I wanted her to plunge her fingers deep into me and bring me to a quick orgasm. There would be plenty of time to experiment with other things and for me to return the favor in a moment. Right now, I desperately needed to get off.

She inserted two fingers further inside me and stroked my G-spot, and our mouths joined together once again. Our tongues swirled and sucked one another while she caressed my insides. But her palm remained stubbornly fixed in place over my mound. I wanted her to move her hand over my aching clit, and I swiveled my hips in a vain attempt to create more friction. But Emma seemed to be holding back, savoring the moment, as if intentionally denying my pleasure.

"Let's move to the sofa," she said, taking her hand out of my pussy and weaving her fingers between mine as she led me to the neon-outlined rectangle at the far edge of the cube. I hardly even noticed the other women as we walked straight by them, my head was so swimming in anticipation of what Emma wanted to do with me on the sofa.

When we got to the neon lines marking the perimeter of the couch, she gently pushed me down onto its surface. When my buttocks rested on the cushion, she kneeled down beside me and kissed me hard on the lips while lowering me slowly onto the couch. Emma lay on her side beside me while she ran her left hand over my breasts and stomach, then she leaned in and sucked my erect nipples. It felt incredible and I hoped she'd soon move lower and administer the same kind of action on my aching clit.

But she seemed content with running her hands over me as she explored every curve and crevasse of my body. When her hand passed over my bare mound, I lifted one of my legs to permit freer access to my pulsating cunny. Instead, she swept her arm under my knee and pulled my other leg up until both legs were pointed straight up in the air. Then she stopped kissing me and lowered her face closer to my hips.

Finally! I thought. She's going to give me attention where I most needed it—in my aching pussy.

She positioned herself behind my exposed ass, then spread my legs apart until they formed a bent V-shape, with my thighs resting against my chest. My entire vulva was now exposed to her and I could feel my wetness trickling down my perineum toward my anus.

Now, Emma, I screamed inside. *Suck my aching twat,* I begged. *Take me into your mouth and lick my clit like you were playing with my tongue earlier. Slip your fingers inside me and fuck my twat like there's no tomor-*

row. Because right now, time is standing still and I'm not sure there's going to be another tomorrow.

Emma paused, and I lifted my head to look in her direction. She looked up at me and smiled with a mischievous grin as the leopard spots flowed over her pretty face. Then she lifted herself up and positioned her hips over top of mine as she rested her thighs on top of mine and slowly lowered her vulva until it touched mine. The feeling when our pussies touched was indescribable.

We were both aflame in passion and soaked through and through between our legs. I could feel her labia interlacing with mine in a different kind of lip lock, and I threw my head back against the sofa cushion in utter ecstasy. I began rubbing my cunt furiously against hers, listening to the sound of our juices commingling as they slurped and sloshed in glorious union. It was dirty and raunchy and sexy, and something I'd been longing to try ever since my last lesbian encounter at the Dinner Party.

Just when I thought it couldn't get any more intense, Emma shifted forward a few inches and our clits suddenly touched.

"Fuck, yes!" I cried out loud as our eyes locked in the strange orange and while shifting lightness.

Her face looked exquisite as we began to grind our pussies together and she fucked me harder. I could feel the hardness of her clit as it flicked and over mine, and I moaned in blissful abandon. I felt the ache deep in my core beginning to build, but I wasn't ready to cum yet. I wanted to savor this moment and play with Emma on the precipice of pleasure as long as I could make it last.

Emma leaned forward and began to kiss me passionately as she began fucking my gaping hole more vigorously. We both moaned into each other's mouths as we savored the union of our most private parts in the soft orange light. Suddenly, Emma lifted her face above mine and moaned an otherworldly sound. I felt a gush of liquid spraying against my open pussy, filling me with her juices. Emma was squirting her wetness against me while she came hard between my legs. Any chance of holding back my orgasm any longer quickly evaporated as I fell over the cliff, spasming a long serious of hard contractions against Emma's sex. While our bodies jerked and spasmed at the height of pleasure, we watched each other gasp and moan in the swirling lightscape.

When our climactic contractions finally subsided, Emma collapsed onto my body and kissed me softly on my lips. For the longest time, we simply lay on our sides with our legs intertwined, kissing and giggling like two little girls.

"That was incredible," Emma whispered in my ear.

"We're not done yet," I said, smiling into her eyes. "This cat still has a lot more fight left in her."

6
____

OVER THE RAINBOW

Emma and I played for another hour or so in the women's dark room, experimenting with different positions and techniques, and we both came many more times. I was tempted to engage with some of the other women in the room, but I wanted to save myself for something else. I exchanged email addresses with Emma and we promised to stay in touch, then I exited the cube.

When I stepped back into the flashing light of the lower level, I glanced over at the men's room. There was something intriguing about watching men have sex with one another, and I was drawn to their shapes moving under a different kind of light effect. As I got closer to the enclosure, I noticed the light looked like little white tadpoles, swimming over the men's bodies while they moved about the room. Just as in all the other rooms, it was beautiful and hypnotic to watch.

Three men were facing each other near the front of the glass, grinding their hips together in a triangle formation. As they swayed their bodies, I could see they all had erections and were rubbing their cocks together in a coordinated frotting action. It was fun watching them slap their swords together like they were Three Musketeers in a playful fight.

Suddenly, the man nearest the glass knelt down and began licking the other two men's penises. It was incredibly erotic to watch him caress their hard-ons with his tongue and lips. It was hard to tell exactly how worked up the men on the receiving end of his ministrations were, but the little white tadpoles racing across their stomachs simulated the effect of sperm shooting out of their cocks.

Then the kneeling man moved up to the heads of their cocks and took both penises into his mouth. I'd heard of double penetration before, but this was an entirely different version from what I'd never seen. As the two men humped their hips slowly together, fucking the kneeling man's mouth, they began to kiss passionately. I was surprised how turned on I was getting watching the action, and I was soon ready to experience some dick of my own in the mixed room. As much as I enjoyed making love to Emma, sometimes all I wanted was a hard, throbbing cock pounding my pussy to its limits.

As I turned toward the cube housing the mixed-gender participants, my kitty beginning to tingle even more strongly. This time, the light effects stretched and curved around the figures in beautiful rainbow-colored stripes. I recognized three figures in the cube: one woman and two men. I stood entranced watching the colored stripes stretch and bend around their curves as they danced and rubbed their bodies together, much like the three men were doing in the men-only cube. But this time, the woman was sandwiched between the men as they bucked their hips against her from opposite sides.

I had to look closely to see their erections under the bands of light, but they were quite noticeable—and *large*. The man facing the woman's front side has his cock pressed up against her belly, while she stroked it sensuously with one of her hands. The man behind her had his tool between her legs and every time he swung his hips forward, I could see its head poke in and out under her mound. With her other hand, she caressed the underside of his cock and pressed it toward her opening. She turned her head and kissed the man behind her as the three engaged in an erotic tribal dance.

Not wanting to interrupt their concentration, my own hand fell to my crotch, and I began massaging my clit while I cupped and squeezed my breasts with my other hand. My mind raced ahead, thinking about all the different positions and permutations I could engage in with these three partners.

After a few minutes of erotic play, the man on the woman's backside angled his hips upward and the woman tilted her ass back to receive him. Their mouths opened in a silent moan as he slid his cock inside her. The man in front continued to hump the woman's belly, but now the woman had two hands free to clasp his cock and give him proper attention. As she and the man behind her rocked their hips together, the rainbow stripes slid over the other man's erection, making it look like a writhing anaconda.

How I wanted that cock inside me!

The movement of the man and the woman who were joined began to speed up and as I drooled from my soaking pussy, he slammed his hips against her ass, forcing her hands to move up and down on the other man's cock. She didn't need to do anything now, other than hold her hands tightly around his throbbing manhood. I was surprised how much of his organ I could see thrusting into the light, even with her grasping it hand-over-hand. It had to be at least nine inches long. As I inserted my fingers into my slit and began humping myself, I imagined directing it into my own quivering tunnel.

The three figures were now moving as one and their pace was accelerating toward an obvious climax. With one final thrust of his hips, the man in the rear slammed his cock deep inside the woman and pulled her hips toward his groin as he came inside her. I moaned out loud as my own climax rolled over me, our bodies heaving from the contractions consuming both of us. The man pulled his throbbing cock out of the woman's pussy and I could see it bobbing in the rainbow light as his seed coursed through his shaft. He leaned over and whispered something in the woman's ear, then left the room.

Now's as good a time as ever to make my entrance, I thought.

I figured I'd better get in there before the remaining couple got too hot and heavy. I wasn't sure if the man in front had come yet, but I sensed he wouldn't be disappointed to have *two* women in the enclosure giving him attention. I opened the door and stepped inside, and they turned toward me. The woman was still holding the man's dick in her hands, stroking it softly up and down. And he was still hard as a rock, in obvious need of satisfaction.

I walked up to the couple and without saying a word, I wrapped my hands around the woman's, feeling the heat emanating from the man's member. She released her hands to permit me freer access and I squeezed his pole tightly. It had to be at least six inches in circumference and even longer than I thought. I could feel him pulsating in my hands, and I leaned in to kiss him. He moaned softly as I flicked my thumb over his slick head, feeling his pre-cum leak onto my hand. The woman leaned forward and joined us in a three-way kiss while her hand cupped the man's balls.

I could feel his passion rising as the two of us gave him a glorious two-way handjob, but I wanted to save him for something else. There was no way I was going to let this beautiful cock go to waste by letting him cum in my hands. I began lowering myself, kissing his sculpted chest and washboard abs. His bush was neatly trimmed with just a bit of stubble on his pubis, and his balls were smooth as a baby's bottom. I really appreciated a man who shaved down there, especially one with such an impressive package.

When my head reached below his navel, I gobbled up the head of his tool like it was my last meal. I could only get about four inches of him inside my mouth, but I savored every bit of it with my swirling tongue. I hadn't sucked that many dicks in my life, but I knew a keeper when I saw one, and this was one spectacular johnson. While I sucked his manhood, the other woman moved behind him, squeezing his balls. Although maybe she was doing something *else* to him back there, because suddenly his hip movements escalated in urgency.

I didn't mind the idea of him cumming in my mouth, but I didn't want to siphon any of his virility before clamping another part of my body around his impressive python. I pulled my mouth off his cock and lifted myself up, licking his sweating torso with my open tongue. When I reached his face, I plunged my tongue into his mouth. The thrusting and swirling action left little doubt that I wanted to be properly fucked by him.

Screw the other girl, I thought. *She'd already gotten her piece of the action—now it was my turn.*

I turned around and began rubbing my slick ass against his dripping pole. Then I slipped his erection between my cheeks and shifted slowly up and down, giving it a tantalizing massage. He pulled back a little and grabbed his cock, trying to steer it into my anus, but I wasn't having any of that. Maybe later, if I was still in the mood, but right now I needed that throbbing monster inside my pussy. I wanted to feel him fucking me the old-fashioned way, filling me with his manhood, stimulating my G-spot, stretching me to the limit.

I reached between my legs and grabbed the sticky head of his prick and directed it toward my wet opening. He was only too happy to oblige, and after I poked it inside the front door, he slowly pushed it in all the way. I gasped at the thickness and depth of his intrusion as I clamped down on his throbbing meat like a bear trap. There was no way I was letting him escape until I was fully satisfied. He reached around and grabbed my tits with both hands, squeezing them gently while he thrust his shaft in and out of my love canal. I could feel my clitoral hood sliding back and forth over my nub as he pulled and stretched my labia with every thrust of his giant cock.

I could have easily come from this movement without any further stimulation, but as if reading my thoughts, the woman circled around and began rubbing her breasts against mine, heightening my ecstasy. As she kissed me passionately, I began moaning and grunting from the pleasure consuming me. My hands wrapped around her waist as I grasped her buttocks in each hand and pulled her toward me with each thrust of the man behind. We both panted in delight as we ground our pussies together.

Never had I felt such intense pleasure from so many different sensations at the same time. This was my first threesome, and it had already far exceeded my expectations. I would have been happy to come this way, sandwiched between two lovers, but perhaps sensing the newness of the experience for me, the woman pulled out of our lip lock and began to move her head down my body.

She cupped and played with my breasts, sucking and flicking my tender nipples with her soft, slippery tongue. I moaned, listening to the popping sound my erect nipples made when they slid in and out of her suckling mouth. I pulled her face into my chest, begging her to continue. But after a few minutes, she pulled away and moved lower. Slowly— tantalizingly—she kissed and nibbled her way down my body until she got to my soaking snatch. She paused and kissed it gently, then nibbled her way down the edges of my labia as the man slammed his cock in and out of me.

"Oh God!" I panted, practically fainting from the intensity of the pleasure building up inside me. The idea of being serviced on both ends by two different partners was driving me insane. I pushed my mound toward the woman's face and tilted my hips so my clit was level with her lips. When her tongue found my button and her lips surrounded me, I grabbed the back of her head with both hands and pulled her tightly toward me.

"Fuck, yes," I panted. "Fuck me," I shouted to no one in particular. I wanted to be fucked from both sides. *Fill me with your cock and flick me with your tongue,* I thought. *I want to soak you with my juices and feel you throbbing deep inside me.*

I slammed my mound into the woman's face and face-fucked her with all my energy as she sucked my clit into her mouth and rolled her tongue over its head. I was seconds away from having the strongest orgasm of my life.

"Yes—*yes!*" I screamed, as I bucked and whimpered from the intense pleasure racking my body. The man sensed I was about to come and I could feel his thrusting beginning to increase in intensity. I felt his hot breath on my back as he panted in unison with me. I looked down at the rainbow stripes washing over our thrashing bodies and closed my eyes, tilting my head back. This was as close to heaven as I could imagine.

When I was finally ready to come, I didn't hold anything back. I screamed like a wild animal, fucking the woman's face while the man slammed his python up inside me in a series of final rhythmic thrusts, spewing his honey inside me. I temporarily lost strength in my legs, but it didn't matter. The man's hard pole had me impaled like a cross, holding me suspended in the air as I gushed all over the woman's face.

When I finally stopped shaking and began to catch my breath, they both pulled away and turned to face me. We pressed together in a sublime three-way kiss, tasting each other's cum in our mouths. I opened my eyes and as I watched the spectrum of colors wash over our faces, and I couldn't help but smile.

I'd finally found my pot of gold at the end of the rainbow.

VOLUME THREE

PAINT ME

$$1$$

CREATIVE LICENSE

It had been weeks since I'd felt the live touch of another woman and I was beginning to feel restless. There was only so long I could go relying on my own devices for fulfillment, even with the help of live online partners. I needed to experience the excitement of a warm body next to me, one who responded to my touch just as I was to hers. I wanted to feel her hot breath on my skin, her moisture on my lips, and her moans in my ear.

One recent day after clearing through the checkout line at the grocery store, an intriguing poster caught my attention on the bulletin board near the exit. It had a photo of a buxom beauty dressed in a Wonder Woman costume with the headline *Looking for a New Adventure?* I stopped my cart and leaned in to admire the girl's curvy figure. Her uniform was so intricately detailed and form-fitting, it almost looked like it was painted on her. The stylized 'W' emblem on her chest arched over her firm breasts and her star-spangled briefs hugged every curve of her hourglass-shaped hips.

I'd never seen a woman in costume look so sexy and striking. As I squinted at the picture ogling her centerfold-perfect figure, I gasped when I recognized the telltale dimples and bulges on her body. At the edge of the black outline surrounding her chest emblem there were two raised nubs located in the center of each breast, and in the middle of her gold belt buckle was a little indentation right where her belly button should be. Even in the crotch of her tight blue shorts, I could make out the tiny appendage of her clitoris poking seductively between her splayed legs. I grasped the handle of my grocery cart, suddenly becoming weak at the knees.

That's not a uniform she's wearing, I thought. *She's naked! That costume is actually painted on her body!*

As I began reading the banner description to see what it was all about, my panties flooded with moisture:

Embrace your inner superhero—join our nude body painting workshop and experience the thrill of living out your wildest fantasies in the flesh. Explore your artistic side using the beautiful human form as your canvas. You can choose to be either the painter-voyeur or the model-exhibitionist. Bring a friend or partner up with one of our like-minded muses at our private studio. Either way, you'll find this to be an unparalleled experience. Find more details at nudebodypainting.com.

By the time I finished reading the ad, the front of my jeans was soaked with a giant wet spot. I found the idea of painting a beautiful naked body up close and having someone do the same to me incredibly arousing. If their customers looked anything like the Wonder Woman model, I couldn't wait to lay my brush—or my hands—on her naked body. This forum was a perfect fit with my graphic design skills. Except this time, I'd be exploring my passion for illustration with live brush and oil.

Holding my cart close to my hips to conceal the stain between my legs, I wheeled the buggy to my car and quickly drove home to gather more information about this intriguing class. When I opened the website, I was greeted with a gallery of colorful men and women bodypainted in a variety of themes. Some were covered in nature motifs with beautiful flowers and foliage covering every square inch of their bodies. Others appeared to be wearing professional uniforms that looked as authentic as the real thing. And there were plenty more superhero costumes, ranging from Batman and Superman to Catwoman and Elastagirl.

In every instance, the designs were so detailed and intricate that it was difficult to separate their naked private parts from the rest of their figures. Extra embellishment was added to their erogenous zones in a concerted effort to disguise their nudity. But as I zoomed in on each picture, it was impossible not to notice the little shadows betrayed by their bare nipples and navels. Most of the men appeared to be wearing a codpiece, but at least one brave model painted as *The Thing* let it all hang out with the creative placement of orange-colored stones coating his genitals.

As I scrolled further down the page viewing more pictures showing artists applying their brushes to the naked figures of their models, my panties clung to my rapidly moistening vulva. I imagined caressing my model's nipples with the soft brush hairs, watching them harden and elongate as I swirled the dye around her areolas. What a turn-on it must be to feel the wet oil being dabbled on the most private areas of your body! I slid my hand down my panties and rubbed my fingers along my slick lips, trying to imagine the sensation.

But I still had many questions about how the program worked. *What happens if the model gets excited while they're being painted? How could anyone not feel aroused with someone caressing your private parts with a soft, moist brush?* I imagined the studio filled with soft moans and sighs as the male models' penises hardened and the female models' hips gyrated from the pleasurable sensations.

And what becomes of the models when the artist's composition is finally finished? I thought. It would be a shame to have to wash it all off before leaving the studio. I'd want to take my newly fashioned super-hero into a private room and have my way with her as I fantasized about her using her superpowers on me. Suddenly, a Live Chat box opened in the lower corner of the website window, and an ellipsis appeared, indicated someone was sending me a message.

Hi, I'm Eva, the attendant typed. *Can I answer any questions you might have about our program?*

I removed my wet hand from between my legs and wiped it on the front of my jeans, then placed my fingers over the keyboard.

Yes, I began. *What happens if I come to the studio alone? How do I pair up with a partner?*

My clit throbbed in anticipation as I watched Eva typing her reply.

We try to schedule even numbers of participants for each session to ensure everybody has a partner. But in the event there's a last-minute cancelation or no-show, the workshop instructor will stand in for anyone who's orphaned.

Stand in? I thought. If the instructor looks anything like the gorgeous Wonder Woman model on their poster, I'd volunteer to be one of the orphans any day.

How long is each session? I asked. *Do both partners get painted by the time it ends?*

We schedule two hours for each session, Eva replied. *Most clients need the full allotment of time to cover a complete body with a detailed design. Although some artists can work more quickly, our customers find it's more relaxing and rewarding to devote all of their attention to one partner at a time. We offer a discount for follow-up sessions to encourage you to take your time and use the full allocation to create a truly memorable experience.*

Memorable experience indeed, I thought. I could only imagine how worked up both the artist and the model would get after two full hours of worshipping their partner's bodies in such close quarters.

Are we allowed to use any design of our choosing?

Absolutely. We encourage our artists to be creative. But if you have trouble finding inspiration, you can choose from a large number of interesting templates we have in our design catalogue.

My mind had already begun racing ahead with risqué ideas for my models.

I'm an experienced graphic designer, so I probably won't need too much help with that aspect of the procedure. But what happens if my partner needs some assistance?

That's what the workshop coach is for. She's available for coaching support during the duration of the session. Even if she's busy with her own client, you can still ask her questions at any time and she can pull away to provide personal help.

I smiled, imagining how far the 'personal help' might go in such a sexually-charged atmosphere.

Are the models always fully naked?

It's generally more fun to have the full canvas to work with, but we don't pressure anyone to be entirely naked. If customers wish to cover up their private areas with tight-fitting undergarments, that is their prerogative. Oftentimes it's difficult to tell they're wearing any clothing once the design is fully blended in.

I pinched my eyebrows wondering how safe it would be to allow paint to invade our private spaces.

What kind of paint do you use? Is it non-toxic and hypoallergenic?

We have three different types of paint, depending on how long you wish for it to remain on your body. The easiest to work with is an oil-based paint that goes on smoothly and is quick to wash off. But some clients like to wear their design a little longer and carry it home under loose clothing to show their friends and lovers. For this, we have a latex-based paint that hardens to a rubbery coating that you can peel off. We also have a vegetable-based paint that enables your partner to remove the coating in a more exciting manner. In all cases, the paint is fully hypoallergenic and non-toxic.

Edible paint? Holy shit! I thought. That would really allow me to let my imagination run wild with my superhero muse. But I wondered if the studio environment would be appropriate if my partner and I wanted to go that far.

How open are the workshop participants to that kind of activity, or is that something that's meant to be reserved for the privacy of one's own home?

Most of our customers find the experience of having their naked bodies painted by someone else to be highly stimulating. Plus, it takes a certain kind of free spirit to disrobe in front of a bunch of other strangers and allow your most intimate areas to be touched in this manner. We find that most clients are quite open to the unrestricted exploration of their bodies before, during, and after the actual painting process. But if you want more privacy, we also have private cubicles and showers in the change rooms for your personal use.

I began to feel my panties sticking to my thighs and looked between my legs, seeing another wet patch forming in the crotch of my jeans. The whole idea of painting nude models in the open space of a group studio was incredibly erotic. The thought of licking my muse clean after I finished painting her with a beautiful design was just the icing on the cake. I quickly wrapped up my online chat so I could attend to more pressing matters.

I think you've convinced me this is something I'd like to try, I typed with trembling hands. *How do I go about making an appointment?*

Just choose an available date and time, then fill in the online booking form under the Appointments tab and make your payment. Feel free to book either a couples session or a solo appointment. Either way, we'll make sure you're partnered up with a like-minded partner. But keep in mind that sessions fill up quickly since we limit each class size to ten participants. Hope to see you soon!

I booked an appointment for next Saturday, then signed out of the chat session and ran downstairs, scrambling through my kitchen cupboards looking for some kind of makeshift body paint. The best I could find was a few small tubes of food dye and a small jar of blackberry jam. Then I smiled when I noticed a large tub of peanut butter in the pantry. I stripped off my clothes and rubbed the batter all over my tits and stomach, watching myself in the hallway mirror. As I swirled the paste into a faux bodice and panty design mimicking the sexy Wonder Woman figure on the bodypainting poster, I spread my legs and rolled my burning clit between my fingers. In a matter of seconds, I came hard imagining myself licking the sticky substance off my moaning partner.

PAINTING OUTSIDE THE LINES

When I arrived at the bodypainting studio on the day of my scheduled appointment, I was trembling in excitement. I still wasn't sure exactly what to expect, but I knew it was unlikely to be anything like any of my previous art classes. I'd done a few nude studies before, but this took the idea of illustrating a naked body to an entirely new level. This time I'd be touching my model up close and personal, using her body as my very own canvas.

As customers streamed into the salon, I sized up each person as a potential partner. Most of the participants wore full-length clothing, so it was difficult to imagine their bodies naked and exposed under the bright lights of the studio environment. But I saw enough curvy hips and shapely breasts under their tight jeans and blouses to rekindle the memory of my body plastered in peanut butter.

Unfortunately, most of the visitors appeared to be already paired up as couples. Three of the pairs were young men and women who were obviously looking for a little adventure to spice up their love life. But one of the couples was a middle-aged lesbian pair who peered at me expectantly as they entered the room. The chunky blue-haired butch eyed me up and down, but her pretty girlfriend smiled at me as her partner led her by her hand. She couldn't have been much older than me, and I felt myself blushing as I checked out her slim dancer's figure in her skinny jeans.

That left me the odd woman out watching the hostess greet each new couple as they entered the studio. She looked to be in her early 30s with long blonde hair tied back in a ponytail. Her bright green eyes and pretty smile reminded me of the actress Charlize Theron, but her figure was all Sofia Vergara. Her full breasts created a deep cleavage in her tight-fitting blouse, and her curvy hips swayed seductively as she greeted each new guest. I glanced up at the clock, remembering the online chat attendant saying each session was limited to ten participants. With only a few minutes left, I squeezed my thighs together in anticipation of being paired up with the instructor.

But just as she moved to lock the front door behind the blacked-out windows, a young girl who barely looked out of her teens squeezed through the entrance. The moment I looked at her, she took my breath away. With shimmering auburn hair, large radiant eyes and pale freckled skin, she looked like the consummate girl next door. Fresh-faced and perky with an infectious smile, I was instantly smitten by her, quickly abandoning the notion of partnering up with the instructor. Besides, I thought, she had a more suitable palette for the design concept I'd been mulling over for my model the last few days.

With all the scheduled participants now accounted for, the hostess latched the front door and moved to the front of room.

"Good morning, everyone," she said, peering around the room. "My name's Molly and I'll be your facilitator for today's class. Thank you all for coming. I think you'll find this workshop to be a unique and exhilarating experience. It looks like everybody's already paired up except for Jade and Brianna, so if you two would like to introduce yourselves, we can get started in just a few minutes."

I looked over in the direction of the pretty redhead and she glanced back at me shyly. She seemed frozen in her corner of the room so I strolled over and introduced myself.

"Hi, I'm Jade," I said, extending my hand slowly.

"I'm Bree," the girl said in a gentle voice. "Pleased to meet you."

When our hands touched, I could feel the perspiration on her palm. I wasn't sure if she was more nervous about the prospect of getting naked in front of a bunch of strangers or from being one of the only orphans along with me. As a show of solidarity, I held her hand as I turned back to face Molly.

"Before I explain some of the logistics and protocols for our workshop," she said, "does anyone have any general questions? I know this can seem a bit daunting at first, since I believe this is a first-time experience for all of you."

One of the couples asked a question about how easy it was to remove the paint from their bodies, and I absent-mindedly glanced around the workshop. There were five distinct stations positioned about ten feet apart, each with a large easel and table carrying an assortment of bowls, paint canisters and different-sized brushes. The easels had a large sketchpad overlaid by a roll of cellophane sheets depicting various characters and images from the public eye. Some of the pictures displayed familiar superhero characters, while others showed famous reproductions of classical portraits from painters ranging from Picasso to Warhol to Vermeer. I smiled, remembering the unique design that I had envisioned from one of my own favorite artists.

"Right, then," Molly said when she finished answering the last of the participant questions. "If each of you wants to stake out a position next to one of the easels scattered around the room, let me explain how to use the materials. You'll find a variety of bowls and brushes at each of your tables, together with a collection of different colored paint canisters. These aren't the typical oil paints you find in the art store. Because you'll be painting on a larger and smoother canvas, i.e. your own bodies, we use a special fluid-acrylic type that spreads and binds more easily to naked skin.

"I suggest that you pour small quantities of each color you wish to use into the empty bowls, then select the fineness of each brush depending on how detailed your design. The broad brushes allow you to cover more area with a uniform pattern, and the thin brushes allow you to apply more detailed designs. There's also a bowl filled with clear water to clean your brushes when changing from one color to another. You also have an easel to draw some preliminary sketches if you wish and a variety of design templates to peruse for inspiration. I'll be circulating around the room and offering assistance whenever you need it, but feel free to shout out any questions as they come up. We've intentionally kept our group size small so I can give you more personalized attention.

"All you need to do now is decide who's going to start off being the painter and who will be the muse. Take your time and have fun. You'll likely find you need the full two hours to finish painting your partner's full body, in which case you can swap positions at our next class. There's a clean smock on each table, which I highly encourage the painter to use to protect your clothing. Now let's get this party started!"

Bree and I stepped toward the nearest painter's station and glanced at each other uncertainly. I didn't have any hesitation about stripping naked in front of other people, but I could tell that she was feeling a bit nervous.

"What role were you thinking you'd like to play first?" I asked.

Bree raised her eyebrows and frowned.

"I'm not much of an artist," she said, peering at my gym-toned body. "I'm afraid I wouldn't be able to do your beautiful figure proper justice."

"Not to worry," I smiled, happy she was giving me an opportunity to touch her first. "I've actually got a little experience in this area, so it might be easier for me to go first." I stared at her little buds poking under her tight t-shirt, trying to contain my excitement. "That is, if you don't mind taking off your clothes..."

Bree hesitated for a moment, glancing down at the floor.

"Do you mind if keep myself partially covered?" she said. "I've got a tight sports bra and some thong panties that shouldn't get in the way too much—"

"No worries," I squinted, disappointed that she wasn't going to give me complete access to her girlish figure. "We can make it work either way."

"Okay. Where do you want me to stand?"

I surveyed our workspace and nodded toward the area in front of a small stool next to the table.

"I suppose right here would work best. The shorter the distance from the paint and the brushes, the less mess we'll make." I paused for a moment, sizing up her figure. "Did you have any particular design in mind that you wanted me to paint?"

"Not really," she said. "If you're an experienced artist, I don't want to get in the way of your creativity. Were you thinking of anything special?"

"I had something in mind that I think perfectly suits you," I nodded. "But I'd rather keep the design a secret until I'm finished. I think it'll be all the more exciting for you to see the finished product once it's on your bare body."

"Okay," Bree said, with a curious grin. "Do you need to prepare anything?"

Sensing that she wanted a little distraction while she disrobed, I glanced toward the bowls and brushes on the side table.

"Why don't I prepare the paint while you get yourself ready?

As I opened the canisters of paint and filled five bowls with the primary colors, I listened to the rustling of Bree's clothing while she stripped. Glancing around the room, I watched each of the other models removing their clothing. Most the women chose to go completely nude, including the pretty lesbian girl on the other side of the room. The solo male model stripped down to a skimpy jockstrap covering his crotch.

Always the double-standard, I thought, shaking my head in dismay. *Perhaps his partner will be able to entice him out of this last bit of protection before they're finished.* I knew that I certainly had similar designs on my muse.

I tied the white smock around my waist then turned around to see Bree standing half-naked with her arms clasped tightly by her side. She was wearing a plain-white, one-piece bra and matching thong panties. Her pale alabaster skin looked so delicate, from a distance another observer might think she wasn't wearing anything at all. Her small but perky breasts thrust firmly against the stretchy fabric, producing two sensuous points where her aroused nipples stood. I glanced down her body and noticed the small cleft in her panties where the tight fabric hugged the indentation of her vulva. I nodded approvingly, realizing her sparse undergarments would blend in nicely with my planned design.

"You're beautiful," I said. "The perfect canvas for what I had in mind."

"You don't think the seams will interfere with your composition?"

"They might distract my *mind* a little," I smiled. "But I think we can make it work."

Bree glanced at my bowls of paint and pinched her eyebrows.

"That's a lot of yellow and black. Are you going to paint me as a leopard?"

I smiled at her and shook my head.

"Nice try, young lady," I said. "You're not going to get it out of me that easily. Though you will be nicely speckled by the time I'm finished."

"More than I already am?" she frowned self-consciously. "Don't you think I've already got enough spots?"

"Don't be silly," I said, noticing the little line of freckles running along the tan lines on her chest and hips. "You can barely see them. But in any event, they'll be all covered up by the time I'm finished. The patches I have in mind are a little more—*stylized*."

"Well now I'm intrigued," she said, spreading her legs, inviting me to begin with her lower half. "Where do you want to start?

"Let's begin at the top with your pretty face. It'll be the focal point of my composition, after all."

"Okay," Bree said, shifting her weight with a worried expression. "I didn't realize—"

"Don't worry, sweetie. I'm not going to cover you up too much. I just want to highlight certain areas of your face to add a little drama to the rest of my scheme."

I dipped a fine-hair brush into the red paint bowl and dabbled a small patch onto my palette plate, then swished it in the water bowl before adding some blue to the compound. Just then, Molly circulated by our table, watching me mix my colors.

"It looks like somebody knows her primary colors," she said, noticing Bree looking nervous as I swirled the purple mixture into my brush. "Did either of you have any questions or concerns?"

I nodded at Molly, happy that she'd arrived at an opportune moment.

"Actually, there was one thing I was wondering about. How *flexible* is this acrylic paint when it dries? I'm concerned about applying it to areas of Bree's face where changes in her expression might crack or break it."

"Good question," Molly said. "While all of our paint is safe to use on the face, if you were thinking of applying it around her eyes or mouth, you might want to consider an alternative material. We have different colors of powdered eye shadow and mascara available, as well as a full range of lip gloss colors."

"That might work a little better," I nodded. "I'll take some pink lip gloss and light purple eye shadow if you have it. And maybe a bit of rose-colored blush for her cheeks."

"Coming right up," Molly said. "I'll be back in one sec."

"*Pink and purple*, hmm?" Bree said, raising an eyebrow. "Are you painting me as a flamingo? Or a peacock, maybe?"

"Ha!" I teased. "Keep guessing—you're just going to have to wait until the end. But I can tell you that I'm not painting you as any kind of animal."

"I figure if I just keep asking these kinds of closed questions, by the time two hours have passed I'll have figured it out simply by the process of elimination."

"You can try, girl. But this is a pretty unique design. I'll be surprised if you've seen it before."

"How do you know I'll like it then?"

"Because it's one of the most beautiful pieces of art every created. And it suits your body tone and shape perfectly."

"So it's a recognizable piece of art? Are you going to paint me as the Mona Lisa?"

"I'm not *that* good an artist," I laughed. "It's pretty hard to match Da Vinci's level of skill. Besides, you didn't sound too thrilled about my painting your face, and that picture is all about the face."

Molly returned placing a small makeup kit on my table and asked if I needed anything else. I shook my head and she circulated around to the next table where the man with the jockstrap was being covered in a liberal coating of black paint.

Batman, I nodded. *Not very original, but I suppose it's every little boy's dream to play their favorite superhero fantasy.*

I flipped open the dish of eye shadow and drew the brush over the powdery paste then stood up directly in front of Bree.

"Close your eyes for a moment," I said.

"Normally I use a soft green," Bree said, lowering her long eyelashes.

"Who's the artist here?" I teased. "You'll have your chance soon enough to mess with me. For now, just stand still and let me do my job."

"I'm looking forward to it," she grinned.

I swiped the brush over each of her eyelids to create a light dusting of lavender color, then reached over to the table for the lipstick cylinder. Bree opened her eyes and smiled at me as I leaned in to apply the gloss.

"I feel like a movie star being primped for the big show. Shall I vamp while you're preparing me?"

I suddenly felt a warm rush between my legs. I was beginning to fall for this girl's personality. Her saucy attitude belied her initial sense of modesty.

"Just shut up while I attempt to make you even prettier than you already are," I said.

As I pressed the tube against her soft lips, Bree opened her mouth, exhaling her cool breath onto my face. My panties suddenly moistened and I flushed slightly.

Bree looked me straight in the eye as her pupils dilated wide as saucers. Apparently, *both* of us were getting turned on by my intimate touch. It took every ounce of my willpower not to close the short distance between us and kiss her on her mouth. The wet gloss hung seductively on her rosebud lips, and I had to bite my tongue to force myself to pull away. When I turned around to retrieve the compact containing the blush, I leaned over at the waist to give her a premium view of my tight ass.

Two can play this game, I thought, turning my face to disguise my widening grin.

When I stood back up with the blush pad in my hand, Bree smiled at me, recognizing how excited I was.

"It looks like one of us doesn't need any help in this department," she said, peering at me through half-closed eyelids.

"You're just getting me all flustered with your sassy attitude. I bet the Mona Lisa didn't give Da Vinci this much trouble while she posed for him."

"He had fewer distractions, as I recall. Wasn't she full clothed?"

"So you have some familiarity with classical art, after all," I said, patting the blush pad gently on each side of her face.

"Just a little. I had to take one course in art history as part of my liberal arts program."

"Where are you studying and what's your major?"

"UC, Public Relations."

My mind suddenly wandered to my last webcam chat with Holly, who was also a student at the University of Chicago. With her red hair and little freckles, Bree even looked at bit like her. I pinched my thighs together imagining her naked with her legs spread apart playing with her wet pussy while I watched her on my computer.

"Is everything okay?" Bree said, noticing my sudden distraction.

"Yes. It's just that you reminded me of someone I know."

"Another one of your muses?"

"In a manner of speaking," I said. "But let's get back to you. I need to concentrate on the matter at hand."

Bree looked at my trembling hand still holding the blush pad and clasped her fingers around my wrist.

"Your hand looks a little shaky right now. Do you need to take a little rest?"

"I'll be fine," I hesitated. "This next part doesn't require the same degree of...personal contact."

I turned back to the mixing table and poured a small amount of red paint into the yellow bowl and blended it with a stir stick. Then I dipped the widest brush I could find in the gold mixture and began swiping the front of Bree's body. As the brush flipped over the edge of her sports bra, it splattered a few drops under her chin. I reached for a towelette on the table and dipped it in the water then wiped her neck with a frown on my face. Bree noticed the other couples painting their fully nude partners, and she grabbed my wrist again.

"You know what?" she said. "This is silly wearing all this getup for a bodypainting class. It's just getting in the way and making a mess. Everybody else doesn't seem to mind getting naked. Why don't I lose the bra and panties? You'll just be covering me up soon enough anyway, right?"

"Um—yes," I said, feeling my heart begin to race at the prospect of seeing her fully naked. "By the time I finish adding all the intricate details of my design, it will be almost impossible to tell that you're actually naked."

"What the hell. Let's do it then."

Bree hooked her thumbs around the side of her one-piece bra and stretched it down and over her body to avoid spilling any gold paint on her face. Then she bent over at the hips and pulled her panties down to the floor, stepping out of them nonchalantly. When she stood back up, I couldn't help ogling at her beautiful figure. Her perfectly bald pussy was framed by slender but shapely hips, and her small breasts were capped with large pink areolas that looked like little cupolas atop her half-domes. To top it all off, her pointy nipples extended almost another full inch from the surface of her skin, echoing the Cathedral of Florence with its pointy lantern atop its peach-colored dome.

Perhaps I should have stuck with a Renaissance-themed design after all, I thought, admiring her classical beauty.

"Still think you can disguise this under all that yellow paint?" Bree said, raising another eyebrow at me.

"I think so. But it's almost a shame to cover you up. You're already a masterpiece just as you are."

"Stop—you're swelling my head," Bree smiled.

"That's not the *only* body part that swelling around here," I joked.

"If you're talking about my funny-shaped breasts, I'm already self-conscious enough about them. I'll be glad when you have them covered up again."

I peered into Bree's eyes, wanting to hold her.

"You shouldn't be the slightest bit self-conscious about your breasts. Believe me, I've seen quite a few in my day, and those are some of the sexiest and prettiest ones I've ever encountered. If I were you, I'd be showing those off every opportunity I could."

"I guess I'm not quite as experienced as you are. I'm still getting comfortable in my own skin."

"Well, let's paint some clothes on you then so you don't feel so uncomfortable."

I dipped the big brush in the gold paint bowl then slowly swiped it over Bree's torso and upper thighs, stopping just below her knees and over the edge of her shoulders. As I watched the hairs of the brush separate over her pointy breasts, I imagined it was my fingers caressing her instead. I was glad that I was wearing a painter's smock to disguise the inevitable wet patch that I was sure was spreading once again in my tight jeans.

"Is that better?" Bree asked.

"Much," I purred. "It's smoother and slicker. Not to mention *sexier*. Which is perfect for the character I'm painting."

"So you're painting a yellow dress on a red-headed model and it's a recognizable portrait of a famous artist. Can you at least tell me in which *century* it was painted?"

"I think I've already told you too much," I said. "If you've taken a course in art history, you could probably narrow it down pretty fast if I told you that."

"What about the *style* of painting? Is it expressionist, cubist, realism, or something else?"

"There's no way I'm giving you any more details. Though if you've seen this painting before, you'll probably figure it out pretty quickly once I start adding the details."

"Do you want me not to look down while you're painting me to maintain the surprise?"

"Yes, please. There must be plenty of other distractions around the room to keep your interest."

"Mmm, yes, I noticed. There are some pretty interesting designs taking shape. You might have some serious competition."

"Well it's not really a contest," I said, dipping my brush into the black paint bowl, "so I'm not too worried about that."

As I sat down on my stool and started to paint the vertical stripes on her stomach, I began to wonder about Bree's sexual orientation.

"But now that you mention it, which ones do you find most interesting?"

Bree took a minute to scan the room, then paused for a long moment peering into the opposite corner.

"Superheroes seem to be a popular theme. There's a Batman, Wonder Woman, Supergirl, and a Catwoman. It looks like we're the only outliers in the room."

I glanced up at Bree's face and noticed her staring intently at one of the models.

"You seem fixated on one in particular. Who are you looking at right now?"

"The two ladies in the far corner. The pretty one is being painted as Catwoman."

"You're not attracted to the naked Batman at the station next to us?"

"He's interesting too. But there's something about that woman's figure. She looks incredibly sexy with her naked body all covered in black."

I dipped a fine hair brush in the red bowl and leaned in to circle Bree's areolas with a flower petal design.

"Do you find yourself attracted to women particularly?" I said, fishing for details.

"I hadn't thought about it very much before today," she said, drawing a slight gasp when I touched her sensitive nipples. "But I have to admit these women look especially sexy dressed up in their naked costumes."

I cleansed my brush in the water bowl, then dipped it in the blue paint and dabbled it softly over Bree's pointed buds.

"Is it turning you on?"

Bree sighed as I circled her nipples with my moist brush, and she began to sway her hips unconsciously.

"Not as much as what you're doing to me right now."

"I'm just getting started," I said. "We've still got a lot of ground to cover. I haven't even gotten to your most interesting parts."

"I'm already buzzing in anticipation."

The further I moved down Bree's body with my brush, the more her hips gyrated in excitement. By the time I began painting the floral arrangement on her mound, I noticed thin rivulets of lubrication streaming down the inside of her thighs.

"Have you ever been with another woman?" I probed.

"Only in my dreams. I've never actually been with *anyone* before."

I glanced up from my stool, surprised to hear that she was still a virgin.

"Is that why you came to the body painting workshop? To explore what it would be like to feel the touch of another woman?"

"Maybe," she said. "I thought it would be a safe place to watch and explore other people's bodies without the pressure of having sex."

"I see your point," I said, facing directly in front of Bree's crotch. "I find it incredibly sexy too." I sensed that she was ready for the last stage of my composition. "Can you spread your legs for me a little bit so I can apply the finishing touches?"

"So soon?" she said. "I'm enjoying this far too much for you to stop now."

"We can always come back for more at the next session. Besides, I have a feeling you might like this next part."

As Bree shifted her legs apart, I pressed my brush between her thighs and drew the soft hairs over her glistening labia. She closed her eyes and moaned softly, tilting her mound upward. I dipped my brush into the bowl of red paint, then flicked it gently over her swollen clit.

"Oh!" Bree panted. "That feels so good. Caress me more with your soft brush, Jade."

Even though I'd covered most of Bree's body and had pretty much finished my design, I lingered for a few moments longer in the sensitive area between her legs. Gently stroking her clitoris with circular motions of my brush, I gradually increased the pressure and speed on her sensitive nub. As I listened to her soft moans and sighs above me, her hips swayed in increasing intensity along with my movements. I was incredibly turned watching her get off from the simple touch of my brush, and I fought the urge to lean in and press my face closer to her.

Suddenly, Bree grasped the top of my head with two hands and began jerking her hips directly in front of my face. I could hear her grunting softly above me, trying not to draw too much attention to our corner of the room. I squeezed my legs tightly together under my painter's smock and enjoyed a long, silent orgasm along with her. I waited until she came down from her climax before withdrawing my brush, then I looked up seeing the flush roll over her face.

"Did you enjoy that, baby?"

"God, yes," she panted. "I want you so bad. I can't wait to touch you at our next session. I've been fantasizing this whole time about how I want to caress you in return."

"We don't necessarily have to wait that long if you want to continue our partnership. I feel exactly the same way about you."

Bree looked down and smiled at me.

"I suppose we should finish up here first. Are you just about done?"

"Just a little bit of final clean up," I said, noticing the yellow paint running down the inside of her thighs. I reached for the moist towelette and rubbed the streaks falling below the hemline of her painted skirt, then reapplied some last-minute touch up where the paint had rubbed off between her legs. As if on cue, Molly moved to the front of the room to address the group.

"It looks like everyone is nearing completion of their compositions," she said. "This is always one of the most exciting parts of the workshop, where each partner gets to reveal their finished work. If you're feeling comfortable sharing, who'd like to go first?"

The Wonder Woman couple raised their hands, then moved their easel out of the way for the rest of the room to see. The model spread her legs and crossed her forearms in the famous pose, as the rest of us cheered. Just as in the poster, the black and gold outline of the "W" emblem across her chest disguised the girl's naked form, but we could still make out the shape of her breasts from the shadows cast by the overhead lights. She was wearing a short blue skirt to cover up her private parts, but she still looked stunning with her painted-on high red boots and epaulets.

"That one looks familiar," Molly said. "Very nice work. I particularly like the golden tiara painted on her forehead. Very convincing. Who's next?"

The Supergirl model stepped forward with a simple blue top and red skirt ensemble and famous red "S" emblazoned across her bare chest. She raised her arm in the Supergirl pose and flapped her cape, giggling her bare breasts under the S emblem.

"We have lots of strong female role models, today," Molly nodded. "I like your use of props to complete the package. Very pretty." Molly turned to the Batman couple and smiled. "I see we have another famous superhero in our midst."

The Batman hunk growled as he assumed the famous pose with his fists clenched by his sides. He'd brought a rubber cowl and cape to match the rest of his uniform and looked every bit the part of the Christian Bale character from the movies. The only distraction in his costume was where his codpiece protruded in his painted-on blue shorts, but we all cheered him on nonetheless.

Next to present was the pretty lesbian woman in the Catwoman costume. Unlike the other models, she was completely nude and painted in black from head to toe. We all ogled her sexy figure, paying particular attention to the sexy cleft between her legs where we could see the slit in her pussy when she spread her legs. Bree wasn't kidding when she said she was the hottest model in the room.

But when it came our turn to present, everyone gasped when I moved the easel blocking Bree's design. We were the only ones with a portrait concept, and everyone oohed and aahed at the intricate composition. I'd been careful to disguise Bree's private regions with floral designs, but you could still tell she was completely naked if you looked closely enough. She seemed to revel at everyone staring at her, but she still didn't know what she'd been painted as.

"Another exquisite piece of work," Molly nodded, admiring our design. "Now I think it's only fair for each of the models to see their partner's handiwork," she said, wheeling a large wardrobe mirror to the front of the room. "If each of you would like to take turns in front of the mirror, I think you'll be pretty impressed with the finished product."

As each of the models stepped up in front of the mirror, their eyes widened at the realism of their designs. They primped and posed as their partners took pictures of them for posterity. Nobody seemed the least bit self-conscious that a bunch of strangers were watching them stand buck naked as they channeled their superhero alter-egos.

When it was Bree's turn to view herself in front of the mirror, she smiled a huge grin when she recognized the familiar image of Gustav Klimt's famous painting titled The Kiss. She looked absolutely shimmering in the gold and black motif, with red- and blue-colored floral arrangements embellishing her golden tunic. Although she was completely nude, the strategic placement of the black and colored patches made it almost impossible to distinguish her private spots from the rest of her body.

"I had a feeling this was what you were painting," she said, turning her body from side to side. "With the gold and black paint and all the hints you were dropping, I knew it had to be Klimt."

"Are you disappointed I ruined the surprise?" I said.

"Not at all. It's a gorgeous design. You're a very talented painter,

Jade. Can you take a photo of me with my phone? I want to remember what this looks like before I have to wash it all off."

I held Bree's phone up and snapped a few pictures, then I handed it to the Catwoman model who'd moved in closer to admire Bree's figure.

"Would you mind taking a picture of the two of us?"

I asked Bree to kneel on a nearby stool, then I moved behind her and dipped my head down over her shoulder and kissed her face just like in the famous original composition.

"What a perfect way to end our class," Molly said, as everyone cheered. "If you'd like to clean yourself up before you leave the studio, we have special lotions in the changing room to help you remove the oil-based paint. Feel free to use the private cubicles if you need any assistance from your partners. I hope to see you all again soon where you can switch roles and paint your other partner with equally pretty bodypaint designs."

As I continued holding Bree in my arms in the kiss pose, I whispered something into her ear.

"Did you need any help removing all this getup?" I asked.

"Yes," she sighed, peering deeply into my eyes. "I want to feel the *rest* of you touching my naked body."

As I pressed my hips against her bare pussy, her tunic design imprinted onto my smock, making us appear as two unified lovers surrounded by the golden fold of her gilded cape.

Soon, my love, I thought, feeling her warm body pressing against mine. *Soon we can dispense with this play acting and be real lovers.*

HIDING IN PLAIN SIGHT

After our session ended, Bree and I showered together in the change room where I helped her remove her body paint. While it was disappointing to remove the intricate design, we enjoyed rubbing out bodies together as we channeled the two lovers kissing in Klimt's portrait. I gave Bree two more powerful orgasms running my fingers over her smooth pussy under the warm shower spray.

While we waited impatiently for our next scheduled body-painting class, we texted back and forth exchanging ideas about what design theme she'd like to use when we switched roles. We searched together online for ideas about how best to highlight my fuller figure while still maintaining a little mystery about my naked form. The trick seemed to be in adding extra detail around the private parts to distract attention from all the extra curves and bulges.

Bree fantasized about painting me as Mystique from the first X-Men movie. She thought Rebecca Romijn's body looked hot and well-camouflaged under the thick layers of dark blue paint. I preferred more playful themes, my favorite showing two hound dog faces painted over one model's huge breasts, with their red noses hiding her erect nipples. But as I scrolled through the nude models on Google Images, all I could think about was Bree's unusually puffy nipples resting atop her perky little breasts. I must have cum a hundred times remembering how it felt sucking on them in the shower of the bodypainting studio.

By the time our next session rolled around, I felt closer than ever to Bree and couldn't wait to feel her caress my naked body with her brush. When we arrived back at the studio on our appointed day, I was happy to see a new lesbian couple had joined our group. Bree seemed to have a special affinity for the female form, and I was hopeful the extra distraction would elevate her interest in deepening our relationship.

As with the first session, Molly greeted each couple as they arrived, then she locked the door and closed the window blinds to preserve our privacy. When she addressed the group, she announced a new theme for today's class.

"Welcome back to our returning couples, and to our new couple, Jenna and Lexi."

I noticed Bree sizing up the young lesbian couple, and when one of the girls smiled back at her, I felt a tinge of jealousy.

"Today," Molly continued, "we're going to work with a different type of paint called liquid latex. It goes on thicker and is more durable, so you can wear it longer and even wear it home to show your loved ones. It also can also be fashioned to look like clothing, so it makes the perfect camouflage if you're looking to create an optical illusion. Some of our clients even leave the studio wearing nothing but their body paint to test the realism of their designs."

One of the young lesbian girls raised her hand with a question.

"Yes, Lexi?" Molly said.

"Is that the same kind of paint that was used to design Mystique's costume in the X-Men movie?"

"As a matter of fact, yes. And if you've seen that movie, you might remember how good a job the paint did hiding the fact that she was completely naked in all of her scenes. I must warn you though, that this paint is harder to remove than the oil-based compound we used in our last session. You'll need to use a special body wash to loosen the film, then peel it gently off your skin. Also, if anybody is allergic to latex, you'll want to avoid contact with it. Otherwise, this new paint form can be a lot of fun to work with. As before, choose a painting station to work at, then decide which of you will be the painter and who'll be the model. I'll be floating around offering suggestions and providing assistance as needed. Just let me know whenever you have any questions or need anything. Have fun and let your imaginations run wild!"

Bree and I chose a spot near the window next to the Batman character from our previous session. He smiled at Bree remembering her sexy Kiss design from last time, and she blushed slightly, turning away.

"So, have you thought any more about how you'd like to paint me?" I asked, stealing her attention away from the hunky guy. "Maybe you didn't have such a bad idea about the Mystique character from the X-Men movie after all."

Bree paused for a moment, glancing at some of the design templates hanging from the easels scattered around the room, then flipped through a few posters on our tripod. She stopped at a picture showing a sexy woman wearing a painted-on business suit. Although the design highlighted every curve of her figure, the lapels and seams of the suit provided just enough camouflage to make it seem at first glance that she wasn't naked.

Bree raised an eyebrow and smiled at me.

"The instructor said that some people choose to wear their designs right out of the studio. Something like this might be kind of fun to test people's reactions outside the workroom. Plus, it doesn't look overly complicated for a newbie artist like me."

I glanced at the design on the easel and felt my pussy beginning to throb, imagining myself walking buck naked down the street dressed as a business executive.

"That could work," I said, trying to conceal my excitement.

Bree noticed my erect nipples poking against my thin blouse, then she peered back up at me.

"If you're going to show this to people outside the studio, did you want to wear anything underneath or do you want to be entirely naked?"

"You've already seen me in my birthday suit," I smiled. "I might as well go au naturel in my new business suit."

"I was hoping you'd say that," Bree said, running her eyes over the rest of my body. "I've barely been able to keep my thoughts off your gorgeous figure ever since we shared that sexy shower after our last painting session."

"Oh?" I said, feeling my panties beginning to moisten imagining Bree fantasizing about me while we were apart. "Did you touch yourself while you were thinking of me?"

"Many times. I couldn't wait to get my hands back on you."

"Or at least your *brush*," I said, glancing at the array of painting equipment on the worktable.

Bree looked into my eyes with a lopsided grin.

"From what the instructor said, you're going to need a lot of hands-on help removing the paint when we're done. It could be kind of fun removing your sexy outfit at the end of the day."

I hadn't thought about that aspect of the procedure until Bree mentioned it. The idea of her peeling off my clothes to reveal my naked body underneath sounded like almost as much fun as the business of painting it on. It would also be the perfect pretense to take her home with me and spend some more quality time with her.

"Okay," I said. "You've talked me into it. Why don't you prepare your materials while I get myself ready?"

As I began to disrobe, I watched the other models around the room removing their clothes. The butchy girl from the older lesbian pair had large pendulous breasts, and I wondered what theme her partner would use to highlight her fuller figure. I resisted the temptation to suggest the hound-dog faces, chuckling to myself imagining how it might look on the chunky woman. The Batman couple had also decided to switch roles, and my eyes widened as I watched his sexy girlfriend undress. She had a pretty ballerina's figure and I couldn't help staring as she wiggled her tight ass out of her skinny jeans.

One station further away, the other couple from our previous class had also switched positions, and this time the young man chose to go fully naked for his bodypainting experience. As I watched his large, semi-erect dong swinging between his thighs, I wondered how his partner could possibly disguise his oversize package with any kind of realistic design.

The new lesbian couple were cute and young, and I would have been happy to see either one of them strip naked and display her body for the rest of the group to see. When the dark-haired beauty stepped out of her loose pantsuit, I was surprised by how large and firm her breasts were. I was glad they'd positioned themselves at the opposite corner of the room where they'd be less of a distraction to Bree. I wanted her attention only focused on me, and I shifted my position a few feet to my left to ensure her line of sight would have minimum diversions.

When she swiveled around on her stool and saw me standing buck naked in front of her, she gasped.

"God, Jade," she panted. "You're even more beautiful than I remember."

"Really?" I said. "It's not like you haven't seen me naked already."

"Well yes, but that was in the close confines of the shower stall while we were standing up washing each other." I watched her eyes dart across my bare mound and flicker between my thighs. "I didn't realize how smooth your skin is. How do you manage to keep yourself so perfectly bare down there?"

"With a little help from my dermatologist," I chuckled. "Laser hair removal is a wonderful thing. If frees you up from having to undergo those frequent painful waxings at the esthetician's office. I'll never have to worry about growing unsightly hairs anywhere in that region ever again."

Bree leaned in to examine me closer.

"And there's no stubble or bumps either. You've given me a perfectly smooth canvas on which to draw my masterpiece."

I looked down at Bree with a mischievous grin.

"If you do a good enough job, I might even let you tear it off me later too."

"I can't wait. But don't distract me. I'm going to need my full concentration to do a worthy job painting this gorgeous piece of sculpture."

She turned to study the picture of the businesswoman on the easel then peered back at me.

"Do you have a preference for what color of suit you'd like?"

"Well, if I'm going to walk out of here in this getup, the least we can do is match the shoes with the outfit. I always carry a pair of black pumps in the car in case I break a heel, so either black or dark blue might work."

"Let's go with navy blue," Bree said. "I'm going to channel that sexy Rebecca Romijn body one way or the other."

I smiled at Bree's flattering comparison.

"You're going to have your work cut out for you disguising my body as well as her makeup artists did, but I'm up for it if you are."

"Do you prefer a pantsuit or a jacket-and-skirt design?"

"Let's go full pantsuit. It'll look a bit more convincing when I spread my legs. That is—if you think you can properly disguise my kitty."

Bree glanced between my legs and noticed my swelling clit poking out between the top of my labia, then peered up at me and smiled.

"That could be a bit of a challenge, but I'm looking forward to giving that particular part of your body a little extra attention." She motioned to her side table filled with bowls of paint. "You're the expert artist here. What colors do I mix to create navy blue?"

I looked at Bree's collection of bowls arranged with the same colors I'd set up from our last session.

"You can either mix black or orange with lighter blue. But you'd need an intermediate step to create orange by mixing red and yellow, so try black first. Pour a little bit of black paint into the blue paint bowl then mix it up to see how it looks. You can always add more if necessary."

Bree did as I suggested, then lifted the contents of the blue bowl for me to see.

"How's this?"

"Still a little too blue," I said. "I think we need just a touch more black to create true navy."

Bree poured a bit more black paint into the blue bowl and mixed it with the wooden paddle.

"How about now?" she said, tilting the edge of the bowl toward me.

"Perfect," I nodded.

"This first part shouldn't be too hard," she said, glancing at my naked body. The only question is what you want to wear under your suit. Do you want to go bare-chested and reveal maximum cleavage, or shall I also paint a blouse under your jacket?"

"Well, if we're going to take this outside, I suppose the less bare skin showing, the better. It's going to be difficult enough to disguise that I'm nude without drawing extra attention to my bosom."

"Okay," she said, not sure how to blend the two elements. "Should I paint the blouse or the jacket first?"

"I think you'll find it easier to paint the blouse first. You can cover the top half of my chest with white paint, then use the blue paint to draw a V-shape over it to simulate the open lapels of the jacket."

"Will you guide me along the way so I don't screw up too badly? I'm going to need a little help around the neck and with the seams to create an authentic-looking shirt."

"No worries," I said. "Just start by drawing a little band of white paint around the back of my neck, then when you get to the front, create a little V to make it look partially unbuttoned."

"What about the collar? How do I create the little flaps pointing down to the sides?"

"I'll help you when you get there. Don't worry about making it perfect. Most of the fun is in drawing it on the skin, remember? Besides, you can always wash off the paint while it's still wet if you make a mistake. Just go with it. Trust your eye."

Bree tensed her mouth into a little frown, then dipped a medium-width brush into the bowl with the white paint. Then she stood up and moved around my backside as I felt the wet brush slide along the back of my neck. She moved slowly at first, trying to create a perfectly straight line around the diameter of my neck, then exhaled heavily when she turned around to face me again.

"Whew," she said. "It's harder than I imagined drawing a straight line on a curvy surface. Now for the tough part."

She paused for a moment, looking at my neckline and large breasts, trying to imagine how a real blouse would look on my chest.

"How much cleavage do you want me to show?"

"Just enough to maintain interest but not enough to draw undue attention to that part of my anatomy."

"Okay," she said, holding the brush with a trembling hand next to my collarbone.

"Just taper the line gently into a closed V," I said. "Remember that an open blouse has a bit of a naturally wavy line anyway, so it doesn't have to be perfect."

Bree inhaled a deep breath, then slowly drew the brush down the front of my chest over the top of my breasts. I tried to remain still while she painted me, but I could feel myself shaking as the most hairs of the brush slid over my bust.

"Now for the other side," she said, repeating the process on the left side of my chest.

When she finished, she stood back and appraised her work, nodding softly.

"I think that looks about right. Now I just need to fill in the side panels and the collar."

As Bree continued to work on me, Molly circulated around the room and joined our group. She glanced at the design Bree had chosen on our easel, then looked at her work-in-progress on my upper body and smiled.

"Looks good so far," she nodded. "Did you need any help, Bree?"

"Actually, yes," Bree said. "You arrived at the perfect time. I'm trying to paint a faux blouse on Jade's chest, but I'm not sure how to create the proper edges to form the points of her collar. Can you help me?"

"Absolutely," Molly said. "The key is to adjust the shades ever-so-slightly to create the illusion of shadows at the edges of each element. Why don't I do the right side for you while you watch, then I'll guide you as you do the other side?"

"That would be perfect, thank you," Bree said.

"If you look closely, you can see that the first coat of white paint has a slight pink tinge to it from Jade's bare skin beneath. All you have to do is paint over the area in question with one or more coats to brighten the whiteness. Let me show you."

Molly chose a finer-point brush from the table then dipped it into the bowl of white paint. Then she leaned in close to me and drew a short V-shaped design pointing down to my left breast. She seemed laser-focused on drawing the design, and I was disappointed not to see her gaze stray at any time down toward my naked breasts. She repeated the sequence a couple of times, painting over the same area to brighten the white color. Then she mixed a bit of black paint with the white on the mixing palette and drew a small outline around the edge of the collar.

"Using just a little bit of light gray color around the bottom edge of the collar simulates a natural shadow effect and makes the fold stand out a little more prominently."

She stood back and surveyed her work then looked at Bree.

"What do you think? Does it look like a realistic collar?"

"Absolutely," Bree said, with wide eyes. "That's incredible how easy you made it look. Can you stay and watch me while I try the other side?"

"That's what I'm here for," Molly said. "I think you'll find it's easier than it looks."

Bree picked up the fine white brush and began slowly drawing it over my right collarbone. I could see that she was holding her breath the whole time as she got redder and redder in the face, then she looked up at me as she drew away. I blew her a gentle kiss and mouthed the words 'you're doing great'. She stood back comparing the two sides and squinted her eyes.

"I can see it beginning to take shape," she frowned. "But it still doesn't look as natural as your side."

"You just need to add a bit of gray shadow around the corners, like I did," Molly said. "You might go a few more centimeters further around the edges though, to mimic the deeper shadow coming from the other side of her body."

As Bree touched up the other side of my collar with the gray brush, I watched Molly's eyes as the darted up and down my chest from my exposed breasts back to Bree's brush. I smiled when I caught her eye and wondered if we'd have a chance to see her naked before we finished our bodypainting program. I remembered Liz mentioning in our original online chat that we might have a chance to work with edible paint at some point, and I hoped that there might be an odd number of participants at our next session so I'd have a chance to see her naked body close-up.

After Bree finished applying the gray shadow around the edge of the collar, she stepped back and furled her brows in disappointment.

"It still doesn't look as natural as your side," she said, shaking her head. "What have I done wrong?"

Molly took the brush from Bree's hand and stepped back in toward me.

"You just need to feather the grayness slightly as you move further from the tips of the collar, like this."

I felt Molly draw the brush gently down the front of my chest closer toward the top of my breast, then she glanced up and smiled knowingly at me as she assessed the design.

"What do you think?" she said to Bree. "Does that look a little more convincing?"

"It's perfect," Bree said. "Can you come back a little later when I get to the jacket lapels and seams? I might need your assistance to create the proper shading with the blue paint also."

"No worries," Molly said. "Just remember to paint over the areas you want darker and use a slightly modified shade to create the necessary shadows. I'll come back in a few minutes to see how you're doing."

After Molly left, Bree looked at me with wide eyes and exhaled through puffy cheeks to emphasize how difficult the painting process was.

"You're doing fine, girl," I said. "If the painting expert says it looks good, I'm sure it will pass the man-in-the-street test. Just keep doing what you're doing and it will come out fine. I'm just enjoying watching your pretty face contort into all these sexy expressions while you're touching me with your little brush."

"Isn't it supposed to work the other way around?" she said. "I want to make your face contort into sexy expressions while I'm touching *your* naked body."

"All in due time," I said. "I'm enjoying the buildup. Believe me, I'm getting incredibly turned on watching you do your handiwork."

"Maybe I can make you feel a little more so as I move lower down your body," she said, winking at me seductively.

Bree moved on to highlight the two sides of the seam running down the separated halves of my blouse, then dabbled a bit of gray into the white paint to draw the buttons on the placket. Then she grabbed the widest brush and dipped it into the navy blue bowl and began swiping it over my breasts.

"Now we're getting to the fun part," she said, peering into my eyes as they glazed over in pleasure.

"Yes," I purred. "Paint me, Bree. Slap that wet brush all over my tits. God, how I wish I could fuck you right now."

"All in due time," she said, mimicking my taunts from our last session. "We still haven't gotten to the interesting parts."

"Mmm, I can't wait," I said, continuing our little game of cat and mouse.

Bree continued swiping the thick brush down the front and back of my body, pausing briefly around my wrists and ankles to draw a straight hemline at the bottom of the sleeves and pant legs. Then she selected a finer brush to draw the V-shape at the front of the jacket outside the edges of the white blouse she'd painted earlier. I could feel the white paint starting to harden as it stuck to my breasts, feeling like a stretchy rubber film on my skin. I looked down and saw that my nipples were swelling, stretching the film into two shiny, frosted teats.

If this is what it feels like for a guy to wear a condom, I thought, *this isn't such a bad feeling.* I was getting more and more turned on as Bree covered my body with this sexy second skin.

When she finished painting the basic outline of the pantsuit, she paused for a moment, studying the picture of the model on the easel. She glanced again at the shading around my blouse collar, then chose another fine-point brush and dipped it in the black paint bowl. Then she leaned in closer to me and traced a diagonal line from my left shoulder over my left nipple, toward the center of my chest.

"Whatever you're doing now, I like it," I sighed, feeling the wet brush tickling my erect nipples as it flicked over my raised points.

"I'm highlighting your jacket lapels, so be still so I can get the lines right. I'm trying to use the black shadow to disguise your big nipples, so no one will know you're actually naked."

"They're not as big as yours," I said, glancing at Bree's chest covered by her splatted apron. "You have the most sensuous, swollen areolas I've ever seen. I can't wait to feel them back in my mouth when we're done with all this."

"It sounds like you've had a lot of girls' nipples in your mouth," she said, glancing up at me briefly.

"Well, not really that many," I backpedaled nervously, as a blush fell over my face.

"Don't worry," Bree said, glancing over my shoulder at the nude model at the next station over. "Your secret will stay with me. I'm kind of glad you've got more experience with girls. It just makes you a better lover, where you can teach me all the tricks."

"You have *no* idea," I said, smiling at her devilishly. "I've only just begun to share some of my girl-loving secrets."

"I'll look forward to that," Bree said, noticing the blue streaks running down the inside of my thighs. "But right now, you better put your dick back in your pants. I need you to stay composed while I finish your wardrobe. At least until the paint dries."

"Yes ma'am," I said, staring at the front of her smock, trying to distract my attention from her pretty face.

For the next twenty minutes, Bree sat facing me on her stool as she used the black paintbrush to outline the front and bottom seams of my suit jacket. I could feel the brush sliding over my skin from the center of my navel toward the edges of my hips. She seemed to be finding her confidence now, moving more quickly as she leaned back periodically to appraise the unfolding design. But when she began drawing a straight line down the front of my mound to highlight the shape of the fly on the front of my pants, I couldn't stop moving my hips as my clit buzzed in anticipation. When she stopped just shy of my throbbing nub, I peered down at her, disappointed.

"I thought you were going to spend a bit more time down there," I said. "My love button is dying for some special attention. Doesn't it need a special disguise too?"

Bree paused, holding her black brush inches from my glistening pearl, trying to decide how to best camouflage the parted folds of my swelling labia.

"Spread your legs," she said. "I think I know just the trick."

I shifted my legs apart and Bree drew a straight line from the crack of my ass to the bottom of the fly seam just above my clit.

"That's it?" I protested. "That's all the attention you're going to give me down there?"

"I don't want you to get too excited. You'll mess up my perfect design. But I'm not quite done yet. Spread your legs a little wider so I can see what I'm doing."

I widened my stance another foot apart and inhaled slowly, thinking Bree was going to tease my love button with her brush from the extra room I was providing. But instead, she tilted her head and drew a fine line down the inside of both thighs all the way to the bottom hemline of both legs. Then she grabbed the gray brush and swiped it gently over the side of my shinbones. When she finished, she stood up and appraised my body from top to bottom. Molly rounded the corner and nodded approvingly at Bree's composition.

"Very nice, Bree," she said, admiring the design. "I see you've taken my guidance well on how to create the appropriate shading to highlight the edges of the lapels and seams. That was very clever the way you drew the jacket lapels over Jade's breasts to disguise her nipples. Did you have any other questions before we wrap up?"

"Just one thing," Bree said, focusing on the front of my chest with pinched eyebrows. "The lapels still look a little flat, like they're, well, *painted* on. I've tried outlining them already with a black color. Have you got any other ideas as to how I can make them look a bit more natural and realistic?"

"I think so," Molly said. "Once again, it's all about using different shades of the base color to create subtle shadows mimicking the natural fall of light on the different angles of the fabric. The lapels naturally curve over a woman's chest, reflecting more light from above. You just need to use a lighter shade of navy to create the illusion of the natural fabric. I'll demonstrate once again on Jade's right side, and you do the left."

Molly dabbled some navy paint into the mixing palette then dabbled a swish of white paint into the mixture to lighten it slightly. Then she took a medium-hair brush and swiped it a few times down the right side of my chest and stepped back.

"See how that highlights the lapel slightly, making it seem to bend and curve naturally in the light?"

"Yes," Bree said. "Thanks for your help. I think I can take it from here."

Molly looked up at the wall clock showing we only had only fifteen minutes left in our session.

"How much more time do you need?"

"Just a couple more minutes, then we'll be done."

Molly handed Bree her brush and she dipped it back into the mixture, then she carefully swiped the brush over the other side of my jacket lapel. She stepped back and nodded at the final result, then reached over for the fine-point brush on the table.

"It just needs one more finishing touch," she said.

She dabbed the brush into the bowl of white paint, then she leaned back in toward my chest and drew a thin horizontal line directly over my right nipple.

"Well it's a little too late for that," I sighed in mock disappointment. "But I'll take whatever I can get at this point."

"I think you'll be happy with the final result," Bree said, smiling into my eyes. "We can always have more fun playing with you later. Right now, I'm excited to show you the finished product. I think you look absolutely stunning in your custom-tailored business suit."

When everybody had finished painting their designs, Molly drew our attention to the front of the room and had each model pose once again for the group.

The chunky lesbian girl had been dressed as a clown, which actually looked superrealistic with her oversized circus shoes, spongy nose, and curly red hair. The batman couple had flipped roles, with the girl painted this time as Batgirl, which didn't seem terribly inspired, but nonetheless looked sexy on her slim and shapely frame. The guy with the big dick was dressed as a fireman, with a thick coil of hose painted over his shoulder. A loose section of the hose dangled down the front of his torso, with the open end strategically positioned directly over his thick organ. I nodded at the creative placement of the brass fitting on the end of the tube used to disguise the exposed glans of his penis. Someone would have to look twice to notice from a distance that he was stark naked. I smiled, thinking how much fun the couple might have with this design after they went home and charged up his firehose with a little extra pressure. The young lesbian couple chose to go with another cartoon superhero theme, this time using the Joker's quirky sidekick Harley Quinn as their muse. Bree and I both lingered for a few extra seconds ogling her girlish figure, recalling the sexy image of Margot Robbie from the recent movie, *Suicide Squad*.

When it came our turn to present, everyone commented on how realistic the suit looked on my body, and when I looked in the full-length mirror, I was floored at how good a job Bree had done. The shadows around the shirt collar and jacket lapels made the design seem to stand out in 3-D relief, and the positioning of the lapel edges and pant seams made it almost impossible for someone standing at a distance to notice my prominent breasts and bare pussy. She'd even added a white pocket square over my breast patch to help disguise my protruding nipples. I'd never been more excited in my life to show my naked body to someone, and I was eager to test how well it would pass the public scrutiny of strangers outside the studio.

"You did an incredible job!" I said, turning to give Bree a big wet kiss.

"Do you really think so? Do you think it's fairly realistic?"

"*Fairly?* I bet I could sit at the end of a boardroom table and hardly anyone would tell I was naked. Let's give it a try and see what people in the street think!"

"You mean walk out of here just like *that*?" Bree said with wide eyes.

"Absolutely. What's the worst that could happen? Get arrested for public indecency?"

"That, and a major traffic pileup from rubberneckers gawking at your gorgeous body."

"Only if they figure out that I'm actually naked. Come on, let's get out of here and have some fun!"

4

————

EN PLEIN AIR

Bree and I pranced out of the art studio giggling like two schoolgirls. I stopped to fetch my black pumps from my car, then we walked arm-in-arm down the sidewalk of the local street. A few oncoming cars passed by without any sign of recognition, then one of the drivers on my side of the street stepped on his brakes and craned his neck into his rearview mirror as he passed by. We stopped at an intersection waiting for the light to change, and someone on the opposite side honked his horn when the lead car paused unusually long at the green light. When we stepped onto the crosswalk, an older woman approaching from the other side smiled at us, then her eyes opened wide when she realized that I was naked.

"This is crazy," Bree said, looking at the stunned look on the faces of passing motorists.

"It's not so bad," I shrugged, turning my head to assess the oncoming traffic. "So far I've only noticed a couple of people recognizing me. This road is too quiet to do a fair test. Let's turn down this busier street and see how many heads turn. It's much more liberating than I imagined walking outside without any clothes."

"It'll only seem liberating until a cop pulls over and throws you inside his paddy wagon."

"You only live once," I said, hooking my other arm through Bree's and pulling her across the adjacent crosswalk. "Let's live a little dangerously!"

As we began to walk along the side of the busy boulevard, most of the motorists passed by without incident, but after a short time, more and more drivers slowed down and honked their horns when they realized what was going on. By the time we approached the next intersection, men were cat-calling at us through their open windows and weaving dangerously across the road. When we got to the light, I heard the sudden screech of tires and the sound of crunching metal behind me. Bree and I looked over our shoulders, and when we realized it was only a minor fender-bender, we scampered across the intersection to the other side.

"I *told* you we were going to cause a traffic jam," she said. "Haven't we had enough fun already? Let's get out of here before someone gets seriously hurt."

I glanced around me, noticing the accumulation of pedestrians staring at us from the other side of the intersection.

"Okay, but where can we go? It's at least a twenty-minute walk back to our car."

Bree heard the sound of a passing overhead train and looked up.

"Let's take the El to the next stop. It'll bring us closer to the studio, and at least get us off the street."

"And be packed in a sardine can with a bunch of leering passengers?" I said, beginning to feel increasingly self-conscious from so many prying eyes upon me.

"It shouldn't be too busy at this time of the day," Bree said. "We'll can find a spot in the corner and I'll stand next to you to provide cover."

She glanced over her shoulder at the two bickering motorists, pulling me toward the transit station entrance.

"Let's get out of here before the police arrive."

The station wasn't as busy as I feared, and we passed through the turnstiles without incident as other commuters hurried up the escalator to catch an incoming train. Bree stood below me on the moving stairs to block the view of other people riding behind, and I crossed my arms over my chest as passengers riding the opposite escalator gawked at my unusually tight-fitting clothes. I was glad we were able to step inside the arriving train as soon as we reached the platform. We found an empty corner of the carriage and sat on a side bench facing away from the rest of the compartment.

"Whew!" Bree giggled, squeezing my hand tightly beside me. "That was a close one. I was afraid that guy from the accident was going to blame you for the crash."

"We're still not entirely in the clear," I said, glancing nervously around the compartment. "What if a transit cop sees us? I'm pretty sure riding in the nude on a public train is against the rules."

"Just be cool," Bree said, noticing the other passengers scattered around the car staring at their phones. "Nobody's noticed you yet, and we're all alone on this side of the car."

She looked down at my crossed arms and legs and smiled.

"You know, I've barely had a chance to look at you from a distance since we left the studio. Do you mind if I sit on the opposite side of the aisle and take a few pictures? It'll be kind of cool to have some photos of a nude businesswoman riding the train to work."

"What the hell," I shrugged. "Might as well milk this thing for all it's worth while the going is good. Just don't leave me alone if more passengers come down this way."

"Don't worry," Bree said, smiling at me reassuringly. "I'll protect you from any peeping Toms."

She stood up and walked over to the adjacent bench seat and reached into her purse. Then she held up her camera and tapped the screen.

"Don't look so stuffy," she said. "Uncross your arms so I can see your pretty tits. There's no point going out in public like this if you're not going to flaunt it a little bit."

I uncrossed my arms and placed my hands in my lap, not knowing where to put them. In my haste to get away from the studio, I'd stowed my purse and other belongings in my car. It felt strange to be sitting in a public venue without my phone or any other personal effects, making me feel even more exposed.

"That's good," Bree smiled, as she tapped her screen to take a few pictures. "Now spread your legs a little bit. Imagine you're riding to work and you're trying to steal the attention of a pretty girl on the other side of the train."

"Like *this* one," I said, nodding toward Bree as I parted my legs.

"Exactly. Imagine she can see between your legs and notices you're not wearing any panties. See if you can get her to squirm in her seat while she looks at your sexy naked body."

I parted my knees further and placed my right hand on my crotch as I began to rub my nub under the dry latex paint. The coating felt strange to my touch, like when I was washing dishes wearing rubber gloves. But this sensation was a whole lot more enjoyable than cleaning dishes. As I felt my button begin to swell under the tight film, the buildup of juices around my pussy made a seductive squishing sound.

"*Yes*," Bree said. "Just like that. You are so turning me on. Can I take you home with me when we're done here? I've been fantasizing about fucking you ever since our first painting session. I want you to teach me all your girly moves."

I smiled at Bree, pointing my toes to spread my legs wider.

"If I wasn't covered in this tight film of paint, I'd show you one right now," I said, wanting to plunge my hand into my sopping pussy and finger-fuck myself while she watched me. But I was thankful to have the coating of paint protecting my bare skin from all the germs on the public transit seat.

Just then, the train roared into the next station and the doors opened as more passengers streamed into our end of the car. I shook my head at Bree, wondering if she wanted to exit at this stop. She noticed a folded newspaper in the corner of her seat and quickly threw it across the aisle to me. Two passengers took positions on opposite sides of each of us, and I unfolded the paper and crossed my legs, holding the tabloid over my chest.

With the paper concealing most of my upper body, neither of the new passengers seemed to notice that I was sitting bare-naked directly in front of them. Bree looked at me and smiled with a devilish grin. I was beginning to enjoy this process of play-acting like a regular commuter, and Bree tilted her head sideways, encouraging me to uncross my legs again. I furrowed my eyebrows, watching the pretty girl next to her clicking her thumbs on her smartphone.

Bree frowned and mouthed the words *'You only live once'* to me.

I lifted my knee and slowly parted my legs, shuffling the paper to distract attention from my shifting position. But the noise caught the attention of the girl next to Bree, and she looked up from her phone and did a double-take when she noticed the deep cleft between my legs created by my swollen labia. I froze in terror, realizing that she'd found me out, then she looked up and smiled at me before tapping on her screen with increased urgency. It was obvious that she was texting someone about what she'd just seen and I glanced at Bree, rolling my eyeballs to my side to indicate that her seatmate had discovered me. Bree looked down out the corner of her eyes at what the girl was tapping on the screen and smiled at me.

'She thinks you're hot!' she mouthed.

Suddenly Bree's brows furrowed and the color went out of her face as she realized the girl was opening the camera app on her phone. She held her fists out in front of her chest and raised them a few inches, signaling for me to cover my face. When the girl tilted her phone toward me, I crossed my legs and spread the paper as wide as I could to conceal my identity. As much fun as I was having playing this little game of striptease, the last thing I needed was for an image of me sitting naked on the subway going viral all over the internet.

When the train rushed into the next station and the doors opened, I stood up and rushed toward the exit. I'd had enough of sharing my body with a bunch of strangers, I just wanted Bree all to myself. She followed me out of the car and we paused on the platform to discuss our next step.

I noticed a taxi dropping someone off at the station entrance below the platform.

"Let's grab a cab and go home," I said. "I think I've had quite enough of this exhibitionist routine. It's time to get out of these clothes and feel your naked body next to mine."

"I was thinking the exact same thing," Bree said. "Do you want to go to your place or mine?"

"I need to go somewhere safe and comfortable. Do you mind coming to my place? We can always go back to the studio to pick up our cars a little later."

"I'm in no rush," she smiled. "Except to feel your bare skin again."

A s soon as we got to my place and I closed the door behind us, I turned around and pinned Bree against the frame. As I pressed my body against her and kissed her passionately, I rubbed my burning clit against her hip.

"Fuck, that was hot," I panted. "That has got to be one of the sexiest things I've ever done."

"No kidding," she said. "Did you see the look on that girl's face when she realized you were naked?"

"I almost had a heart attack when I realized she was trying to take a picture of me. What was she typing on her phone?"

"Something about this hot babe sitting naked in front of her on the train. She told her friend you were gorgeous and that you were turning you on."

"Did that get you turned on too?"

"Are you kidding me? I almost came when you started touching yourself."

"Let's go upstairs," I said. "Help me get this stuff off so I can properly make love to you. I'm damp as a dishrag under all this plastic coating."

"Can we leave it on just a little longer?" Bree asked. "I want to fantasize about the business executive having her way with me before you go back to your normal identity."

She lifted her finger to my mouth and pulled my bottom lip down.

"You still have a few open bare patches where we can have some fun."

"As long as you help me peel this off all the *other* spots where we can have even more fun."

I took her by the hand and led her upstairs to my bedroom, then laid her atop my comforter.

"Now it's *your* turn to spread your legs," I said. "I've been dreaming of sucking your pussy ever since I covered you in yellow paint at our first workshop. Let me show you what it feels like to be properly made love to by a woman."

"Yes, boss," Bree grinned. "Teach me the right way to do the job."

I pushed Bree's torso down on the bed, then began to unbutton her blouse. It was lightly splattered with blue paint around the collar, and I smiled remembering how pretty she looked as she concentrated on painting me.

"The first thing to remember," I said, getting back into character for our play-acting scenario, "is to not rush an important task like this. The key is to tease your subject, so her arousal level slowly builds up until she's begging for you to touch her."

Bree looked at me with a playful expression.

"What if she's *already* seriously turned on from all the foreplay we've just been through?"

I paused, peering at her with a lopsided grin, then I grabbed the two sides of her blouse and ripped it apart, revealing her bare breasts.

"Then you dispense with any unnecessary effort and seize the opportunity when it reveals itself."

"Hey!" Bree protested in mock indignation. "That was one of my most expensive blouses. Now you're going to have to give me a raise."

"Oh, I'll give you a *raise*, alright," I sneered, leaning down to suck her puffy areolas into my mouth.

As I sucked on her teats, I could feel them swelling in my mouth, and after a few moments I lifted my head and stared at her unique double-domed breasts.

"That's my girl," I panted. "God, how I love your pointy breasts. Do you like it when I suck on your pretty tits?"

"Yes," Bree sighed. "Show me how to properly lick a woman's breasts. I want to learn everything from you so I can return the favor when it's your turn."

"Mmm, yes," I smiled. "Soon enough. But since this is your first time, I think it's only fair that I spend a little more time with you. Lie back while I worship your beautiful temple."

I placed my mouth back over Bree's swollen nipples and circled my tongue around her tips as I felt them harden and press further into my mouth.

"That feels so good, Jade," Bree moaned. "Don't stop. Suck my big pink nipples. Hold me like the lovers in Klimt's painting."

"I couldn't touch you the way I wanted while I was painting you," I said, moving up to kiss her lips. The brush can only accomplish so much. You've got to lose yourself in your painting in order to truly appreciate it's beauty."

"Yes, Jade," Bree panted. "Lose yourself in me. I want to feel you become one with me just like the lovers in the painting."

Seeing the flush in her pale cheeks, I bent down and began kissing her down the front of her torso. As I passed her breasts, I reached out one last time and squeezed them gently, rolling her thick nipples between my fingers. I could have spent all day playing with her tits, but her gyrating hips told me she wanted my attention elsewhere.

When I reached her navel, I unfastened the button at the top of her jeans then I unzipped her pants and pulled them off her legs. She was wearing gold-covered lace panties, and I smiled remembering what it was like to touch her there while I painted her at the studio.

"You shouldn't have," I purred, looking at her bare skin under the lacy threads.

"This time you can *remove* the yellow from my body rather than covering me with it."

"That's exactly what I was thinking," I said.

As I curled my fingers under the top of her panties, she lifted her hips off the mattress and I pulled them softly down her thighs. This was the first time I'd seen her pussy fully exposed from below, and I gasped when I saw how delicate it looked. She had the prettiest puffy folds of symmetrical lips running along both sides of her slit and not a single hair follicle in sight. With her pale, perfectly bald skin, her cunny almost looked like a little girl's, and I felt the latex covering sticking to my snatch as my pussy began to water like an open faucet. I could see the head of her clit poking out from its sheath, throbbing in the glistening overhead light.

"God damn, Bree," I panted. "Just when I thought you couldn't possibly get any sexier. That's the prettiest pussy I've ever laid eyes on."

"I'm glad you like it. I spent a lot of time today getting myself properly prepared. I know how you like it smooth and bald."

"I do," I said. "It's as smooth as a baby's bottom."

"Lick my bare pussy, Jade. Show me how to make love to a woman."

"Oh, Bree," I said. "You have no idea how much I've wanted to do this. Just lie back and enjoy."

I lowered myself onto the bed between Bree's legs and began kissing her thighs up toward her mound. The closer I got to her pussy, the wetter her skin became as her lubrication streamed down her legs. I moaned, remembering the image of the yellow paint running down the inside of her thighs when I brushed her bare vulva in the workshop. I lapped up her sweet nectar and closed my eyes savoring the fresh scent.

When I reached her pussy, I flattened my tongue and licked the front of her slit like an ice cream cone up and down a few times, as Bree made soft mewing sounds. Then I closed my lips around her soft labia and sucked her flesh into my mouth. Bree spread her legs wider for me, and I nibbled my way up toward the apex of her folds. When I finally reached her burning clit and closed my mouth around her, she gasped and pressed her mound into my face.

"Oh God," she moaned. "It feels incredible to feel your lips around me. I'm going to come, Jade. Hold me close."

I was surprised that Bree was ready to climax so quickly, but I knew that this was her first time experiencing cunnilingus, and I was thrilled she was so turned on by my touch. Her hips jerked softly against my face as she grunted above me, and I pressed my tongue against her bud, feeling it tremble in my mouth. I held her gently while she came down from her high, then I pulled myself up beside her and peered into her blushing face.

"That was fast," I said.

"I've never felt anything like that before," she said. "That's way better than doing it by hand."

"Even with a wet brush?" I said, smiling into her eyes.

"Well you were giving me a little more focused attention down there this time. Speaking of which, I promised you more of that at the studio. Can I return the favor now?"

"By all means," I said. "But I think you'll have to help me off with my clothes first. I'm probably covered in who-knows-how-many germs from the subway seat."

Bree peered back at me and smiled.

"Maybe I only need to remove a little flap over your strategic areas. Let me enjoy this little fantasy for a little longer."

I kissed Bree softly, feeling the wetness building up in my crotch.

"Okay, but I have a feeling you won't need any special moisturizer to loosen things up down there. I'm already soaking wet between my legs."

As Bree wiggled her body down beside me, she kissed and licked the sticky paint covering my torso. When she reached my breasts, she squeezed them gently and flicked her tongue around my nipples just I'd done with earlier.

"What does it feel like underneath all this paint?" she asked.

"Kind of strange, actually. I can feel you touching me, but everything is kind of desensitized."

"That's not what your *nipples* are telling me," Bree said, noticing my teats pushing up against the stretchy film.

"Maybe this is what it feels like for a guy wearing a condom," I mused. "He can get hard, but it doesn't feel the same as going au naturel. I've always enjoyed the touch of bare skin far more."

"We can arrange that," Bree smiled, noticing my hips beginning to gyrate in excitement.

She lifted herself up and positioned herself between my thighs, then paused for a moment to study her handiwork.

"It almost seems a shame to take this off," she said. "I drew the paint seam so perfectly right over your crot—"

"If you don't tear these off me soon," I interrupted, "I'm gonna jump you and fuck you, pretty pants or not. I'm dying to feel your sweet mouth on my bare lips."

Bree looked up at me with a devilish grin.

"I'm just playing with you. You told me earlier that the key to making love to a woman is to tease her until she's begging for you to touch her."

"You're a quick study, girl," I smiled back at her. "But I think you've gotten me properly warmed up. Now get down there and show me some love."

"Yes boss."

She spread my legs further apart, then she dug her fingernails into the sides of my vulva and drew them down toward my bottom. I could feel the rubbery film stretching, then I felt a rush of cool air as the seal broke over my wet pussy. It was an exhilarating feeling being exposed in this raw condition to Bree, but I worried that the lack of fresh air to my covered pussy over the last couple of hours might create an unpleasant smell.

"It feels so good to let my pussy breathe again," I said. "But it must stink down there after being all closed up this long."

Bree moved in closer and began to peel the layer of film away from my perineum.

"Not at all," she said, inhaling a deep breath through her nose. "You just smell...*sexy*."

"At least it should be *clean* down there," I said. "Nothing else has touched me since I showered this morning."

"Let's see if we can remedy that situation."

When I felt Bree's lips touch my pussy, I moaned as I tilted my hips up to meet her lips.

"God, I needed this so bad," I hissed. "I feel like I've been freed from a cage. Suck my pussy, baby. Make your boss cum with your pretty lips."

She proceeded to nibble and tease my labia as I'd shown her earlier, then she placed her lips over my raging clit and sucked me into her mouth.

"Yes, Bree," I panted. "Suck my clit. It feels so good."

Bree circled my pearl with her tongue, then she began flicking it up and down in a repeating pattern. I lifted my head and pulled her head up gently.

"Don't forget to mix it up a bit, baby," I said. "A girl likes to feel like she's being worshipped down there, not trilled by a teenage boy. Pretend you're licking a lollypop. Sometimes you suck on it, sometimes you lick it, and sometimes you roll it around in your mouth. It's the *variety* that turns your partner on."

"Sorry, Jade," she said, looking up at me with her wet face. "This is all so new for me. I'm glad you're teaching me. I want to learn how to satisfy you. Keep telling me what you like while I lick you."

She placed her face back between my legs and rolled my nub around her mouth, alternating between licking and sucking. As I began to feel my passion rising, I rolled my hips on the bed and moaned in excitement.

"That's perfect, Bree," I panted. "I'm getting close. Make love to me with your mouth."

I reached down with my two hands and pulled her face tighter against my pussy. It didn't take long for me to reach the point of no return, and I lifted my hips off the bed as I cupped Bree's face in my hands.

"I'm going to come for you baby," I groaned. "I'm gonna cum so hard in your mouth."

When the wave finally poured over me, I whinnied like an injured animal from the pleasure rolling over me.

"Uhhn," I moaned. "I'm cumming, Bree! Taste me, baby."

As the explosion of built-up lubrication inside my pussy poured out of me, I felt my juices spraying against the side of my thighs and all over Bree's face as I held her tightly against me. My contractions lasted for almost a full minute while I jerked and heaved my hips in the throes of climax. When I finally collapsed my body back onto the bed, Bree lay transfixed watching my vulva continue spasming until I exhaled heavily, signaling the end of my powerful orgasm.

"That was so hot!" she exclaimed, shimmying up excitedly beside me. Her looked like she'd devoured a messy watermelon. "I didn't know a girl could squirt like that. You almost *drowned* me with your juices."

"Sorry, baby. I can get pretty wet when I'm turned on. I think I had quite a bit pent up inside me from all the foreplay leading up to this. When you made me cum so hard, it just gushed all out of me."

"So I did a pretty good job for my first time, boss?" she said, smiling at me.

"Yes, baby," I said, peering into her pretty green eyes.

I placed my mouth over her glistening lips and tasted my sweetness coating her face.

"And next time," I said, remembering that we'd be using edible paint at our next painting session, "I'll be the one eating you all up."

5

FORBIDDEN FRUIT

I made love to Bree all afternoon, bringing her to multiple new highs worshipping her tender body. I wanted her to spend the night, but she was beginning to experience cramps from all the powerful orgasms she'd experienced, and she had mid-term exams the next day. In the intervening days leading up to our next bodypainting class, we texted back and forth like lovestruck teenagers, teasing each other about what we planned to do at the next session.

I went online and scrolled through hundreds of images of nude bodypainting models, but by the morning of our class, I still wasn't sure what theme I'd like to use. It was Bree's turn to be the model again, and I was looking forward to playing out our fantasies in front the whole class. I wasn't sure how far Molly would allow us to explore our partners in full view of the other participants, but I had a feeling the addition of edible paint would create some strong temptations.

When Bree and I arrived at the studio, three of the couples from the last session were already there and they asked us about our experience testing our business suit design in the street. The young lesbian couple seemed particularly interested in where we went, and when we told them about our train experience, their eyes widened in excitement. Everybody seemed more charged up than usual for today's class, but I noticed the fireman stud from the previous session kept tapping his phone while he glanced out the front window impatiently. As we neared the appointed start time, Molly asked where his girlfriend was and he said they'd had a fight and wasn't sure she'd attend. When she offered to step in to be his painting partner for today's session, he took one look at her sexy body and nodded sheepishly.

At ten a.m., she looked outside the front door then latched it shut and slowly pulled the blackout blinds over the windows. I was glad she was being more careful than usual, because I knew if any passersby had any inkling as to what was going on inside, they'd be pressing their noses to the glass. When she was certain we had complete privacy, she went to the front of the room to address our group.

"As I mentioned at our last class, today we're going to change things up with a different type of paint. This time, we're going to use a special type of edible paint that will allow you to have a little more fun when I comes time to clean up. But I should warn you that this paint isn't quite as durable as the oil and latex paint we used previously, so it can get a bit messy and runny if you leave it on for too long.

"Also, in the interest of sharing the spoils with everybody, I encourage you to switch roles halfway through the session so that *both* partners will have a chance to be participate in the fun. As always, all your necessary materials are laid out for you at your respective painting stations, and you've got additional design ideas to browse through on your easels."

Molly looked over at the fireman stud and smiled.

"It looks like Brett will be on his own today, so I'll be pairing up with him for today's session. But if any of you need any help at any time, just give me a shout and I'll pull away for a few moments. Before we get started, do you have any questions?"

One of the young lesbian girls put up her hand.

"Yes, Lindsey?"

"What exactly is the edible paint made from? I mean, how safe is it to—*eat*?"

Molly nodded her head with the familiar question.

"You might be surprised to find that it's made from the same ingredients as store-bought Jello pudding. It's a blend of milk, sugar, cornstarch, butter, and vegetable-based food dyes, totally non-toxic and safe to eat. Although it might be a little cool to the touch at first, since it's been kept refrigerated to keep it from spoiling. But that just makes it all the more titillating to apply. Were there any other questions?"

The girl from the Batcouple pair raised her hand timidly.

"Yes, Kate?"

"Are we allowed to, you know, *sample* our creations from time to time as we work on them?"

Molly's lips curled into a sly smile.

"That's the whole point of using edible paint. Half the fun is in removing it once you've finished your design. We realize that some of you may find it difficult to contain your excitement as you're being painted. If you want to explore your creation more closely at any time, we've tried to provide a safe and open environment to do so."

Molly paused as she looked around the room.

"But if anybody is going to feel uncomfortable about seeing others touch their partner's body in this way, now is the time to say so. We don't want anyone feeling self-conscious about either watching or being watched as we explore this fun facet of the bodypainting experience. Of course, if you want some additional privacy, you're also welcome to use our private change rooms in the rear."

Molly paused to make eye contact with each workshop participant to be sure everyone was comfortable with the rules of engagement.

"Does anybody have any more questions before we get started?"

Everybody looked at their partners and nodded with crooked grins on their faces. Bree and I moved to the nearest painting station and flipped over a few design panels on the easel to generate ideas. The themes seemed to be divided between the main food groups. Most of the male models were painted in fruit or vegetable themes, with the strategic placement of various tubers and legumes used to disguise their hanging genitalia. Many of the female models were painted in dessert themes, with cherry-topped sundaes and other sundry pastries used to disguise their private parts. But we both paused when we saw a picture of the sexy Latin actress Carmen Miranda wearing a skimpy costume of grapes and berries with a fruit bowl perched atop her head.

"What do you think?" I said, looking at Bree. "Are you hungry for the main course, dessert, or a little appetizer?"

"As much as I like the idea of licking all those yummy-looking pastries off you, I think the vegetable and fruit themes might be a little easier to paint."

I glanced at the picture of Carmen Miranda and nodded.

"You might be right, but remember what Molly said. This session isn't so much about trying to create a perfect design as it is about having fun and enjoying the cleanup process. It's just going to get all smeared off soon enough, anyway."

"Mmm," Bree smiled, thinking back on how we rubbed our bodies together when she was at my place. "I like the idea of smearing it off each other. Who should go first?"

I turned to the front of the room and saw Brett beginning to strip in front of Molly.

"Why don't you go first so I can guide you along the way? I have a feeling Molly's going to have her hands full for most of this class. Besides, I've got a little surprise embellishment that I have planned for the end."

"Oh?" Bree said, widening her eyes in curiosity. "I thought you'd already showed me all your tricks when I was at your place."

I smiled at her with a raised eyebrow.

"A good lover likes to mix it up from time to time, remember? Plus, I like to save the best for last. Kind of like the cherry atop the ice cream sundae."

"So you were thinking of painting me in a dessert theme? I've been dying for you to lick my cherry again."

"You'll have to wait and see," I said. "Just try not to melt until I finish. This particular surprise will require a stiff upper lip, so to speak. Go get yourself ready while I strip."

"Yes, boss."

As Bree popped the lids off the glass jars of pudding paint, I glanced around the room to see how the other partners were progressing. The Batgirl at the next station over had chosen a meat theme to paint on her hunky boyfriend as she began to paint sinewy slabs of steak over his bulging pecs. The young lesbian couple was going with the pastry theme, as I watched one of the girls lean in closely to paint pretty pink cupcakes over her girlfriend's breasts.

The middle-aged couple had chosen a playful seafood-based theme, as the slender one began to paint an image of a school of fish swimming across her partner's undulating chest. Molly was painting another meat locker theme on Brett's gym-toned fireman's body. I glanced down at his thick Johnson swaying between his legs and noticed it twitching as she began moving her brush down his body.

"So, what'll it be?" Bree said, swinging around with her brush in her hand. "Citrus fruit up top and strawberries down below?"

"Sounds about right," I smiled. "Melons to cover my big parts and berries to cover the little ones."

"What do you think about grapefruits to cover your breasts? They're pink and sweet, and about the right size."

I paused, remembering some of the images I'd seen while surfing online to get ideas before the workshop.

"That could work," I said. "But did you know there's a special type of fruit grown in Southeast Asia that looks almost exactly like a woman's bare breasts? It's called milk melon, and it's incredibly erotic. Here, let me show you."

I reached into my purse on the floor and pulled out my phone, then tapped on my screen a few times.

"See?" I said, turning the screen around for Bree to view the images.

The picture showed a bamboo trellis with long flesh-colored bulbs hanging down from the vine. At the bottom of the spoon-shaped plants was a swelling with a darkened circle in the center that looked amazingly like a bare breast.

"It might be kind of fun to paint a bunch of these on my chest to make me look like I have multiple boobs. It would be hard to distinguish the real ones from the fake ones."

Bree took a look at the screen and jerked her head back in amazement.

"That's a *real* fruit?!" she asked. "They look exactly like a woman's breasts!"

"Yes, except for their elongated shape. But that just makes them look all the more erotic, like some kind of Salvador Dali painting."

"No kidding," Bree said. "Talk about a surreal image. I'm not sure if this is going to make you look more sexy or *creepy*!"

"It won't seem so creepy when you're sucking on those fake breasts once they're painted on my chest. Get to it girl. The clock is ticking."

"Okay," Bree said. "Just help me figure out how to blend the paint to create that unique color."

"Place equal parts of red, yellow, and blue on the mixing plate, then mix them together. You'll want to make it slightly darker than my skin tone so they stand out more clearly on my chest. If you need to lighten it, just add a bit of white to the mix."

Bree mixed the paint as I suggested, then dipped a medium-width brush in the blend and held it up to my chest.

"Here's goes nothing," she said. "Are you sure you're ready to have three breasts?"

"The more the merrier," I chuckled.

"All the more to suck on," Bree smiled.

She leaned in began slowly drawing the brush down from the base of my neck toward the center of my chest. When she reached the top of my cleavage, I could feel her moving the brush in circles as she stared intently at the design. Then she swiped the brush up and down the center of my chest a few times and stepped back and glanced at my phone to compare it to the photo.

"That was easier than I thought," she said. "It about the right color, and it stands out in nice contrast to the rest of your skin. Now I just need to add the fake nipple. Red and white makes pink, right?"

"You got it, girl."

Bree mixed the new shade, then used a finer-point brush to paint the darker nipple in the center of my new breast. She circled over it a few times to create the proper shading and shadow, then stepped back and nodded.

"Not bad, if I do say so myself," she said. "It almost looks like your real breasts."

"Just a lot more pendulous," I chuckled.

"Good point," Bree said. "We'll need to touch up your real ones a little bit to create the surreal effect from the image."

Bree leaned back over the mixing table and dabbled the brush in the flesh-colored paint, then turned around and began painting some lines above each of my breasts. Each time her brush reached the top of my tits, she paused and feathered the paint to blend in with the lighter shade reflecting from the lights overhead.

"I kind of wish we'd gone with the grapefruit theme," I frowned. "You're barely even touching my actual breasts this time."

"That's part of the *look*, remember? We're trying to mimic fake boobs alongside your real ones. They'll get plenty of attention later when I suck *all* of your breasts when we're done."

Bree proceeded to paint a few more faux breasts on the top and side of my chest, then she stepped back and compared her design with the photo one last time.

"I think I've got the gist of it," she nodded. "It looks pretty much just like the melons in the photo. Shall I paint the bamboo shoots behind them to simulate the look of a trellis?"

I looked up at the clock and noticed that forty-five minutes had already passed.

"I think you better move on to the lower part so we don't run out of time. I'm dying to feel your brush again on my clit. Besides, we still have to allow a bit of time at the end for the fun part."

"Oh yeah," she said. "For the *surprise*."

Bree glanced at the picture of Carmen Miranda on the easel, then began mixing a darker shade of pink to simulate the color of cherries. As she began painting the belt of hanging fruit around my waist, I glanced around the room again to see how the other teams were doing.

The Batcouple had almost finished painting the hunky guy in their deli-case theme, with mouth-watering cuts of ham, turkey, and beef covering his shredded abdomen. His girlfriend had cleverly angled a turkey roast over his crotch so that one drumstick extended down his thigh while the other one rested over his throbbing organ. I glanced over to the other side of the room, where the young lesbian girl sat on the edge of the mixing table with her legs spread apart as her partner kneeled in front of her painting a white cake with strawberries over her mound and pussy.

"Hurry up, Bree," I said. "I'm starting to get hungry. I can't wait to eat you all up."

Bree smiled at me as she dipped the fine-point brush in the pink paint mixture, then she sat down directly in front of me and began painting strawberries around my vulva. When her wet brush touched my clit and she began swirling it around in little circles to paint another berry, I sighed in pleasure.

"Keep doing that and you're going to make me come," I said.

"I better stop then," she said, smiling up at me. "I wouldn't want to ruin the buildup. I'm supposed to make you *beg* for it, aren't I?"

"I've taught you too well," I cursed.

Bree stood up and stepped back to appraise her creation, then she took a quick glance at the picture on the easel.

"Not quite as intricate as Carmen's dress, but I think it'll do in a pinch. You definitely look edible."

"Okay, *your* turn," I said, shifting her to the other side of the easel. "Now it's my chance to have a little fun with you."

"Were you thinking of painting me in a similar style?" Bree asked.

"With a slight variation," I said, winking at her. "I think I'll continue with the fruit theme, just with some different types of exotic fruit."

Bree looked at me curiously.

"Does this have something to do with the surprise you mentioned earlier?"

"Maybe," I smiled. "But just like with your Kiss painting, you're just going to have to wait until the end to see what it looks like."

"Damn, Jade, you're such a tease."

"Just like I taught you. Don't you find it makes for a more intense climax?"

"Yes, but maybe you can be a bit easier on me this time. It took three days for those abdominal cramps to go away after I last saw you."

"A lot of women would give their right arm to experience orgasms that powerful."

"I suppose you're right. I guess not *all* girl cramps are bad."

As I began painting my design on the front of Bree's body, she looked around the room, and I noticed a little stream of fluid running down the inside of her right thigh. She seemed particularly intent on watching the pretty lesbian couple in the far corner, and I wondered just how far along they'd gotten in appreciating their design. After another thirty minutes, I finished painting my composition and stepped back to admire the final product.

Molly had placed full-length mirrors on the opposite side of each workstation easel, and I motioned for Bree to step toward the back of the Batcouple's tripod to assess her completed design. When she looked in the mirror, she smiled at the level of detail I'd put into my concept. The horn of cornucopia tilted down the front of her chest, spilling it's bounty of fruit onto her bare mound and pussy.

"Mmm," she said. "I like how the bowl of fruit points to my kitty. But what's that purple-colored fruit right at the base of the bowl?"

"That's an eggplant."

"Isn't that a vegetable? It looks a bit like a—"

"Penis?" I chuckled, recognizing the familiar shape. "It's definitely a fruit. A very *tasty* fruit when cooked in the right way. But yes, it also makes a very sexy dildo when you're in a pinch."

I reached down into my purse and pulled out a real, eight-inch eggplant. Bree's mouth opened wide when she realized what I had in mind.

"You're kidding?" she said. "You put that thing *inside* you?"

"This one's big enough to fit inside *both* of us," I grinned.

Bree opened her eyes as big as saucers.

"You've been holding back on me," she smiled.

"Hey, a girl doesn't want to reveal *all* of her tricks on the first date."

Bree shook her head as she pinched her eyebrows at me.

"You weren't thinking—*right here*?" she said.

I looked around the room and saw that each of the other couples were locked in a passionate embrace as they kissed and licked each other's bodies. The lesbian couples were already grinding their hips together and we could hear the moaning of the Batcouple behind their easel. Even Molly and Brett were getting into it at the front of the room, as her head bobbed over his drumstick that was pointing straight up in the air.

"Looks like everybody's gotten a head start on us," I said, placing my hand on her chest. "Lie down on the table so I can properly fuck you."

Bree paused, as she pushed back against me gently.

"Don't you want to see your creation first? Take a look in the mirror at the design on painted on you."

I stepped in front of the glass and gasped when I saw Bree's work. The fake milk melons blended in perfectly with my own artificially elongated tits, giving the impression of multiple swelling breasts covering my chest. I glanced down and nodded at the way she'd woven the strings of cherries around my waist to look like a hanging skirt, then strategically placed strawberries around my thighs to disguise my pussy.

"Very impressive, young lady," I said. "I particularly like the little touch where you added a dab of chocolate-colored paint at the tip of the strawberry right over my clit. Very clever—and very sexy."

"Can I lick it off you before you do me?"

"By all means," I said. "I've been dreaming about you eating my pussy this whole week."

Bree stepped toward me and reached out to cup my breasts, then leaned down and took my left nipple into her mouth. I tilted my head down and looked at the bizarre sight of many fake tits on my chest and moaned.

"Yes, Bree," I painted. "Suck my tits. *All* of my tits."

She lifted her head and began licking the tips of my faux milk melons and purred.

"Mmm," she said, smacking her lips. "They taste wonderful. So sweet."

She licked each of my fake melons clean, then placed her head over my right breast and circled her tongue around my areolas as she rolled my erect nipple around in her mouth like a lollypop.

"You're such a good student," I sighed, recalling how I'd taught her to mix up her technique.

"I studied hard," she said, popping her mouth off my rigid nipple.

"I bet you did," I said, placing my hands around her hips and swinging her over to the edge of the painting table. "Now let me have a little fun with *your* sweet fruit."

I moved the paint materials to the side of the table, then lifted her up onto the edge and kneeled down in front of her. Spreading her legs wide, I drew my tongue up the side of her thighs then licked her dripping slit from the edge of her rosebud all the way up to her steaming clit.

"Fuck, Jade," Bree grunted. "That feels so good. I want to feel you inside me."

I looked up at her and smiled, then slipped two fingers inside her tunnel as I puckered my lips over her nub and sucked her into my mouth. As I began to thrust my fingers inside her, she grabbed the back of my head and began to rock her hips into my face. I could taste the sweet smell of sugar filling my mouth as the dark purple paint began to stream down my face.

"Yes, Jade," she said. "Fuck me with your fingers. I'm so close—"

I pulled my fingers out of Bree's cunny and glanced up at her with my stained face.

"Not yet, baby. I want to feel you pressing up against me when you come. Lean back a bit more."

Bree tilted her back down toward the table and rested her weight on her two elbows as she watched me position the big eggplant in front of her pussy. I slowly inserted the slender end in her opening, then I moved in closer to her and lifted my right leg onto the table beside her. I pressed the thick end of the tuber into my hole and pressed my hips forward as the fruit disappeared inside both of our holes. When our vulvas merged and we felt our clits touch, Bree threw her head back and squealed.

"Oh my God, Jade," she yelped. "That feels incredible. Fuck me with your big purple dildo."

I grunted in pleasure, as much from the incredible sensation of the squash sliding inside me as from Bree's dirty talk. I angled my hips up and began thrusting harder against her hips as we ground our clits against one another. Bree's eyes suddenly glazed over as I realized she was on the verge of coming from the tip of the eggplant rubbing against her G-spot.

"Fuck, Jade," she suddenly screamed. "I'm going to cum! Fuck me with your big cock. Oh God—I'm cummming!"

As I watched a deep flush roll over Bree's pale chest while she bucked wildly against my hips, I listened to the sound of moans and sighs filling the rest of the room. This was one workshop I'd never forget, I thought, as I pressed my mound against Bree's, squirting red and purple paint all over her belly.

VOLUME FOUR

THE THERAPIST

1
———————

"Every time I see you, I want to tell one of those bad gynecologist jokes," I said to my sex therapist friend Hannah at our weekly luncheon.

Hannah rolled her eyes as she took another bite of her salad. Her practice seemed to be the never-ending butt of jokes among our friends, but she'd learned to take the digs with good humor.

"Well you know I'm a far cry from a gynecologist, but I could use a little laugh today, so if you really need to get it out of your system, lay it on me."

"Ok, so this old lady goes to see her dentist," I started. "When her appointment is called, she sits in the chair, lowers her underpants, and raises her legs..."

"Uh huh," Hannah murmured, lifting a glass of soda water to her lips to signal her disinterest.

"So the dentist says," I continued, 'Excuse me, but I'm not a gynecologist.'"

I paused long enough for Hannah to begin swallowing her water. "'I know,' said the old lady. 'I want you to take my husband's teeth out.'"

Hannah lurched forward, spewing her soda water all over her salad as she raised her hand to her mouth, coughing loudly.

"Are you okay?" I said, glancing at the surrounding restaurant patrons alarmed by the sudden commotion at our table.

"Y–yeah," Hannah gagged. "The water just went down the wrong way. I wasn't expecting that punchline."

"Pretty good, right?" I smiled.

"Better than most, I'll grant you," she nodded. "But I don't know why you guys always make fun of my practice. *Someone* has to help all the sexually dysfunctional people out there."

"I know," I said, frowning sheepishly. "It's just hard to imagine what goes on in your office when people talk candidly about their sex lives."

"You'd be surprised," Hannah said, taking another swig of water to clear her throat. "In fact, I was thinking of inviting you to one of my sessions sometime."

I pinched my eyebrows and shook my head, surprised at her offer.

"As a *patient* or as an observer?"

"You don't need any help with your sex life," she said. "You're already miles ahead of me with all your wild escapades and adventures. I'd like to present you as more of a role model for what a healthy, sexually uninhibited person looks like."

"What would you have me *do* exactly? Don't you have to protect patient-doctor privilege? I thought you guys had to keep everything at arms-length, so to speak."

"I've been experimenting with some different strategies lately," Hannah smiled. "Let's just say I've been trying out some more *active* therapeutic techniques."

"No way!" I said, widening my eyes as I rested my cocktail on the table so as not to spill it. "Isn't that against the rules? I thought you had to maintain a certain degree of professional distance or risk losing your license."

"I still do. The only difference is now I encourage them to practice some of the prescribed self-empowerment techniques in my *office* instead of at home, so I can coach and guide them more actively. Besides, everybody signs a waiver before we take it to the next level."

"Holy shit!" I said, shaking my glass incredulously. "While you *watch* them touch themselves intimately?"

"Sometimes," Hannah nodded. "But most patients prefer to be concealed behind a protective screen when they first start the process."

"So you basically guide them through a facilitated *masturbation* session?"

"In a manner of speaking, yes. I find most patients need a little more active engagement to get them over the hump becoming comfortable enjoying sex with another person. You'd be surprised how many sexually dysfunctional women there are out there."

"So most of your patients are women?"

"Yes—I find them much more interesting to work with."

"Oh my God," I panted, beginning to feel my panties moisten under my tight jeans. "I'd love to be a fly on the wall in one of these sessions. How do you manage to stay focused when things start to heat up? Don't you get aroused while these women pleasure themselves?"

Hannah shifted uncomfortably in her chair, signaling for the waiter to bring her another cocktail.

"I do. At first, I just kind of squirmed in my chair and squeezed my legs together in frustration. But I've discovered a more animated way to keep myself stimulated while I watch my patients enjoying themselves."

My eyes flew open as the fluid in my cocktail glass began to tremble.

"You stick a *vibrator* down your pants?!" I said. "Isn't that kind of noisy? How do you hide that from your patients?"

"It's not just *any* vibrator," Hannah said with a crooked grin. "Our friend Cheryl from the local Babeland store introduced me to a new kind of toy. It's designed by a woman to mimic the touch and movement of real fingers and lips. It doesn't buzz so much as *hum* as it undulates both inside and on the outside of your vulva."

"Jesus!" I squealed, furrowing my brow in frustration. "Just when I thought I had the full collection of the latest toys. What does this thing look like?"

Hannah opened up her purse and passed me a large finger-shaped device attached to a hollow cone at the base.

"I just happen to carry one with me wherever I go," she said. "See for yourself."

I peered at the strange-looking object, stroking the soft silicone surface gently.

"It sure doesn't look like anything I've seen before. How does it work if it doesn't vibrate?"

"The long finger-shaped appendage goes inside you and bends in a series of come-hither motions against your G-spot. Give it a try by tapping the control button on the base one time."

I pressed the button and the finger began waving toward me like some kind of animatronic alien finger.

"*What the fuck*?" I said. "That's insane! It moves just like a real finger. And it hardly makes a sound."

"That the best part. You can use it anywhere. Even in a crowded restaurant. You should give it a try. Pretend that you're reclining on a couch in my office."

I glanced around the table to make sure no one else had seen the strange device that I was fondling at the table.

"It's tempting," I said, peering into the orifice at the top of the cone. "But what's with this little hole near the bottom of the device? What goes on there?"

"See for yourself," Hannah smiled. "Tap the button a second time. You might be in for a bit of a surprise."

I tapped the button again and a long, tongue-shaped object pushed up out of the hole and began undulating like a hypnotic snake against my palm.

My eyes grew wide as saucers as Hannah nodded at me with a huge smirk.

"Like I said," she grinned. "It's not a vibrator so much as a *replicator*. Doesn't it remind you of a real finger and tongue?"

"In a weird, perverted, *ET* kind of way–yeah."

Hannah lowered her gaze and nodded toward my midsection.

"You've got to feel it down there to really appreciate it. Go ahead–give it a try. No one needs to know besides us girls."

"Seriously?" I said. "Right here?!"

"Why not? There's a long skirt surrounding the table. You can loosen your pants and insert it inside you without anyone knowing. Let me have a little bit of fun watching you pleasure yourself for a change. We haven't been together that way in quite a while."

"I have to admit," I huffed. "I *am* insanely horny right now. I'm dying to try this thing out. But what are you going to do while I amuse myself?"

"I'm going to eat my salad like we're having a normal luncheon. This is all about *you* girl, don't worry about me. Knock yourself out."

"I can't believe I'm thinking about doing this," I said, watching the tongue slither back into its hole as I turned the toy off temporarily.

"It should be pretty easy to insert it if you're already properly worked up," Hannah said, lifting her glass to her lips.

I glanced to both sides of our table to make sure nobody else was watching, then reached under the tablecloth and unzipped my jeans, pulling them down to the floor. I could feel my juices already pooling on the wooden chair between my legs as I lowered the device under the table.

"Just be sure to position it so the hole is over your clit," Hannah whispered.

"I'm all over that," I nodded, slowly inserting the bulbous tip into my opening.

It slipped inside my slit smoothly, and I gasped as I pushed it all the way up inside me.

"It's not like just *any* old finger, is it?" Hannah grinned.

"No," I panted. "It's longer and fatter than most."

"It's designed with the ideal shape and form to stimulate your G-spot. If you've got it pressed all the way inside, turn it on to see what it feels like when it's animated."

I glanced around me nervously, watching the other restaurant patrons lost in conversation with their partners.

"Are you sure I'm going to be able to control myself in full view of all these customers? What if I break out into a Meg Ryan in front of all these people?"

"That'll be up to you to keep things under control as much as you can. But if not, what's the worst that can happen? Just like in the movie, everybody will want to know what you ordered that made you so happy."

"Very funny," I said, fumbling to find the control button on the base of the unit resting over my mound.

I pressed the button and began squirming in my chair as the long pointed finger began caressing me like no lover I ever had.

"Uhnn," I groaned, feeling the unusual stimulation inside my pussy.

"Not too bad, is it?" Hannah smiled. "Imagine all that going on while you're watching one of my patients pleasuring themselves."

"Is that really *possible*?" I said, getting even more turned on at the thought of watching one of her clients playing with herself in Hannah's private office.

"I've been thinking about it for a while," Hannah nodded. "It's the logical next step in the process of learning to become fully functional in a paired relationship. I've already had a few of my patients suggest they'd like me to guide them through their first encounter with another partner."

"You know how I like to *watch*," I groaned, as my eyes began to glaze over from the delicate sensation of the long finger rubbing up against my G-spot.

Hannah crossed her legs under the table and began to bob up and down as she flexed her buttocks and thighs together watching me get off.

"I do," she said, lifting her cocktail glass off the table and sliding her tongue around the rim suggestively. "Try the tongue action now."

"You're such a tease," I hissed, reaching under the tablecloth and tapping the control button one more time.

When I felt the flexible appendage push out of the hole and begin rolling over my hard clit, I bent over my place setting, grasping the handles of my chair tightly.

"That's it, babe," Hannah purred. "Feel the rhythm. Close your eyes and imagine it's your fantasy partner licking your pussy. Surrender to the feeling..."

"Is this how you do it with your clients?" I panted. "Talking to them all sexy while they play with themselves?"

"Sometimes," Hannah smiled. "Or sometimes I just let them do most of the vocalization while they tell me what they're doing behind the screen."

I spread my knees further apart imagining myself in one of her sessions.

"Do they ever get to the point where they're comfortable letting you watch them?"

"That's the ultimate goal. I've had a number of clients reach that level already. But I'd like to try taking it one step further. That's where you come in–"

"Tell me, Han," I moaned, beginning to lose myself in the fantasy. "Tell me what you want me to do with your sexy patients."

"We'll start out slowly at first," she instructed. "We'll just have you listen to them moan and purr as they begin the process of self-discovery behind the safety of their protective screen. But you'll have to be quiet at first to not distract their self-focus."

"At *this* point," I said, beginning to feel the pleasure spreading over my entire body. "That might be enough. With this amazing device doing its thing, I could probably get off listening to the sound of running water."

"That's the intent," Hannah laughed. "At least for my clients. But in order for them to become truly uninhibited and be able to function competently, the next step would be for the two of you to emerge from your hiding places and become comfortable watching each other in a face-to-face setting."

"*Fuck, yes,*" I panted. "If I can help another soul learn to enjoy the full pleasures of lesbian sex, count me in!"

"I know *you* won't have any trouble participating in this next phase of the process," Hannah smiled. "Just try to keep some of your more extreme methods in check for a while so you don't scare away my customers."

"I promise to keep my big dildos at home if you insist," I smirked.

"Once we get them feeling comfortable touching themselves and achieving climax in this voyeur scenario, the last step will be for the two of you to join together on the same couch and explore each other with more direct contact."

"Can I break out some of my favorite moves then?"

"If you find your partner is responding appropriately. Just be careful to always be gentle and focused on her needs. If you get to the point where she feels comfortable getting more inventive, by all means–"

"Oh, I've got the *means* alright," I moaned, imaging myself straddling one of her patients with her legs splayed wide apart as we ground our pussies together and I watched her come all over me. "How soon can we set this up?"

"I've got a certain patient in mind. She's young and never been with another woman before. She's had some unfulfilling experiences with men and confided that she's always fantasized about being with a woman. We'll just have to ease her into it carefully. Are you up for the opportunity, assuming she's game?"

"You know I am," I grunted, pressing harder down against the artificial tongue. "But first, tell me more about this girl..."

"She's nineteen, a sophomore in college, with a cheerleader's body–"

"She's athletic then?"

"Oh yes," Hannah smiled. "Tight ass, firm tits, and legs that could wrap all the way around you while you tribbed her virgin pussy–"

"Oh God, Han," I moaned. "I can't take it any longer. Sign me up– I want to taste her sweet pussy in my mouth..."

"Yes, Jade," Hannah purred. "Let it go, hun. Surrender to the feeling–"

As I imagined the co-ed writhing in ecstasy sitting on my face, the pleasure generated by the lifelike sex toy suddenly peaked, and I bit my lip as I began convulsing in my chair. I'd never fought so hard to remain quiet during a powerful orgasm in my entire life. There was something about the experience of cumming surrounded by scores of oblivious restaurant patrons that made the experience all the more erotic. While I twisted and squirmed in my chair, Hannah smiled as she raised her glass in toast to me.

"Congratulations, Jade," she said. "You've just passed the first test with flying colors."

2

______

With every passing day after our luncheon, I grew increasingly excited about the idea of participating in one of Hannah's guided therapy sessions. When she finally called me back, I almost dropped my phone fumbling to answer it.

"Han?" I answered the phone expectantly.

"Are you sure you're up for this?" Hannah asked.

"Are you kidding me?" I said. "It's all I've been thinking about since I last saw you."

"I've got another session scheduled with my target client for this Thursday at eleven a.m. Are you available?"

"With the young co-ed?"

"Yes."

"Absolutely!" I gushed.

"Ok," Hannah said. "We're going to have to set this up carefully. I don't want to put too much pressure on either one of you during this initial encounter. I think it's better if she doesn't even know you're there at first. I'll talk to her while she begins to explore her body behind the safety of the protective screen, then broach the subject of introducing a potential partner at the next session."

"Okay," I said. "But where will you hide me?"

"As strange as it may sound, I think the only safe place to be sure you're not discovered is in my closet. You can open the door a crack and listen if you promise to be absolutely quiet the entire time. That way, I can protect her identity in the event she doesn't wish to escalate things to the next level."

I shook my head at the idea of spying on her like a peeping Tom, but the dampness in my panties betrayed my true feelings.

"I'll feel like a bit of a lech hiding in the closet, but if that's what it'll take to make sure she's comfortable, I can work with that."

"Okay then," Hannah said. "Meet me at my office at 10:45 and I'll get you situated. And remember–not even a peep."

"I promise to be on my best behavior," I smiled. "If I can stay silent surrounded by a hundred restaurant customers, I think I can handle one uptight schoolgirl."

"And don't bring any toys either. I don't want to take the chance she'll hear anything other than my soothing voice."

"Not even your special vibrator that doesn't make any noise?"

"I'm not sure I can trust you with that thing. Besides, it's already going to be put to good use while you're in the closet."

"No fair!" I protested. "*You'll* be the one having all the fun!"

"I'm sure you can find other ways to amuse yourself," Hannah said. "You'll have plenty of chances to get more actively engaged during the next session. Just don't trip over anything in there when things start to heat up."

As soon as Hannah hung up, I rushed into my bedroom and positioned my dressing room mirror in front of my clothes closet. Then I opened the door a crack and imagined it was the schoolgirl I was watching while I jilled myself to a quick orgasm.

This should be interesting, I thought, quivering in the darkness. *I just hope her patient will find it as erotic as I do, knowing someone else is on the other side of the curtain.*

On the day of the scheduled session, I arrived fifteen minutes early as requested, while Hannah reiterated the ground rules and gave me final instructions. She made me promise that I wouldn't open the door until her client was safely behind the protective screen. She knew she was already pushing the boundary of professional ethics, and she wanted to make sure that her patient's identity would be protected until the girl felt comfortable introducing another person into the mix.

When I got into the closet, I pushed the coats to one side to produce an open space for me, then I peered through the louvers as I heard a soft tap on Hannah's office door. The slats were angled downward, so I could only see the floor a few feet ahead of me, but that was enough to get my heart racing in excitement already.

"Good morning, Haley," I heard Hannah say as two shadows crossed the floor in front of me. "Can I get you a coffee or tea? It's a bit chilly out there today, and you probably need to warm up."

"I'm fine, thank you," a young woman's voice spoke softly. "I'm pretty nervous about today's session and I don't think I should be holding any hot beverages in my trembling hands."

"There's no need to worry," Hannah assured the girl. "We're going to take things slowly, at your own pace. May I take your coat?"

"Yes, thank you," the girl said.

I heard the rustling of clothes then the sound of footfalls moving toward the closet. The door on the opposite side of the closet opened and Hannah reached in to fetch an open hanger, then she hung the girl's coat over the crossbar. I could smell her perfume on the garment, and my pussy twitched when I realized how close she was to me on the other side of the door. But neither Hannah nor I so much as made eye contact, to protect the secrecy of our little ruse.

"Have a seat, please," Hannah said, and I heard the sound of the girl reclining on the office divan.

"If you remember from our last session," Hannah continued, "we talked about trying something a little different today. You shared your discomfort about touching yourself intimately based on your prior family history, and that you thought it might be helpful to have me coach you through a private session. Are you still feeling comfortable taking it to this next level?"

"I think so," Haley said. "But you mentioned the possibility of my having a bit more privacy. I'm not sure I'm ready to have you watch me just yet."

"Of course," Hannah said. "It'll be easier for you to concentrate on exploring your body and focus on what you're feeling without any outside distractions. I can move the linen screen between the two of us to protect your privacy, but I'd also like to place this long dressing mirror in front of your couch so you can watch yourself and begin to get more comfortable with your body. Will that work for you?"

"I suppose so," Haley said, hesitating. "Do you have any expectations for today's session? I mean, in terms of achieving climax or anything like that?"

"None whatsoever," Hannah said. "This is all about you becoming comfortable in your own skin and beginning the process of self-exploration. The only desire I have is that you learn to relax and accept the beauty of your own body. This is a journey, not a destination. You need to learn how to love *yourself* before you can begin to think about loving someone else."

Oh, she's good, I thought. If only every girl could have this kind of advice when they're first experiencing the strange feelings of puberty and early adulthood. Far too many parents make their kids think sex is dirty and that enjoying any kind of carnal pleasure before marriage is sinful. For a moment, I reflected back on my own awkward attempts at sex with my first husband, realizing how much time and pleasure I'd forsaken until I learned to explore my sexuality on my own and with other like-minded women.

I listened to the sound of furniture moving across the floor as Hannah positioned the mirror in front of Haley's settee then placed the curtain between their two chairs.

"Does that make you feel more comfortable?" Hannah asked the girl.

"Yes, thank you," Haley said.

"Good. Now first, I just want you to look at yourself fully clothed in the mirror. Look at your pretty face and the curves of your figure and recognize that you're a beautiful woman who was designed to enjoy the natural pleasures of your body. And that this is also part of the natural process of pairing with a partner and enjoying the shared union that is part of the human experience."

"Okay..." Haley said with a hesitating lilt.

As I listened to her soft voice, my mind raced imagining what she looked like lying on the divan, watching herself in the mirror.

"But first you need to get fully comfortable in your own skin," Hannah said. "And begin to experience the pleasures that you've been naturally endowed with as a healthy young woman. Unfortunately, our society has learned to cover up our bodies as if they're a shameful thing we should hide. I want you to see your body as a beautiful thing and recognize the pleasures it can deliver to you, both when you're alone and with a partner."

Damn straight, I thought, feeling the blood rushing to my pussy as I reflected back on my own first tentative explorations of my young body that led to my first climax.

"Now I want you to take off your blouse and your bra,'"Hannah continued. "And lie back against the chair as you examine your body and begin to explore some of your erogenous areas."

I heard the sound of soft rustling behind the screen, followed by awkward silence.

"Can you see your naked torso in the mirror in front of you?" Hannah asked.

"Yes..." Haley said softly.

"Look at your breasts and examine their shape. Did you know that every woman has her own unique shape? Some have large breasts, some have small breasts, some have pointy breasts, and some have floppy breasts. It's all part of the female expression and what makes you unique."

More awkward silence.

"Do you like the shape of your breasts, Haley?" Hannah said.

"I suppose so..."

"I want you to cup them in your hands and feel how soft and pleasant they feel to be held and coddled. A woman's breasts are a beautiful thing, and they serve many purposes. Besides feeding a newborn child, their shape is meant to attract other partners whose bodies you can likewise enjoy and appreciate. And of course, your breasts can be a source of intense internal pleasure for yourself. Did you know that some women can climax just from the feeling of their babies suckling on their teats?"

"I had no idea," Haley said.

While Hannah talked the girl through the process of self-examination, I mimicked her movements and gestures, trying to imagine how she felt and how her body was responding. I unbuttoned my blouse and opened my bra, feeling an electric charge race through my body as I felt the fullness of my breasts in my hands.

"Now I want you to pinch your nipples gently between your thumbs and forefingers as you cup your breasts and roll them between your fingers, telling me what you feel."

"It tingles a little bit," Haley confessed.

"In a good way?"

"Yes–I think so."

"Do you notice any changes to the size and shape of your nipples?"

"Yes," Haley said. "They're growing larger and firmer."

"That's another one of the amazing reactions our bodies experience when our erogenous zones are properly stimulated. Do you like the feeling when you touch your breasts in this way, Haley?"

"Yes," she panted softly.

The girl's visceral reaction to touching herself sent a chill down my spine as I felt myself getting wetter and wetter by the moment.

"Look at your body in the mirror as you touch yourself. Do you see your chest flushing and your breasts subtly changing shape?"

"Yes."

"That's from your blood rushing to the area to provide more oxygen and nutrients to feed the increased stimulation. Isn't it wonderful how our bodies naturally respond when we stimulate it in a pleasant way?"

"Mmm," Haley purred.

"Now I want you to bend your head down and lift one of your breasts toward your mouth. You've been blessed with larger breasts than most, and if you can suck and lick your nipples, I want you to tell me how it feels."

Soon after, I heard the sound of liquid sloshing and the smacking of lips. I knew that Haley was sucking her plump nipples, and the thought of it sent rivers of fluid running down the inside of my legs. I was glad that I'd chosen to wear a dress instead of jeans so I'd have freer access to my pussy in the tight confines of Hannah's closet.

"How does that feel?" Hannah asked.

"Heavenly," Haley sighed. "I've never really explored my body in this way before."

"You'll be amazed at all the ways you and your partner can create exciting sensations like these using different techniques and body parts to explore the different areas of your body. Look up at your nipples in the mirror every now and then, but don't let me stop you from continuing your exploration."

I could hear the sloshing and smacking sounds increasing in frequency and pitch, along with Haley's moans and sighs. I had to bite my lip to keep from moaning myself, as I imagined what she must have been feeling at this moment.

"What do you see and feel?" Hannah asked.

"The dark ring around my nipples is getting smaller and my nipples are getting harder the more I lick and suck them."

"Mmm, that's good," Hannah said.

I could tell Hannah was getting just as turned on as I was from the exchange, and I wondered if she'd turned on her vibrator yet.

"Mix up the way you stimulate your nipples," she said. "Try circling your tongue around the perimeter and flicking it over the ends of your nipples every now and then. Most of the pleasure in exploring our bodies is discovered from the many different ways we can stimulate ourselves and others. Squeeze your breasts with your hands, pinch your nipples, suck and play with them as you lose yourself in the moment."

"It feels good," Haley panted. "I think I'm ready to try some of those other new techniques you mentioned now."

I smiled when I realized Haley was losing herself in the process and beginning to surrender to the pleasurable feelings flooding her body.

"Let's get comfortable seeing your *entire* body in the nude then," Hannah continued. "I want you to take off the rest of your clothes and throw them to the side. There are so many other ways to give yourself pleasure."

I heard some more rustling of clothes, this time more urgent-sounding, and the telltale sound of clothes dropping to the floor. It was obvious to me that Haley was getting more and more worked up and that she no longer cared if her clothes got a little wrinkled or dirty.

After the rustling sound stopped, Hannah paused for a moment to let the silence in the room escalate the sexual tension. Her professional technique was working for more than just her client, as I froze with my hand still as a statue against my dripping pussy while I imagined the pretty schoolgirl looking at her naked body on the chaise lounge chair.

"Are you fully naked now, Haley?" Hannah asked.

"Yes," the girl said.

"Examine the curve of your profile for a moment. See the way your waist tapers and the swelling of your hips above your long, shapely legs. Do you think you're beautiful, Haley?"

"Yes," she said. "I feel good all over."

"Good," Hannah said. "Now I want you to spread your legs and knees apart a little bit so you can examine your private area. Can you see your skin glistening on your vulva and on the inside of your thighs?"

"Yes," Haley panted.

"That means your body is enjoying the stimulation you've provided so far and that you're feeling aroused viewing your own body. Can you see the slit between your legs?"

"Yes–"

"I want you to run your hands gently down the front of your torso, feeling the softness of the skin on your abdomen..."

"My tummy is trembling," Haley said.

"That's a natural reaction to the excitement you feel as you caress yourself and move closer to your magical place."

"Magical place?"

"You'll see what I mean soon enough. Can you see the natural hairs covering your private area?"

"Yes," Haley said.

Both Hannah and I guessed that a girl this young and innocent wouldn't have learned yet to trim her pubic hair in the manner of the modern custom.

"I want you to run your fingers through your bush and tell me what you feel."

For a moment I envied the virgin schoolgirl with her natural muff. It had been a long time since I'd felt the wonderful feeling of my pubic hairs being caressed and stroked in this way. By way of consolation, I raised my slippery fingers up from my crotch and spread my juices over my bare mound.

"It feels kind of ticklish," Haley said from behind the screen. "But in a good way. I feel all warm and tingly inside."

"That's your body's way of saying it's enjoying the sensation of being touched this way. Now the blood is rushing to an entirely different area of your body. Can you feel yourself becoming wetter and wetter around your opening?"

"Yes," Haley said. "It's a good thing you put a blanket down over your chair. Otherwise, I'd be making a mess of your pretty office."

"That's perfect," Hannah said. "I'd like nothing more than for you to make a mess of my office. That just means that you're enjoying the experience and that your body is reacting the way it was meant to."

"I can feel things beginning to heat up down there," Haley grunted. "And there's other changes too–"

"Spread your legs further apart now and tell me what changes you see. And what you *feel*."

"I can see my lips are getting wetter and darker. And my little bean is getting plumper and harder. I feel like I'm tingling all over now..."

"Move your hands between your thighs and feel the slippery wetness as you caress the sides of your labia. How does that feel?"

"It feels *good*," Haley panted. "It's so warm and wet. I'm feeling some other sensations now..."

"Isn't it wonderful how good you can make yourself feel just by gently exploring your body and appreciating your natural beauty?"

"Yes, Dr. Marshall."

"Please, call me Hannah. At this point, we don't need to stay so informal, plus it will make it easier for you to vocalize what you're feeling. Now, I want you to explore a very special place on your body. Trace your fingers up along the edges of your labia until they meet at the top, then touch your little nub and tell me what you feel."

"*Huh!*" Haley gasped. "Oh, that feels–different. It's a much more intense type of tingling now."

By now I was rubbing my button furiously as I imagined Haley playing with her clit for the first time. As I peered through the slats trying desperately to catch any sight of her shadow or movement on the reflective floor, I could hear the soft sound of my own juices as I became more and more excited by the sensory deprivation of being locked in the closet.

"Yes," Hannah said, encouraging Haley on. "We women are lucky to be endowed with the most sensitive organ on the human body. Our clitorises are bestowed with more than eight thousand nerve endings–more per square inch than even on the end of a man's penis. Rub your fingers softly over your jewel and close your eyes as you savor the feeling."

"Oh God," Haley moaned. "That feels so good. I had no idea I could make myself feel this way."

"We're just getting started exploring all the possibilities," Hannah said, her own voice starting to become ragged. "Run your fingers over your clit, trying different movements. Sometimes it's nice to pinch it gently between your fingers, and sometimes it feels good to rub your fingers in circles over your button. Can you see anything *else* changing in your vulva as you rub yourself this way?"

"Yes," Haley groaned. "My lips are getting puffier, and they're beginning to separate a bit."

"*Fuck me,*" I groaned under my breath, wishing I could be looking into the same mirror that Haley was viewing at this precise moment. *How I'd love to fuck her sweet little pussy right now.*

"That's perfectly normal and healthy," Hannah purred. "That's just your body's way of saying that it's ready to accept another partner into the equation. Do you think you'd like to try that someday soon?"

"Maybe," Haley said. "But right now I'm having too much fun all by myself. I'm beginning to feel some different feelings now. The tingling is getting much more intense. It almost feels like I have to pee or something..."

"That means you're getting closer to reaching the apex of your pleasure," Hannah said, shifting in her chair. "Close your eyes now and focus on your body as you surrender to the pleasure. Don't worry if things start to get pretty intense. Just lose yourself in the process..."

"Yes, doc–I mean Hannah," Haley squeaked. "I feel it now. It feels like a wave is falling over me. A big, beautiful wall of pleasure engulfing me..."

"Yes, Haley," Hannah mewed. "Let it consume you. Surrender to the passion inside your body."

"Oh God! Oh God!" Haley whimpered. "It feels so good. Something is happening. I feel it coming over me–. Uhnnn! Uhnnn! Uhnnn!"

As I listened to Haley having her first powerful orgasm, I lost all control and began squirting over the floor of Hannah's closet as my pussy clamped together in multiple contractions while I leaned against the wall to steady myself. I'd never heard anything so erotic in my entire life, and my whole body was trembling at the thought of meeting her face-to-face at our next session.

When Haley finally stopped moaning and silence filled the room, I could hear Hannah shifting again in her chair. I wondered if she'd been unable to control herself and had had a powerful orgasm of her own listening to Haley. With that lifelike sex toy embedded in her pussy, I couldn't imagine how she'd able to hold back.

"How does it feel to experience the natural pleasures of being a woman, Haley?" she said.

"Oh my God," Haley panted. "I had no idea I had this inside of me. I want more–"

"There's so much more for you to experience, young lady. I encourage you to experiment with more self-exploration before our next session. Of course, the ultimate pleasure of being a woman happens when you get to *share* this pleasure with another partner. Do you think you might be ready to try this at our next meeting?"

"Um–maybe. But how will that work? I don't think I'm quite ready to jump right into an intimate relationship with a complete stranger."

"With your permission," Hannah said, "I'd like to invite another patient to the session who's expressed similar feelings about being with another woman. We can start slowly at first with the two of you just watching and talking to one another before we consider taking it to the next stage. You should always feel completely comfortable with your partner before agreeing to share this kind of intimacy."

"That does sound interesting," Haley said. "Would we be separated by protective screens again?"

"Only if you both want it that way. But something tells me you're ready to discover for yourself how much higher it can elevate the experience watching another woman pleasuring herself with you at the same time."

"Yes," Haley said. "I think I might like that."

"Let me know before your next session if you'd like to meet this new girl. Because she's definitely ready to meet you."

No shit, I muttered under my breath as my pussy continued spasming over my fingers firmly embedded inside my hole.

I had no idea know how I'd be able to keep it together for a whole week before I met this girl again. I smiled as my juices streamed down the insides of my thighs.

I'll just have to practice as much as I can in the meantime to get ready.

____

The intervening week before Haley's next scheduled session felt like the longest week of my life. I couldn't stop thinking about what she looked like and how she'd react to watching me respond to Hannah's instruction the way she had. I spent long hours lying on my couch with my dressing mirror propped up in front of me, fantasizing that it was Haley watching me instead of myself.

I must have cum a hundred times contorting myself into different positions trying to make myself look as sexy and alluring as possible. I didn't want to take any chance that she wouldn't respond positively to me in this shared therapy session. Beyond my desire for her to enjoy the experience to the fullest extent possible, I didn't want anything getting in the way of her moving on to the final step in her journey of sexual awakening. Every time I thought about actually touching her, my pussy throbbed and I had to tear my clothes off once again to quell the yearning desire within me.

When the appointment day finally arrived, I spent most of the morning trying on different outfits I thought might strike the right balance between sexually enticing and emotionally guarded. After all, Hannah was presenting me as another repressed patient who'd reached out for help overcoming her fear of intimacy with other women. I finally decided on a pleated mid-length skirt with inch-high pumps and a creamy silk blouse that hugged my breasts just enough to highlight the fullness of my bosom.

Hannah had asked me to arrive at her office five minutes after the hour so she could prep Haley first and confirm that she still wished to proceed as intended. The plan was for her to send me a quick text with either a smiling or frowning emoji to signal her readiness. When I still hadn't heard anything by 11:15, I shifted uncomfortably in her waiting room, wondering if Haley had gotten cold feet.

I couldn't blame her if she had. This whole idea was highly irregular and must have been kind of frightening for her. It was a far cry from meeting someone the natural way, getting to know them over a period of time before deciding to initiate intimate relations. But if she was too afraid to approach another woman the traditional way, I had every intention of making this experience as comfortable and uplifting as possible.

When my phone pinged and I saw the smiley-face symbol in my message thread, I stood up and nervously smoothed out the wrinkles in my blouse. I chuckled at the realization that I was just as anxious as the young schoolgirl at the prospect of our chaperoned playdate. Hannah stuck her head out her office door motioning me inside, and I straightened myself out and walked confidently into her office.

The girl was standing a few feet to Hannah's side, smiling nervously at me when our eyes met. I was surprised how young she looked in her skinny jeans, tight t-shirt, and Keds sneakers. She had long blonde hair, big bright eyes, and the plump skin of an adolescent who hadn't lost any of her youthful collagen. I must have looked ancient almost fifteen years older than her, as I pulled my shoulders back trying to lift my chest and press my breasts against my tight blouse.

Hannah turned toward the girl, arcing her arm toward me.

"Haley," she said. "This is Jade. In spite of your difference in age, I think you'll find you actually have a lot in common. I've brought the two of you together today to share some of your mutual experiences and learn to become more comfortable expressing your intimacy in the presence of another woman."

Hannah peered at the two of us and smiled.

"Would you like a drink before we get started?"

"Have you got some *tequila* behind your bar?" I joked.

"That might not be such a bad idea to help you both loosen up," Hannah chuckled. "But unfortunately, all I have to offer is coffee or tea."

"I'll have a coffee with a bit of cream and sugar then," I said.

"Tea is fine," Haley nodded.

"Cream and sugar also?" Hannah asked.

"Yes, thank you."

As Hannah turned to prepare our drinks, I moved closer toward Haley and extended my hand. She looked even prettier up close, with thick natural eyebrows and long dark lashes.

"Pleased to meet you, Haley," I said. "Hannah's told me so much about you. You're even more beautiful than she described."

Haley reached out and clasped my hand softly, and I could feel the nervous dampness in her palm as we touched for the first time.

"Thank you," she said. "You're very pretty also."

Her eyes blinked as she stole a glance down my body, peering at the cleavage formed by my push-up bra peeking out of my loosely unbuttoned blouse. My breasts were at least full size larger than hers, and I stood three or four inches taller in my elevated pumps.

"You remind me a little of Marilyn Monroe in that white blouse and skirt," she said.

"That's very kind," I smiled. "I could never hold a candle to her, though I feel a certain affinity given my own little seven-year-itch. It took me at least that long to break free of the oppressive bonds of my first marriage."

"Have you married again?"

"No–I guess I'm still discovering myself. I've kind of been looking

for a change of pace lately. I never felt fully satisfied in my relation-
ships with men."

"I've never felt comfortable approaching *either* gender, actually.
My parents were pretty strict about the whole dating thing when I
was growing up–"

Hannah returned from her kitchen and handed each of us a
steaming mug.

"I see you two are beginning to get more comfortable," she said.
"I'm glad to see you hitting it off so quickly. Would you like to get
more comfortable?"

Haley and I turned to see two long chaise lounge chairs facing
one another about ten feet apart, angled slightly toward Hannah's
armchair positioned at the apex of the triangle. I smiled when I realized she'd done this intentionally to facilitate her own enhanced
viewing of the two of us once we got loosened up.

We walked toward the settees and I paused, motioning for Haley
to take the one on the left side. Both chairs were covered in a long
throw blanket, and I kicked off my shoes before sitting back against
the curved backrest, crossing my ankles on the end nearest Haley. It
felt awkward holding my coffee in this semi-reclined position, and
when I leaned over to rest it on the floor beside me, Haley did the
same.

"How are you both feeling today?" Hannah said as she sat in her
chair in front of us, crossing her legs sexily with her pointed pumps
bouncing gently in our direction.

I had little doubt she was wearing her special sex toy under her
prim business suit, and I envied her for a moment, knowing she'd
have a leg up on the two of us for the rest of the session.

"Good," Haley said, with a gentle lilt.

"Better *now*," I said, smiling toward Haley.

"You've both expressed interest in exploring a same-sex relationship, but also about your reservations initiating the process given
your previous experiences."

I nodded, realizing there was more than a hint of truth in her statement, even though I'd long since resolved my reticence about being with other women.

"The purpose of this session is to give you both an opportunity to become more comfortable in the presence of another woman, and to the extent you feel ready, to begin to explore the boundaries of your sexuality in the safe confines of my office. Is this still something you both feel comfortable proceeding with?"

I looked at Haley and she peered back at me, as we both nodded gently.

"Okay," Hannah said. "At first, I'd just like the two of you to gaze into each other's eyes for a moment and pause as you take a moment to acknowledge each other as willing partners and make a silent connection..."

I smiled at Haley and saw a soft flush spread over her cheeks as her pupils began to widen while she peered back at me. Even though neither of us said a thing, the longer I looked at her the more excited I got as my chest began rising and falling from my elevated respiration rate.

"Now, I want each of you to take a minute to look over each other's bodies without making any judgements or feeling self-conscious that you're checking each other out. Take a moment to appreciate the different shapes of your respective figures, and listen to how your body is reacting as you soak each other up."

I was happy to be given free license to leer at Haley's youthful figure, and as my eyes drifted down her body, I could feel my panties begin to moisten in excitement seeing the girl of my dreams reclining directly in front of me. Her breasts looked like they were painted on her body, sitting high and firm under her tight t-shirt. She had a narrow waist and slim but shapely hips, tapering to slender hourglass-shaped legs, looking all the more toned resting gently on the firm surface of her settee.

She in turn ran her gaze all over my body, pausing to stare at my full breasts pushing up against the flimsy silk fabric of my blouse. For a moment, I wished I'd decided to go braless, so she could see how she was turning me on as my nipples pressed against the soft fabric of my lace bra. After a few seconds of lingering, her eyes traced a line further down my body, pausing at the bottom of my skirt's hemline, as if hoping to catch a glimpse into the shadow between my closed legs. When her gaze reached the bottom of my feet, I wiggled my toes playfully, and she did the same with her cute sneakers. Even though we hadn't said a thing to each other for several minutes, I felt like we were already beginning to bond over our strange circumstances.

"Take a moment to revel in the beauty and diversity of the female form," Hannah whispered. "Recognize that everyone is built differently, and that these differences contribute to making each of us all the more interesting and alluring. Can you see the natural beauty within each of your own bodies and in those of your partner?"

"Yes," Haley nodded, tracing her gaze once again up to my pointed breasts.

"Absolutely," I enthused.

"Let's take this to the next level then," Hannah said. "If you feel comfortable, I'd like each of you to remove your tops and lie back in your chair while you admire one another in your undergarments."

As I slowly began unbuttoning my blouse, Haley leaned forward, pulling her t-shirt over her shoulders. When she lifted it over her head, her blonde locks fell down over the front of her cream-colored sports bra. I was a little disappointed to see her covered up so tightly, but her bra only seemed to accentuate the firmness of her perky tits.

When I unfastened the last button on my blouse, I pulled my arms out one side at a time then leaned back against the soft backrest. It felt electrifying to rest there in my lacy bra as Haley ran her eyes lustily over my exposed chest and abdomen. My brassiere was low-cut enough that she could see the tops of my dark areolas, and they puckered slightly as my hard nipples began to lift the fabric away from my skin.

"Now look at each other's bodies more closely," Hannah intoned. "Examine the shape of each other's breasts, the curvature of your waists, and the smoothness of your stomachs. What do you see that appeals to your feminine senses?"

"I like the fullness of Jade's breasts," Haley purred. "And the way the top edge of her bra angles sexily down toward her cleavage."

"Yes," Hannah said, stretching the S out the end of the word. "Being a sensual woman means we can dress up in different ways to tease and excite our partners as a precursor to more intimate relations. What do you see in Haley's body that you find most attractive, Jade?"

I paused for a moment, examining her tight belly and the subtle striations in her stomach.

"I like the line running down the middle of her abdomen from the bottom of her bra to her belly button. I wish I could be that lean and sexy once again."

"That's the beauty we share as women of different generations. Some women are more lean and chiseled, while others are more full-bodied and curvy. It's all part of the magnificent palette of the human form and what makes it so interesting for each of us to experience. Are you beginning to imagine what lies further underneath?"

"Yes..." Haley said, her cheeks flushing a crimson red.

"Oh, very definitely yes," I sighed, wishing I could jump out of my seat and tear Haley's sports bra off with my own hands.

"If you're ready then, you may remove your brassieres and begin to get more comfortable being naked in the presence of one another."

Haley hesitated for a moment, looking at me to make the first move. Fortunately, the bra I'd chosen to wear had the closure at the front, and as I pressed my fingers together unhinging the clasp and spreading the cups apart to reveal my naked breasts, I heard Haley gasp a few feet away. Her reaction only excited me more as I peered down at my tits, seeing that my nipples had already hardened and extended to their full extent. I pulled my bra off my back and threw it on the floor, and my whole body started buzzing as Haley stared at my torso with wide eyes.

Within a few seconds, she felt emboldened enough to remove her own sports bra as she pinched her thumbs under the lower band and pulled it over her head in one swift movement. Her breasts jiggled softly on her chest and I marveled at how perfectly round and symmetrical they were. They looked bigger than I imagined when I saw her fully clothed, and I began to salivate as I leered at her creamy skin and her light-colored areolas. They'd already begun to bunch up in excitement, protruding like two erasers on the end of a pencil.

Hannah paused just long moment to give each of us a chance to soak up each other's bodies. I could see Haley's eyes darting excitedly between my points as a light dew formed at the top of her chest between her breasts. This just accentuated the youthful look of her glistening skin, glowing like a sexy goddess. As my mouth watered at the thought of taking her moist nipples into my mouth, another part of me began to grow rapidly wetter.

"What are you feeling as you look each other's naked bodies?" Hannah said, interrupting our thoughts.

"I'm thinking how much I want to touch Haley right now," I confessed.

"There'll be plenty of time for that soon enough," Hannah said, admonishing me gently. "What are you feeling at this moment, Haley?"

"I'm just..." Haley panted, her moist lips parting slightly. "I'm just amazed at how gorgeous Jade's tits–I mean *breasts* are. She's looks like a supermodel to me."

"It's okay to use informal terms to describe each other's bodies," Hannah nodded. "It helps to desensitize the experience and lose yourself more readily in the feelings of arousal that you're experiencing. Are you beginning to recognize how each of you are responding to the sight of watching one another in this manner?"

"Yes," Haley said as she locked her eyes on my tingling teats.

"You have *no* idea," I smiled, peering at Haley's quivering tummy.

"I'm happy you're both responding so positively. That means you're attracted to one another and that you're becoming more comfortable with the idea of exploring a different kind of union. Are you ready to take it to the next level?"

"I think so..." Haley hesitated.

"*God* yes," I panted, feeling the wetness in my panties beginning to run down the crack of my ass.

"Why don't you both take off your lower garments now, but keep your panties on for the moment? Part of the attraction with foreplay is taking our time to build the desire and teasing our partners by withholding those things we most crave. Take a moment to look at your naked bodies, but not completely undressed yet."

I leaned forward and unclasped the latch at the back of my skirt, then lowered the zipper and pulled my skirt down the front of my legs, throwing it playfully on the floor. Haley locked eyes on me as she unfastened the front of her jeans, wiggling sexily on her divan while she pulled her pants down, then flipping off her sneakers and throwing everything on the floor beside her.

She was wearing plain white low-cut panties that stretched at least four inches below her navel. I could see the dark outline of her bush under the thin fabric, and my pussy twitched knowing I'd soon get to see her completely naked. She leaned back and fixed her gaze on my crotch while I teasingly separated my feet a few inches. I was wearing matching lace panties and the light color must have shown the giant wet spot that had formed in the fabric. But I couldn't yet see any sign of wetness in Haley's underwear, since she still had her legs closed in a protective posture.

"How does it feel to view another woman like this, nearly naked?" Hannah asked. "Are you noticing any new reactions in your body as you watch your partner disrobe?"

"Yes," Haley panted. "I'm beginning to feel that same tingling sensation I experienced at our last session. It feels like my whole body is on fire..."

"How about you, Jade?" Hannah said, smiling at me. "How do you feel sitting in front of Haley almost naked?"

"Very sexy," I said. "I'm feeling things I haven't felt in a long time."

"So it would appear," she said, glancing at the wet spot between my legs. "Now I want each of you to spread your legs a little further apart to witness the effect you're having on one another. Take a moment to recognize the reaction each of you are experiencing as you become more and more aroused looking at one another's bodies."

As I spread my legs further apart, Haley pulled her feet up a few inches, then angled her knees down onto the divan to reveal the white swath of fabric running between her legs. I could see the indentation of her slit in the tight cotton and the telltale darkness of a small wet spot in the middle of her panties. Seeing her reveal this little slice of her private anatomy raised my excitement level even higher as the wet spot in my own panties slowly spread all the way from one side to the other.

While Haley stared at the widening dark spot between my legs, I noticed her chest begin to rise and fall as she started breathing more heavily. It took every ounce of my willpower to stay seated in my settee and not sprint over to her side and take her for myself. Hannah was right about one thing. All this slow buildup was driving me more crazy with desire and just increasing my longing to touch her.

"Can you see how each of you are responding to one another the more you reveal of yourselves?" Hannah said. "Are you beginning to become more comfortable with the idea of watching another woman being intimate and moving closer to a more formal connection?"

"Yes," Haley sighed.

"*Fuck*, yes," I gushed.

"Let's remove our remaining entrapments then and revel in the naked glory of the female body. You may both remove your last vestiges of clothing if you feel comfortable. Take a moment to soak up one another's bodies and connect with your feelings. A healthy sexual relationship starts with feeling comfortable in both your and your partner's nakedness."

I raised my hips, practically tearing my panties off as I pulled them down my legs and tossing them on the floor. While I kept my legs slightly parted, Haley wriggled out of her little white panties and dropped them sexily on the floor beside her. This time, she parted her legs the same distance as mine as we both stared at each other's wet slits shining in the bright overhead lights of Hannah's office. Haley's light pubic patch formed a perfect triangle over her mound and I clenched the fabric on the divan beside me trying to keep my hands from straying any further.

"There now," Hannah purred. "That wasn't so bad, was it?"

"No," Haley said. "It was actually easier than I imagined."

"How about you, Jade? How do you feel seeing your partner fully naked in front of you?"

"I'd hardly call it *easy*," I groaned. "The hardest part is remaining still on my sofa. My hands want to wander all over the place right now."

"If that's what you feel like doing, don't let me stop you from enjoying the process. I encourage each of you to begin touching yourselves while you verbalize how you're feeling. Communication and openness are the first two essential ingredients in any healthy relationship."

As I watched Haley separate her legs further apart, I lifted my hand to my breast and squeezed it tightly while I lowered my other hand to my crotch and began to circle my button. Normally I'd take more time to tease myself, but at this point I was so horny I needed to get right down to business.

Watching me touch myself and begin to moan softly seemed to encourage Haley, as she moved her hand to the inside of her thighs and began to flutter her fingers over her button. While we both began to moan and roll our hips over our divans, Hannah began to bob her foot more forcefully over her knee and cleared her throat.

"Yes," she mewed. "It's a beautiful thing watching another woman pleasuring herself. Focus on one another as you listen to the reaction of your own body and that of your partner. The biggest turn-on is seeing your partner respond excitedly to your touch."

I wasn't sure if she was talking more about what *she* was feeling at this precise moment, or referring to what we were experiencing. It must have been even more exciting for her watching two sexy women touching their naked bodies only a few feet in front of her. With her special sex toy working its wonders underneath her business suit, I imagined she'd have experienced multiple climaxes facilitating these sessions.

"Don't forget to communicate how you feel," she said. "Tell your partner what she's doing to you right now."

"I'm so excited watching Jade touch herself," Haley said. "I never thought a woman could look this sexy and beautiful before. The feelings inside are even more intense than last time–"

"And *you*, Jade?" Hannah said. "How is your body responding seeing Haley get excited watching you?"

"Oh my God," I groaned. "I want her so bad. I want to touch her and taste her and feel her trembling in my arms."

"Soon enough," Hannah smiled. "For now, I just want you both to learn how to satisfy one another at a distance without the added pressure of direct engagement. Focus on what you're feeling, and surrender to the pleasure engulfing your bodies. As before, feel free to experiment with different forms of stimulation. You can begin learning from one another even before you come together."

I spread my legs further apart and inserted two fingers from my other hand into my hole as I began to rub my clit more quickly.

"Mmm, yes," I panted. "You're so beautiful, Haley. I'm imagining you touching me..."

"Yes, Jade," Haley said. "I want to touch you and feel your wetness. You're making me so hot right now."

Haley mimicked my technique, awkwardly inserting the middle finger of her left hand into her slit while she pumped it in and out as she began jilling herself more rapidly. Our hips began to slowly lift off our divans and our mouths opened in pleasure as we moved inexorably closer to orgasm.

"Yes, baby," I purred. "I want to watch you let it go. Imagine me sucking your jewel as you come in my mouth–"

"Oh God," Haley squealed as she arched her hips higher in the air. "It's *coming*! Suck my pussy, Jade!"

Suddenly, Haley fell back onto the surface of the divan and she hunched over, jerking her body back and forth while she pressed her fingers deeper inside her pussy. Seeing her come just inches away from me was more than I could take. I suddenly flipped over on all fours and pounded my cunt as my tits wobbled excitedly over my chest. Within seconds, my orgasm washed over me like a tidal wave as I began squirting long streams in Haley's direction. While I peered at her between my legs, I saw her mouth gape wider apart as she watched me writhing uncontrollably on the chair in front of her.

I glanced over at Hannah for a moment and saw her slumping rhythmically in her own chair as she watched the two of us cumming with our fingers deeply embedded in our pussies. I smiled, knowing she had her *own* special finger stimulating her G-spot as she surrendered to an entirely different kind of lover.

4

———————

After we all came down from our highs at Hannah's therapy session, she asked Haley and me if we were ready to proceed to the next stage in our intimacy journey. Knowing this meant we'd be allowed to touch each other, we both quickly agreed, but since we'd used up all the allotted time in the day's session, Hannah scheduled our next meeting for the following week. When we parted, Haley and I kissed each other on the cheek, but that was enough to keep me going until we met next time.

In the intervening week, I ran through all kinds of scenarios imagining how I'd like to touch and caress her. It was kind of fun not using any toys for a change, since I knew those would be off base during our next encounter. Hannah didn't want any artificial stimulation getting in the way of Haley learning to enjoy sex in the natural manner. That was easy for *her* to say, I thought, remembering how she'd responded watching Haley and me writhing on our divans while she let her special sex toy do all the work for her. But I knew she was right, and as I lay on my sofa dreaming of all the ways I could stimulate Haley, I came many times remembering what she'd said to me when she experienced her first orgasm in the presence of another woman.

This time, I thought, *she won't need to pretend that I'm touching her when she comes next to me.*

On the day of our next scheduled session, we arrived at Hannah's office a few minutes early, which gave her a chance to prep us and set the ground rules. The most important thing, she said, was to go slow and make sure our partner felt comfortable before pushing any further.

I looked around her office and noticed that the two settees had been pushed to the side, and I looked at her inquisitively.

"Where did you want us to relax?" I asked.

Hannah smiled as she led us into another room with a four-poster bed. The drapes had been pulled and a series of candles were lit around the room to set the mood. I could smell a hint of lemongrass from some burning incense on the night table, and I nodded at Hannah's preparation.

"I thought you might like something a little more comfortable to relax on this time," she said. "Plus, I suspect you'll need a little more room to maneuver as you begin to explore each other's bodies. I wanted to make sure you felt as cozy as possible before proceeding to the next step. Why don't you give it a try and see what you think?"

I strolled up to the bed and ran my fingers over the linens. The high thread count made the bedding feel like silk, and I got goose-bumps imagining what it would feel like to lie next to Haley on the sumptuous surface.

"What do you think, Haley?" I said. "Do you think this will be suitable for our purposes?"

Haley stepped forward and ran her hands over the sheets, then turned toward Hannah and smiled.

"It feels like I'm in a five-star hotel," she said. "I've never experienced anything so luxurious in my entire life."

"I wanted you to feel completely relaxed in preparation for the next step in your journey of sexual awakening."

"What about *you*?" Haley asked. "Where will you be while Jade and I are resting on the bed?"

Hannah turned to a reclining chair resting in the corner of the room.

"I'll be sitting in the shadows not too far away. I want there to be minimum distraction while you and Jade explore each other's bodies."

"So you'll be with us for the remainder of the session then?"

"If that's what you prefer."

"You were very helpful last time," Haley nodded. "Plus, it somehow seems more erotic knowing you'll be watching us."

Hannah paused as she peered at the two of us with a sly smile.

"I'll try to be less involved this time while I give each of you a chance to experiment with what turns you on. But I assure you that I'll be enjoying the process almost as much as you will."

She walked to the other side of the room and lay down in her chair, crossing her legs.

"To get you in the mood, sometimes it can be more exciting to let your partner take your clothes off before you lie down. Who'd like to begin?"

Haley and I peered at one another, and a blush fell over her cheeks. It was obvious that she wanted me to make the first move, which was fine with me since I'd been undressing her with my eyes from the moment we came in the door. She'd chosen to wear a more formal outfit today, with a collared blouse, wool pants, and suede loafers. Whether she was trying to mimic me or she was trying to project the image of more sophisticated woman, was unclear. Either way, I liked the look, and I felt my heart beating faster as I imagined unbuttoning her blouse.

I stepped forward and reached out my hand to her, and she met mine with her opposite hand, squeezing my fingers gently. I tilted my head down, and she closed her eyes, anticipating my kiss. Pausing an inch from her mouth, I felt her cool breath on my skin, and my pussy twitched when I realized I was about to touch her intimately for the first time.

When our lips touched, she puckered them like they used to in old-time movies. I smiled, realizing that this might have been the first romantic contact she'd ever experienced and that she still hadn't learned the art of erotic kissing. I lifted my hand and cupped her face as I moved closer, pressing my body against hers. She unconsciously tilted her pelvis, pressing her hips against mine. I parted my mouth and nibbled her flesh, feeling the fullness of her lips.

She sighed as we pressed our breasts together, and I circled my arm around her, caressing the indentation of her lower back. I was dying to plunge my tongue into her, but I remembered Hannah's admonition about going slowly, and instead I turned around and sat down on the bed with my knees straddling her hips. While Haley peered down at me, I began to loosen the buttons of her blouse from the top. As I began to spread the panels apart, I smiled when I noticed that she was wearing a lacy bra like the one I'd worn at our last session.

I leaned in and kissed her exposed belly with my moist lips, reaching up to cup her breasts as I squeezed them gently. She began to moan and reached behind my head to run her fingers through my hair. I'd almost forgotten how to properly make love a woman with all my recent escapades, and suddenly I was happy that I'd agree to participate in Hannah's guided session.

Maybe I'd needed this as much as Haley did.

As she pulled my head tighter against her belly, I reached behind her and unfastened the clasp at the back of her bra, pulling it gently over her shoulders. Her brassiere fell below her breasts, and I lifted myself up, licking her pointy tips. Her nipples were hard and warm, and as I sucked them into my mouth one at a time, she gasped, pulling my head harder against her body. As I began to roll my tongue over her tips, I moved my hands to the front of her chest and squeezed her breasts more tightly. They felt full and firm in my palms, and for the first time since I'd entered the office, I became conscious of the warm feeling in my pussy. My juices had been flowing for some time now, and the feeling of wetness between my legs made my nipples harden.

Haley was running her fingers through my hair more wildly now, and I took this to mean that she was ready for me to take it to the next step. I traced my hands down the front of her belly, unclasping the button at the top of her pants, then I slowly pulled the zipper down to reveal a pair of black lace panties. Seeing her wearing sexy lingerie got me even more turned on, and I slipped my fingers over the waist of her pants and began to pull them down over her hips.

My heart pounded as I felt them tighten up when they reached the widest part of her hips, realizing just how curvy and tight her ass must have been. As I pulled them further down her thighs, Haley lifted her feet and kicked off her loafers, stepping out of her jeans. I pulled her blouse off her back, and her brassiere fell softly onto the floor. Now she stood inches away from me, almost naked and quivering in excitement.

Hannah must have sensed Haley's trepidation, as I heard her shift in her chair for the first time and clear her throat.

"Sometimes it's even more erotic to have your partner remove her clothes while you *watch*," she said. "Would you like to undress Jade yourself Haley, or watch her do so herself?"

"I've been dreaming of seeing her naked again this whole week," Haley said. "But I'm not as experienced as Jade in the art of undressing another woman..."

Taking Haley's cue, I stood up off the bed and stepped back a few paces to give her a chance to take in my full figure. I smiled at her as I began to slowly unbutton my blouse. I'd decided to go braless for today's session, and as it became apparent to Haley that I was naked under my shirt, I saw her eyes widening in excitement. After I unclasped the fourth button, I let the silky fabric fall on top of my breasts while I breathed in and out deeply. As my nipples began to harden, pressing against the soft fabric, Haley's lips begin to separate.

I teased her for a moment longer, bringing my hands together and pushing my tits closer together. She panted looking at my cleavage, and I felt my pussy getting wetter seeing her rising excitement. When I undid the last button and threw my blouse on the bed beside me, I watched the flickering light casting sexy shadows over Haley's mounds. I wanted to step forward and trib her pointed nipples with my own, but I reminded myself that this session was all about her.

The more slowly I could build her desire, the more I knew she'd enjoy the moment when we finally came together.

Damn, I thought. It had been a long time since I'd been this patient in seducing another woman. Apparently I needed Hannah's guided lessons just as much as Haley.

As we stood facing each other in the hypnotic shadows, Haley glanced down my midsection and a small curl formed on the side of her lips. For the same reason she'd chosen to dress more maturely, I'd chosen to wear jeans so she'd feel more comfortable seeing me as a peer. But the problem with the tight jeans was that they revealed the widening wet spot between my legs far more easily than when I wore my skirt.

"It looks like you're getting just as excited as me," Haley smiled, locking her eyes on my dark stain.

"Sorry," I shrugged. "I guess I lubricate a little more easily than most women."

"Mmm, I like that," Haley purred. "I can't wait to feel you. I'm beginning to get wet too."

I glanced down at Haley's legs and saw the shimmering slickness on the inside of her thighs.

"Perhaps it's time for the two of you to get more comfortable on the bed," Hannah interrupted from the darkness.

I'd almost forgotten she was there, but far from finding her intrusions irritating, I was glad she knew when we needed a little prompt. I slipped off my jeans, then lay down on the bed with my arm cocked sexily against the side of my head in a come-hither look to Haley. She didn't hesitate to join me on the other side of the bed, and we quickly melted into each other's arms. As I felt her press her body against mine, I kissed her with an open mouth, and this time she parted her lips and allowed my tongue to probe her cavity. Our breasts mashed together, and as we intertwined our legs, we both began to moan passionately. I pulled my leg up, pressing it against her pussy, and she responded by grinding her hips against my thigh.

By now, she'd joined me in thrusting her tongue into my mouth, and as we writhed together on the bed, I grabbed her ass and pulled her closer. The passion with which she was tongue-fucking me made me think she was ready for different kind of tongue lashing, and after a few minutes I disengaged and began nibbling my way down the front of her body. The only sound I could hear from the other sound of the room now was the soft rusting of Hannah shifting in her chair and the occasional soft sigh. I wondered if Haley sensed how much she was enjoying herself watching us, but at this point my only concern was satisfying the pretty girl lying beside me.

As I nibbled on Haley's teats and swirled my tongue over her areolas, she arched her back and pressed herself more firmly against me. It was apparent to me that she'd lost all of her inhibitions about being with another woman, and I hummed my approval as her body responded to my touch. I traced the little indentation running down the center of her tummy with my tongue, and her stomach quivered the closer I got to her private area as she began to roll her hips in anticipation of my touch.

When I reached her panties, I pulled them over her hips while she lifted her ass off the bed. Her bush felt as soft as fur and I rolled my cheeks over it, reveling in it's sexy scent and plush thickness. Beads of lubrication rested on her muff like morning dew on a spider web, and I paused to suck them into my mouth, tasting her sweet honey.

The further down I lowered myself, the further she spread her legs apart, until my shoulders were comfortably nestled between her legs. For a moment, I paused with my head cocked above her clit as I closed my eyes and inhaled her sweet, perfumy scent. After a few moments, she began to shimmy her hips impatiently, eager to feel my touch in her special place. Instead, I dribbled some saliva out of my mouth and let it fall on top of her inflamed jewel. When she felt the unexpected moisture on her button, she groaned and lifted her hips closer to my face.

"Oh God, Jade," she whined. "You're driving me crazy. I want to feel your touch so bad. Take me into your mouth like you said you would last time. Suck my pussy with your pretty mouth."

Her dirty talk just turned me on all the more, and I lowered my head to encircle her burning clit.

"Oh God–Oh God," Haley panted. "That feels so good. Lick my little man with your lips and make me feel like you did when I watched you last time."

Little man, I chuckled to myself. I hadn't heard that expression used by a woman before to describe her clit, and I wondered if this was a euphemism her parents had used when she was younger. But it didn't matter to me–I was just thrilled that she was expressing her desire for me and telling me how much I was turning her on.

As I hummed in delight, I began circling her button with the tip of my tongue, and she began groaning more loudly. While I mixed up my technique between sucking and licking her pearl, she placed her hands behind my head once again and pulled me harder into her crotch. As her breathing began to get more ragged and accelerated, I knew that she was getting close to the point of no return. I was tempted to pull back for a few seconds to prolong her torment, but then I realized there'd be plenty more time to tease and play with her after she released her pent-up sexual tension. She began to lift her hips off the bed as her body became rigid in a tight lock, and I slipped my fingers inside her and began to stroke her tenting G-spot.

"Oh God, Jade," she hissed. "Don't stop. I'm going to cum. *Yes!*" she grunted. "I'm cumming in your mouth!"

Suddenly, I felt the walls of her pussy clamping down on my fingers in rhythmic contractions as she humped her hips against my face while holding me tightly against her. I paused for a moment to feel her body spasming as I peered up and watched her pretty face contorting into paroxysms of pleasure. After what seemed like a full minute of tensing her body in a prolonged and powerful orgasm, she finally dropped her hips down onto the bed, panting loudly to catch her breath.

With the room suddenly quiet, I heard gentle squeaks coming from the other side of the room as Hannah shifted rhythmically in her chair. It was obvious to both of us what was going on in the dark, and we smiled at one another as I pulled myself back up to look into Haley's steamy eyes.

"That was beautiful, Jade," she sighed. "Thank you for making me feel like a woman for the first time in my life. I can't believe how skilled a lover you are. I'm afraid that I'll never be able to meet your expectations–"

"Remember that there are no expectations or targets in this first direct encounter between the two of you," Hannah breathed deeply, collecting herself. "Jade–why don't you show Haley how she can satisfy you. Sometimes it's more fun for the *receiver* to take the lead."

I knew immediately what Hannah meant, and as I lifted myself up off the bed, I looked into Haley's eyes and nodded.

"Why don't you lie there for a little longer and let me do most of the work?" I said.

I raised myself up on all fours and straddled her face with my knees on either side of her head, and she looked up at me with wide eyes and smiled. As I ran my fingers gently through her silky hair, I began to lower myself until my dripping pussy hovered inches over her pouty lips. She flicked her tongue out awkwardly trying to bat my clit, and I cupped her cheeks, lowering myself a little further until my nub pressed against her lips.

"Just open your mouth a little bit and nibble on me for a moment," I said. "Sometimes when you're making love to a woman, less is more. Let me ease into it while I watch your pretty face."

Haley did as she was told, and as she sucked my hard nub into her mouth, I closed my eyes and groaned.

"Yes, baby," I purred. "Just like that. Suck my button and roll it around in your mouth. I like the feeling of your mouth on my body."

As Haley began to roll her tongue over my bulb in a similar manner to the way I'd kissed her earlier, I smiled. She was a quick study, and I felt myself growing closer to her with every passing moment.

"Yes, Haley," I encouraged her. "Just like that. Feel my hard clit in your mouth. I'm making love to your mouth while I watch you. I'm going to cum for you soon."

Haley's head nodded excitedly, and her eyes began to widen as I pressed my pussy harder down onto her face. I could feel the passion rising within me but I didn't want to drown her in another torrent if I came too hard, so as my orgasm began to take hold of me, I lifted my hips and pointed my pussy over her tits while I squirted my juices all over her heaving chest. As she peered down at me between my legs, I saw her face twist into another silent orgasm. Apparently, I'd excited her so much with my waterworks that she hadn't needed any direct stimulation to come once again.

As we both groaned and shook our bodies together on the bed, I heard the sound of gentle sloshing coming from the direction of Hannah's chair. I peered over at her and noticed that her pants were unbuttoned while she rubbed her hands sensuously over her naked mound.

"That was very good, ladies," she sighed. "You're making excellent progress. It's time for the last step in your pair bonding. Now I want you to touch each other at the same time and experience the joy of coming together. Jade, I'm guessing you have a bit more experience in this area."

"Perhaps just a little," I smiled, as I shimmied my hips over Haley's slippery torso toward her quivering pussy. I paused for a moment when I reached her bush once again and tilted my pelvis back and forth over top of her bush, feeling the soft hairs tickling my clit and wet opening.

"Would you like me to make love to you now, Haley?" I purred.

"Isn't that what we've been doing all this time?" she said.

"Not quite *this* way," I smiled. "I think you might find this brings us even closer together and feels even more amazing. Lift your knees up higher and spread your legs for me."

Haley looked at me confused for a moment, and I nodded reassuringly. When she pulled her knees almost up to her chest, I pushed her thighs apart and peered at her inflamed gland, poking its head out of its hood. I kneeled over top of her and slowly lowered my body until the bottom of our thighs rested on one another. Her eyes widened when she realized what I intended to do, and a sly smile formed on my mouth as our clits touched for the first time. As I began to grind our hips together providing direct stimulation to our most sensitive areas, she threw her head back and groaned . I didn't know if she'd even conceived of two women touching themselves this way, but the look of pleasure on her face indicated that she was quickly losing herself in the process.

As I shifted my weight forward and back, stroking her hard clit and rubbing our sopping pussies together, she began to whimper and toss her head from side to side. Seeing her enjoying the tribbing action so much just made me want to fuck her harder. I transferred more of my weight onto her thighs, and she began to rock her hips in concert with mine. The feeling of our nubs rolling over one another as our slits smacked against one another was the most exciting feeling either one of us had experienced. Before long, she began moaning more urgently, and I saw a flush begin to spread over her chest as her nipples contracted even more firmly.

"Yes, Haley," I groaned, seeing the look of ecstasy roll over her face. "Let it go baby. Let me feel you cum with me while I make love to you."

"Yes, Jade," Haley grunted. "I feel it coming. I'm going to cum so hard against your pussy. Fuck me harder."

That was all I needed to hear as I pressed my hips harder down onto her vulva and began humping her more forcefully. When I heard her pussy begin to make sexy gassy sounds, I knew she was cumming again, but this time I stayed connected to her while my own orgasm took hold of me. The sound of my juices spraying onto her gaping hole as she moaned in euphoria was the sexiest thing I'd ever heard. As we came together listening to the sound of our pussies spasming in the height of ecstasy, I leaned forward and kissed her passionately. Haley had come a long way since her first awkward guided session with Hannah, and as our pussies continued twitching against one another, we both sighed in contentment.

Soon after, we heard Hannah moaning softly in her chair, and we turned our heads to see that she'd pulled her pants down all the way and was ramming her long dildo in and out of her pussy.

"I'd have to say you've both graduated with flying colors," she panted as her body jerked softly in her chair.

Haley and I looked at each for a moment with the same thought, nodding our heads in Hannah's direction.

"I think maybe Hannah needs a little therapy session of her *own* now," I smiled.

VOLUME FIVE

THE HOUSESITTER

1

———————

As I finished packing my bags for my two-week vacation to Bora Bora, my heart pounded with excitement. I hadn't been away from home for this long in years, and I could already feel the warm sea breeze on my face. Even though it was early March in Chicago, I'd chosen to wear light Bermuda shorts and open sandals so I could enjoy the tropical lifestyle the moment I stepped off the plane. I was ready to leave the melting snow and biting wind-chill of the midwestern winter far behind.

But I was anxious for another reason. I was about to leave the security of my valuable home and the care of my beloved tabby cat in the hands of a teenager I barely knew. I'd seen her grow up over the years as the daughter of my best friend, but this was the first time she'd be responsible for managing an entire household on her own. Granted, her mother lived only a half-hour away, but there was still a lot of mischief a high school senior could get into left to her own devices for so long. I had visions of her holding wild house parties and her friends trashing the place while the neighbors looked on disapprovingly as the cops raided the place.

The only comfort I had was knowing I'd be able to monitor the property 24/7 using my recently installed security system. With five

Wi-Fi-enabled cameras installed at key locations in and around the house, I'd be able to watch and listen for any unusual activity directly from my iPhone. I was a bit concerned about invading my housesitter's privacy, but I'd already informed her of the setup and both she and her mother seemed okay with the arrangement.

Besides, it wasn't as if I'd be spying on her in private areas like the bathroom and bedroom. I just wanted to make sure that the main points of ingress and egress were protected and that high-value areas of my house could be watched. I'd had the system installed for *her* safety as much as my own.

Or so I'd convinced myself.

As I carried my suitcases downstairs, I heard the soft chime of the doorbell. I looked at my watch and saw that I had four hours before my flight departure.

Good girl, I thought. She's already demonstrating responsibility by arriving on time for our scheduled briefing. Even though I'd emailed her intricate instructions, there were still a few important details I wanted to go over.

But when I opened the door, I wasn't quite ready for what I saw. The cute freckle-faced teenager I'd known in her youth had blossomed into a beautiful, curvy, full-figured woman. Wearing tight stretch jeans and a form-fitting sweater, she reminded me of the statuesque actress Christina Hendricks from the TV series Mad Men. I hadn't seen her for quite a few months, and she seemed to have a whole new confidence about her.

"Hi Jenny," I stammered, catching my breath. "Please, come in. Do you need some help with your bags?"

"No thanks, Mrs. Jackson," she smiled, lifting her small suitcase, stepping into my vestibule. She had flushed cheeks from the cold weather outside and she rubbed her hands together to warm them up as I closed the door.

"You must be freezing in those light clothes," I said. "Didn't you bring a jacket?"

"I wasn't planning on leaving the house very much," she said. "I've got lots of homework to keep me busy during the school break."

I nodded my head, knowing she was gearing up for college in the fall.

"Yes, I suppose so," I said. "But at least the garage is heated, and you'll have the full use of my car while I'm away if you need anything. So hopefully you'll have minimal exposure to the elements."

"Thanks," Jenny said. "I'll take good care of your property, I promise."

"It'll be good training for college," I smiled. "Is this the first time you've been on your own for this long?"

"Other than the occasional babysitting gig, yes."

"I've stocked up the fridge and left instructions for everything in the kitchen, so hopefully it won't be too much trouble. Why don't you bring your bags and leave them at the bottom of the stairs while I get you up to speed?"

Jenny followed me down the hall and dropped her bags at the landing to my stairs, then I led her into the kitchen and swung open the pantry door.

"The most important thing is making sure Oscar is properly fed and keeping his litter box clean. I've pulled out two cans of cat food and a bag of kibble and placed them on the kitchen island. All the other instructions are on the fridge door."

Oscar jumped up on top of the island when he heard the familiar rustling of his kibble bag, and Jenny rubbed his shoulders while I continued the briefing.

"I give him two scoops of kibble in his dish by the door in the morning and try to keep his water dish at least half-filled with fresh water at all times. Then another half-can of wet food around six p.m. and a few mouthfuls of kibble whenever he seems needy."

"He seems pretty amenable," Jenny said, listening to him purr as she gently stroked his back.

"He's pretty low maintenance," I nodded, happy to see Oscar warming up to her so fast. "Give him a little bit of cuddling a few times a day and he's pretty happy. Let me show you where I keep his litter box."

I led Jenny to my main-floor laundry room and opened a closet door revealing a large bag of cat litter.

"His litter box is under the laundry sink. If you clean it once every couple of days, it will keep the smell under control. Just scoop up any clumps you see with the little ladle and place it in this covered waste can. If it gets full, the trash collection comes every Tuesday and Friday, but honestly it should be fine for the two weeks you're here. If the litter gets low, refill as necessary using this bag."

I pointed to a cat toy resting atop one of the shelves.

"If you feel like playing with him every now and then to keep him from getting bored, he loves playing this little cat-and-mouse game."

I picked up the toy fishing rod and dangled a stuffed mouse above his head while he playfully batted at it. After I placed the device on the dryer, Jenny picked it up and pulled the mouse along the floor in front of Oscar's face as he chased after it. I couldn't help noticing her round ass in her tight jeans as she wiggled her hips to simulate the mouse scurrying along the floor.

"Perfect," I smiled with a slight flush in my face. "You two will be best friends in no time. Of course, you're welcome to use the washer and dryer at your leisure. The controls are pretty self-explanatory."

"I'm used to doing my own laundry, so no problem," Jenny nodded.

I led her back to the kitchen and placed my keys on the island countertop.

"These are the keys to the house and the car. Instructions for the TV remote are on the table beside my sofa. You're also welcome to use my computer in the office if you need to print anything or do some extra homework. The login password is Oscar123."

I glanced into my backyard and motioned to the pool.

"One other thing. I've uncovered the pool a bit early and turned on the water heater, so if you feel like a refreshing swim or want to use the hot tub, feel free any time."

Jenny looked outside and widened her eyes looking at the rippling turquoise water.

"Wow," she said. "I wasn't expecting that. I'm afraid I didn't bring any swim clothes..."

"I've got some swimsuits in my bedroom dresser upstairs. You're welcome to use those." I glanced at Jenny's large breasts and chuckled. "Though I'm not sure you'll fit into them very comfortably."

"I'll find a way to make do," she smiled.

"Okay then," I said, suddenly aware of the twitch in my pussy. "Everything else is pretty self-explanatory, but if you have any questions or run into any trouble you can text me on my phone. I should have it with me most of the time, but if there's an emergency you can also call my neighbor Betty, whose number is on the fridge."

"I hope you won't be looking at your phone *too* much while you're on vacation," Jenny smiled. "Isn't that the whole point of going on vacation? To get away from all those everyday troubles?"

"Of course," I said, pulling my cell phone out of my purse. "I don't intend to, but I wanted to remind you that I've got cameras set up in various places throughout the house to keep an eye on things. I'll be checking in periodically to make sure you're not having any wild parties or burning the place down."

"Not to worry, Mrs. Jackson," Jenny chuckled. "Between the pool, the TV, and the computer, I've got plenty of other things to keep me amused."

I smiled at her, admiring her voluptuous figure.

"There are no cameras in the private areas like as the bedroom and washrooms, so you don't have to worry about your personal privacy." I pointed outside the kitchen door, where a small wireless camera hung from the eavestrough. "But just so you know, one camera keeps an eye on the backyard, and there's also one at each of the exit doors, and one at the top and bottom of the central stairway, all of which can pan and tilt to provide wide coverage of each area. So you might want to keep your clothes on while you're scampering around the house."

"No problem with the cameras," Jenny smiled. "I'm used to having my parents keeping close tabs on me already."

"I'll bet," I said, trying not to undress her with my eyes. "You must be dying to head off to college in a few months. All those cute boys and toga parties–you'll think you'd died and gone to heaven."

"I'm not really into all that..." Jenny said, shrugging her shoulders.

"Not even *boys*? There'll be a whole new set of rules once you get onto campus."

"We'll see," Jenny said, glancing at my cleavage in my tight cotton blouse. "I'm sure there'll be plenty of other distractions when I get there."

"Um, yes," I said, momentarily taken aback by her sudden change in demeanor. I heard a honk from the driveway and glanced at my watch. "That must be my taxi. Did you have any more questions before I head off for the airport?"

"I think I'm good to go," Jenny said. "Enjoy your trip and don't worry about Oscar or your house. Everything will be just like you left it when you come back."

"Thanks, Jenny," I said, leaning in to give her a peck on the cheek. "Thanks again for looking after things while I'm away. I've transferred four hundred dollars to your account for the initial deposit. I'll pay the second installment when I return."

"Sounds great," Jenny said, cradling a purring Oscar in her arms. "But if everything turns out to be *this* easy, I might have to issue a refund."

"You're going to need every penny you can earn for college," I said. "It's the least I can do."

I carried my bags out to the driveway and the taxi driver placed them in the trunk, then I nestled into the back seat. It wasn't until I sat down that I realized how wet my panties had become. I wasn't sure if it was the feel of Jenny's skin on my lips that had gotten my juices flowing, or her comment about having other distractions at college. Had her glance at my cleavage projected an interest in something other than *boys*?

Either way, something told me that I'd be checking my phone more often than either of us expected while I was on my little South Pacific excursion.

2

———————

By the time I checked in for my flight and cleared through security at the airport, it was already starting to get dark. When I got to the waiting area at my departure gate, I picked up a magazine and tried to distract myself while waiting for the flight to board. But I couldn't stop thinking about Jenny. I was absolutely floored by her transformation from a skinny freckle-faced freshman to a stunning, statuesque high school senior. Not only did she have a figure that made my mouth water, but some of her reactions suggested she was just as interested in me as I was with her.

Did her comment about not being into boys and her frequent glances at my cleavage signal she was attracted to women, like me? And when I mentioned that she might not fit into my bathing suit and she responded by saying that she'd find a way to 'make do', did that mean she was intending to swim in her underwear or–God forbid–in the *buff*?

The more I thought about it, the wetter my panties became as I squirmed uncomfortably in my chair. I glanced up at the display board behind the gate agent's desk and saw that I still had fifteen minutes before the plane began boarding.

What the fuck, I murmured, pulling my phone out of my purse, tapping on the home security app. It won't hurt to check up on her before I depart for the first leg of my flight to Hawaii. If only to make sure Oscar's water bowl is filled.

Yeah, *right*, I smiled, knowing full well that I just wanted to catch another glimpse of her sexy body.

When the app opened, it showed two side-by-side panes displaying the camera locations inside the house. Seeing no sign of Jenny in either picture, I tapped on each one and toggled my finger across the screen to angle the camera to pan the upstairs and downstairs living areas.

Okay, I said, tilting my head. *Maybe she's in the bedroom or the bathroom getting ready to turn in.*

I waited a few minutes, but still seeing no sign of activity, I swiped my thumb to the left to view the two cameras covering the outside doors. She wouldn't have any reason to be outside in the cold weather, unless she'd stepped outside to have a smoke. But she didn't strike me as the type. Shaking my head in dismay, I swiped to the last two images displaying views of the backyard and the garage.

Still no sign of Jenny.

What the hell, I cursed. Where is she hiding? She couldn't have taken off so soon after I'd left. The car was still parked in the garage, so I knew she hadn't gone out for more provisions.

I was just about to tap the playback feature on the inside cameras to track her previous movement when I noticed a shadowy figure moving around the pool image. A curvy girl wearing a terry-cloth robe walked toward the shallow end of the basin, then dropped her robe on the patio and stepped into the steaming water.

"*Holy shit!*" I exclaimed, recognizing her hourglass figure and her long, corkscrew hair. *She's naked! And she's going to skinny dip in my pool!*

The outdoor security camera had detected her movement and turned on the security lamp, illuminating her body like a pale apparition against the reflecting surface of the pool. Covering her breasts with crossed arms over her chest, she slowly lowered herself into the water then began doing gentle breast strokes across the thirty-foot-long pit.

As I watched her silvery body gliding through the water like a translucent nymph, I suddenly became aware of the moisture building up between my legs. Even though I could only see the back of her body partially obscured by the swirling water, I could clearly make out the cleft in her ass and the exquisite curvature of her hips as she flapped her legs in and out in a gentle whipping motion.

Jesus Christ, I panted, imagining she was scissoring her legs against something *else* right now.

When she reached the end of the pool and turned around to swim the opposite length, I could see her pretty face illuminated by the bright spotlight as her head bobbed up and down in the shimmering water.

Oh my God, I muttered under my breath, scarcely believing what I was seeing.

I began to spread my legs unconsciously, imagining her burying her face in my pussy as I watched her beautiful ass rising and falling in the tumbling surf. I placed two fingers on the screen and pinched them together, zooming in on her figure slicing through the water. As she swam back and forth across the pool, I traced her motion by drawing my finger slowly across the screen to turn the camera in lock-step with her movement.

I was so mesmerized by the intoxicating scene on my phone, I barely heard the announcement over the public address system for the last call to board my plane. I looked up, and noticing the diminishing line of passengers streaming onto the jet bridge, I picked up my bags and scurried to the end of the queue.

Fuck! I cursed under my breath, trying to balance my iPhone in my hand while I fumbled with my boarding pass.

I just prayed that I'd be able to access the airport's Wi-Fi signal from inside the plane so I wouldn't have to miss another second of watching her sexy figure.

When I nestled into my seat by the window, I turned my body away from my seatmates and pulled my phone close to my breast so I could watch her without any further interruption. The last thing I needed was for someone to catch me leering at her like I was watching some kind of porn video. But just as Jenny paused by the pool-side ladder preparing to lift herself out of the water, the flight attendant announced over the p.a. system that we had to turn off our electronic devices in preparation for take-off.

You've got to be kidding me, I cursed as I watched Jenny reach up onto the handles.

"Madam?" a flight attendant said, leaning over the aisle. "Please turn off your phone and connect your seat belt. We're about to take off."

I peered up at her with my mouth agape, as if supplicating divine intervention. The timing couldn't have been worse. Just as I tapped the power button on the side of my phone, I saw the top of Jenny's dripping breasts rise out of the pool before the screen faded to black. Gritting my teeth in frustration, I checked the information folder in the back pocket of the seat in front of me to learn how to connect to the airplane's inflight Wi-Fi network. I didn't want to miss one more unnecessary second of spying on this sexy vixen if I could avoid it. Even if she'd gotten dressed by the time I got back online, I could still use the replay button to watch the entire scene from start to finish over and over.

Thank God for modern technology, I said to myself, noticing a large wet spot had formed in the front of my shorts.

Forty-five agonizing minutes later, after the plane had reached cruising altitude, I heard a chime and looked up to see that the seat belt sign had been turned off. It was now okay to power back up my electronic devices. I pressed the power button on my phone, tapping my foot impatiently while I waited for the home screen to light up.

When I saw the familiar apps appear on the screen, I tapped the settings icon then clicked the Wi-Fi function to join the air carrier's proprietary inflight service. They were charging an outrageous $24.99 for a full-flight pass, but at this point I would have paid ten times that amount to get back online. After entering my credit card information and agreeing to the terms, I saw the three delta-shaped bars alight on the top left-hand side of my phone screen.

Okay, we're back in business, I huffed, clicking the home security app until it opened up to the pool-cam view. But when the image appeared, there was no longer any sign of Jenny anywhere in the backyard.

Of course she would have gone back indoors after coming out of the pool, I said to myself. *It's freezing cold at this time of the day in Chicago!*

I was about to tap the replay button so I could watch her naked body slicing through the water again when my finger paused over the glass.

Unless...

Could she have jumped in the hot tub to relax and stay warm after her late evening swim? Could I be that lucky?

I swiped my thumb down to tilt the camera closer to the front of the house, and my heart skipped a beat when I saw Jenny submerged in the churning water with her arms outstretched over the rim. Her body was turned away from the neighbors' yards, directly facing the camera. The top of her tits poked out of the swirling water like two pink balloons, dancing atop the churning eddy.

She had a quiet, blissful look on her face, but I could see her body shifting under the opaque surface of the water. For a moment, I thought it was just the action of the powerful jets pushing against her body from all directions. But there was something about the way she was moving her shoulders and adjusting her position on the seat that led me to believe there was something more going on.

Could she possibly be...?

I knew from plenty of personal experience just how pleasurable it was to position the jets directly in front of my pussy. With the powerful rush of water flowing over my clit, there was nothing quite so heavenly as the feel of the warm water caressing my most sensitive part. When Jenny lowered her hands under the water and angled her arms toward her crotch, there was no longer any doubt.

She was playing with herself under the water!

As I watched her lean her head back against the top of the hot tub and her mouth begin to part open, I suddenly felt a rush of heat and wetness to my own aching pussy.

She certainly didn't waste any time making herself comfortable in my house, I smiled.

But I could tell from her position in the tub that she was missing the ideal placement to receive the most direct stimulation.

Move two feet to your left! I wanted to shout at her while I stared at my phone screen. *There's a jet perfectly positioned to stimulate your clit! You haven't lived until you've come from one of those things!*

I remembered that I'd added a two-way audio feature to each of the cams so I could send a warning message to any potential burglars caught by my motion sensors. For a brief moment, I considered turning it on to encourage her to take full advantage of the hot tub's special features. But this was no *burglar*–this was my young housesitter who must have thought I was far out of earshot by now flying over the Pacific Ocean.

Besides, even if I could reach out to her this way, how could I possibly hope to carry on such an intimate conversation without attracting the suspicion of my fellow passengers sitting only inches away?

But it didn't take long for Jenny to figure it out. Her arms stretched out to her sides as she searching for the precise location of each of the water nozzles. When she leaned forward a few inches and felt the jet shooting up from the edge of the bench a few seats over, she froze for a moment as her eyes widened in excitement. It only took a few seconds for her to move directly over the pulsating stream as she slumped her body lower into the water.

Suddenly, her mouth gaped open as she felt the powerful jet pulsing against her sensitive nub. I knew immediately what she was feeling, and I ached to be lying next to her, feeling her body shaking as she reveled in the rising pleasure administered by the powerful spray. She tilted her head further back against the rim, then her elbows flared out from her sides as she squeezed her tits under the swirling water.

Fuck me, I cursed, wishing it were *my* hands caressing her gorgeous melons instead of her own. I dreamed how I'd ravage her in the sensuous whirlpool while hidden from the prying eyes of my neighbors under the cloak of the swirling water.

I sat captivated as Jenny's mouth gaped progressively wider from the intense pleasure building inside her. When her climax finally washed over her, her head began jerking back and forth while her face scrunched up into the most exquisite form of ecstasy. I almost came along with her, squeezing my thighs tightly together trying to keep my body from writhing in sympathy with her next to my oblivious seat mates.

After she stopped trembling in the swirling water, Jenny lay back against the seat of the hot tub and slumped her shoulders in delirious exhaustion. She had the cutest flush on her face, and for a brief moment, I thought she glanced up at the security camera perched only a few feet away from the tub.

Had she suspected that I was watching her the whole time? Did she notice the movement of the camera as I traced her movement in the pool and the hot tub? Or heard the soft whirring of the camera as I zoomed in on her face when she came?

If so, what was already the most stimulating thing I'd witnessed in a long time, suddenly became even more arousing. I needed to release my pent-up sexual tension, and fast. I peered over at the lavatory sign nearest me and noticed that it was vacant. I waited a few minutes until Jenny stepped out of the hot tub, revealing her glorious glistening body, before I asked to be excused.

The moment I locked the lavatory door behind me, I tore off my clothes and thrust three fingers deep inside my sopping pussy, fucking myself furiously. It must have taken less than ten seconds for me to pop off with the most powerful orgasm I'd had in months. As I stood quivering over the sink with my hand embedded in my snatch, I looked up at the mirror and smiled.

I suddenly knew that I wouldn't be so alone on this trip after all.

3

When I returned to my seat, I switched over to the indoor cams and noticed that Jenny had gone upstairs, flitting back and forth between the master bedroom and bath. She'd changed into flannel pajamas with a Little Mermaid pattern, and I smiled at the contrast of the girly cartoon images with her sexy, curvy figure. The upstairs camera was installed at the top of the stairs, but she'd left the bedroom door ajar just enough for me to angle the camera to see the edge of the bed.

When she emerged from the bathroom, she picked up a book from the nightstand and propped up the pillows to provide a comfortable reading position. Then she sat down on the bed and began reading with her legs crossed over one another. As she wiggled her bare toes while she read, I zoomed in the camera to examine her face more closely.

Her auburn hair fell softly against her pale cheeks in gentle ringlets, highlighting her speckled cheekbones. She had large eyes with brilliant green irises, framed by dark eyebrows arching seductively over long lashes. And her slender nose had a slight upturn at the end, accentuating her puffy rosebud lips and cleft chin. Wearing virtually no makeup, she looked like a fashion doll from a Bergdorf Goodman department store.

The perfect model of young, sensual beauty, I thought.

While she read her book, her gaze stayed focused just below the line of sight of the camera down the hall. As much as I wanted to zoom out to take in more of her breathtaking body, I was afraid the noise might attract her attention and she'd catch me spying on her again. But after a while, she placed the book beside her on the bed and peered around my bedroom, looking for another distraction.

Much to my horror, she leaned over and pulled open the drawer to my bedside night stand. The noise of the drawer gave me an opportunity to zoom back out, and I saw her eyes widen as she peered inside at the contents. I'd thought about hiding my sex toys in another location, but I hadn't imagined she'd be bold enough to go fishing around in my personal effects.

Cheeky girl, I smiled, noticing my breathing rate becoming more raspy.

I kept a whole treasure trove of toys next to the bed, and it must have looked like a veritable candy store to a young teenager just turning the corner into adulthood. She pulled out each device one at a time, examining it closely before placing it on the side of the bed beside her.

The first one was the long and sturdy Magic Wand, my trusty industrial-strength vibrator that delivered a powerful and sustained jolt directly to the clitoris. She held the handle vertically in her left hand and gripped the flexible ball at the top, bending it forward and back with her other hand. Then she pulled out my tiny Pocket Rocket and twisted the end, feeling the nubby head beginning to buzz softly in her hand. When she reached in and removed the salami-sized, two-sided silicone dildo that I used whenever I had a special friend over, I grimaced in embarrassment. She grasped the double-headed penis at each end and bent it forward and back into a U-shape, pinching her eyebrows and shaking her head in dismay.

It must have been a shock to her young sensibilities to discover all the naughty ways a woman could stimulate herself with the wide assortment of sex aids on the market. Or maybe she was just trying to fathom how the demure Mrs. Jackson, who she'd known since childhood, had become such a perverted sex addict.

Not so demure now, am I little girl? I smiled, feeling my juices beginning to flow again in my tight Bermuda shorts.

She reached back into the drawer and pulled out a strange-looking device that looked like a balled fist with two fingers pointing up in a V-shape. Jenny held up my familiar JimmyJane vibrator and inserted her finger between the two appendages. Then she tapped the button on the base and smiled as the little digits fluttered against her hand.

Mmm, yes, I nodded toward the screen. *It feels even better when you place your clit between the vibrating fingers.*

I was getting increasingly worked up watching my young housesitter play with each of the devices, wondering when she was going to try them in the manner they were intended.

She placed the JimmyJane vibrator down on the mattress, then removed a U-shaped object from the drawer and looked at it with a wrinkled brow. She grasped the two ends of the We-Vibe toy and gently flexed it open a few inches. Then she began tapping the buttons on the outside of the device to feel the different vibration settings on each side.

Did she even know which end to put inside? I wondered. She didn't look like she'd had much experience using vibrators. For all I knew, she'd only seen those hard plastic phallic-shaped dildos still prominently displayed in most sex shop windows.

At least she's got a full two weeks to experiment with them, I smiled.

Knowing the best was yet to come, I saw her lean over and extract one of my favorite sex toys, the Rabbit. Shaped like an oversize erect penis, it had a transparent shaft with circulating beads and a protruding thumb-shaped arm with two soft silicone rabbit ears that fluttered against the clitoris. Jenny picked it up and tapped each of the control buttons on the base, watching with amazement as the head of the dildo wobbled like a spinning top while the chrome beads rotated in the middle of the shaft and the rabbit ears fluttered softly against her palm.

Yeah, girl, I smiled. *That one will put you over the top in no time.*

I was intrigued why Jenny hadn't started to experiment with any of the toys by removing her clothes, but I was thrilled that she was showing so much interest in my special collection.

She turned her head toward the open drawer and pinched her eyebrows, peering at the last item in the drawer. When she pulled it out, I smiled, recognizing the distinctive shape of the Ose vibrator. Shaped like a giant flexed finger with a flat base harboring a mysterious hole, she must have wondered how in God's name it worked. But as she began tapping the buttons on the base of the unit, her eyes widened as she watched the long finger begin to flex in a come-hither motion.

But it wasn't until she pressed the button controlling the *lower* part that her eyes really opened in shock and amazement. As it began to pulse in her hand, she drew it closer and squinted at the little hole, watching it pucker in and out like some kind of animatronic mouth. Which is exactly what it was designed to simulate. This was one of my favorite vibrators for exactly that reason, and for a moment I was disappointed that I hadn't packed it for my trip.

But when I saw Jenny pull down her pajama bottoms and spread her knees apart, I quickly forgot about my own needs as I zoomed in to inspect her sex. I gasped when I saw that she'd shaved herself entirely bare, and my pussy spasmed when I saw her glistening pink folds framing her pretty flower.

When she picked up the Ose vibrator and pointed the finger toward her hole, I shifted uncomfortably in my narrow airplane seat, dying to rip off my clothes and spread my legs far apart while I fucked myself watching her. When she inserted the wand into her slit, I groaned audibly, and the woman sitting next to me turned her head, momentarily distracted from the book she was reading.

But when Jenny thrust the device deep into her pussy and tapped the buttons to activate the two human-like functions, I sat up and cleared my throat, trying to keep myself composed. But the rivers of lubrication running down the inside of my thighs made it clear I was anything but composed. I pulled a magazine out of the seat flap in front of me and placed it on my lap to conceal the rapidly darkening wet spot in the crotch of my shorts, turning the phone screen even further away from the prying eyes of the passengers around me. Even though I'd be absolutely mortified if anyone caught me watching the video, there was no way in hell I could stop now, even if the air marshal tried to force me to put it away. They'd have to send in a virtual *army* to wrench this live feed out of my hands.

With the Ose vibrator now pulsing at full speed against Jenny's pussy, she pulled her knees up closer toward her chest and spread her legs further apart. The sight of the fluttering object planted between her legs as she threw her head back against the pillows was driving me insane with desire. But when she unbuttoned the top of her pajamas and began twisting the teats on her voluptuous tits, I couldn't take it anymore.

I excused myself once again, saying I had an upset stomach, and headed back to the lavatory with my phone in hand. As I waited impatiently for the occupant to come out, I inserted my earbuds into the port on the bottom of my phone and tapped the screen to engage the audio function. I could hear Jenny moaning into my ear, and I flapped my legs impatiently, desperately wanting to get into the private room where I could relieve myself.

When the passenger finally opened the door and began to step out, I practically ran him over squeezing into the chamber, slamming the door shut. I placed the phone on top of the sink and pulled my shorts down to my ankles and thrust two fingers into my snatch, pulling the base of my hand hard up against my throbbing clit. As I watched Jenny's knees beginning to flutter with increasing urgency and a deep flush begin to spread over the top of her bosom, I couldn't hold it any longer. As my orgasm washed over me like a tidal wave, I gushed all over my hand and fingers, shaking like I was having an epileptic seizure.

Soon after, Jenny's body also began to convulse as she groaned in the throes of her own powerful climax. As I watched her firm melons bouncing on her chest and her face flush a deep shade of crimson, I moaned along with her until we were both completely spent and exhausted. Then I peered down at my dripping thighs and drenched shorts lying on the floor, wondering how I'd ever be able to return to my seat in such a messy condition. There was no way I could wear these same shorts drenched in my lubrication and God knows how many other people's dried urine from the lavatory floor. There was only one way out of here.

Opening the door a crack, I waited until a female flight attendant passed by, then I quietly called out to her. She turned toward me with a puzzled look and came closer to my door.

"I'm so sorry to bother you about this," I said. "But I've had a bit of an accident and I'm afraid I won't be able to wear these shorts again for the rest of the flight."

She widened her eyes and nodded knowingly. Apparently, I wasn't the only passenger who'd run into this predicament before.

"Can I ask you a huge favor?" I said. "Could you retrieve my carry-on bag from the overhead storage compartment above seat 15F? It's tan colored and has a name tag for J. Jackson."

"No worries, Mrs. Jackson," she said. "I'll be back with your bag in just a moment."

When she returned with my case, I placed it on top of the small vanity and wiped down my legs with a moist towelette. Then I stepped out of my soiled shorts and threw them in the waste receptacle.

I won't be needing those anymore, I murmured to myself. The hard part would be keeping my dick in my pants for the *rest* of the flight to Hawaii. I knew that I'd have to find another distraction to keep me busy so I didn't soil another pair of shorts.

No more Jenny videos until I get to my own private room, I said.

But my mind was already swimming with all the new entertainment possibilities over the course of the next two weeks.

Who needs tropical beaches and chilled mai tai's when you've got the most beautiful, sexy lingerie model at your beck and call whenever you need her?

4

———————

After changing into fresh clothes, I returned to my seat by the window. Even though I was dying to see what Jenny would do next, I dared not reopen the camera app for fear of making another mess. For the rest of the flight to Hawaii, I kept myself distracted watching a movie. A very tame, family-oriented movie. I didn't want to risk viewing another sexy scene that might rekindle my new obsession with my young housesitter.

When we landed in Hawaii, I had to change planes for the next leg of my flight to Bora Bora, so there wasn't any time to check the home security monitors during the brief stopover. By the time I boarded the aircraft, I was so exhausted, I slept the rest of the way to my final destination. When I landed in the archipelago, I took a taxi to my hotel, where a porter escorted me to an overwater bungalow overlooking a turquoise lagoon. I hadn't eaten for eight hours, so I unpacked my bags then headed to the dining room for a sumptuous seafood dinner.

By the time I returned to my room half-intoxicated on margaritas, I was ready to power up my phone and resume watching my new favorite playmate. But with the five-hour time difference between Bora Bora and Chicago, Jenny was already fast asleep, nestled under the warm covers of my bed. It hardly mattered though, since by now I had almost a full day's worth of video to play back any time I wanted.

I tapped the home monitoring app on my phone and toggled back to the upstairs view. I'd left the camera pointed in the direction of the bedroom, so I hoped there'd be plenty more footage of Jenny amusing herself with my toys. But I was disappointed to see that after coming so hard using the Ose vibrator, she'd put the rest of the instruments away before turning in.

I guess after having two powerful back-to-back orgasms, she needed a rest, I smiled. *Or maybe she was just pacing herself, leaving room to enjoy the other devices another day.*

I came three more times replaying the erotic scenes from the hot tub and my bedroom, over and over. When I finally satiated my lust, I took a relaxing dip in my room's private plunge pool, watching the sun set over the quiet lagoon.

I could get used to this, I thought, taking in the blissful scene.

The only thing missing was a partner to enjoy it with. Maybe I'd bring Jenny back with me next time. The only problem was her mother, who just happened to be my best friend. I didn't want to risk damaging our longstanding relationship. Even if Jenny *had* recently turned eighteen and could make her own decisions.

I fell asleep that night feeling the warm ocean breeze wafting through my veranda window, dreaming of Jenny's naked body gliding through the coral waters of my lagoon. When I woke up, it was already past noon Chicago time, and I flipped over my phone to see what she was up to. I found her sitting at the kitchen island with some school books propped open, making notes in her journal.

Good girl. You don't want to waste your entire spring break playing around the house. You'll need good marks to get into your choice of college in the fall. There'll be plenty of other distractions to keep you amused when you get there.

I walked down to the breakfast bar in the hotel and helped myself to a large serving of eggs Benedict with a side of fresh pineapple and lox. I almost felt sorry leaving Jenny with a fridge full of microwave dinners and pre-cooked casseroles. But something told me she'd find *other* ways to keep herself satisfied while I was away.

I needed to find something to keep my mind off what was happening back home, so I signed up for a snorkeling expedition to a nearby reef. When we arrived there, I marveled at the variety of colorful sea creatures, from striped angelfish to iridescent snapper and giant speckled grouper. I loved swimming among the docile nurse sharks and stingrays, even hitching a brief ride on a large sea turtle. After returning to my room and noticing that I was already a bit sunburned, I pulled off my wet bathing suit and propped myself up in my bed.

When I checked in on Jenny, at first I couldn't see any sign of her in the main rooms of the house or in the backyard. It took a few minutes of angling the upstairs and downstairs cams before I saw her seated in my office, quietly tapping on my keyboard. Although the door was slightly ajar, the line of sight from the ceiling-mounted camera to the office only allowed me to see half of her body.

I remembered leaving my login code if she needed to print anything, but the audio feed didn't indicate any sign of activity other than soft tapping on the keyboard. I hesitated for a moment, thinking I'd give her some peace and quiet and check back later in the evening. Maybe I'd catch her using another one of my sex toys when it was closer to bedtime.

But then I remembered I had *another* app on my phone that provided direct access to my home computer. It was useful when I needed to access important files remotely, but I hadn't used it for a long time. I clicked on the app, and it opened showing my live screen with Jenny's cursor hovering near the top of the web browser. She clicked on the bookmarks tab and began scrolling through my list of saved web addresses.

Forgetting that I'd arranged everything into themed folders, I was mortified when she clicked on the folder for my favorite lesbian porn videos. I used these whenever I felt particularly horny and needed a distraction, but I never intended for anyone *else* to find my private stash. She double-clicked on a link labeled *hot tribbing*, and a window opened showing two naked girls scissoring on an oversize bed. Jenny tapped on the speaker icon at the bottom of the screen and slid the volume bar to the right, and I heard soft moaning wafting out into the hall.

Unsure if it was Jenny's voice or the sounds of the girls on the video, I toggled back to the camera monitoring app. Jenny's left leg was spread far apart with her jeans pulled down to her ankles as she rolled her hips sensuously on the chair. Unable to see what she was doing from the rear position of the camera and with her back turned away from me, I cursed at my inability to watch her more closely. Desperately wanting to see what she was doing while she watched the video, I scanned the remote access menu and noticed a camera icon.

When I clicked the button, my iPhone screen divided into a split window with the tribbing video on one side and Jenny's face on the other. I could only see the top half of her body from the fixed position of the webcam atop my laptop, but that was more than enough. Her cheeks were flushed as she squeezed one of her breasts with her right hand and extended her other arm between her legs in a rhythmic motion.

Holy fuck! I groaned. She was playing with herself while watching a lesbian porn video!

There was no longer any doubt in my mind that she was sexually attracted to women. As I watched her face twist into increasing contortions of pleasure, my eyes darted back and forth between the scene playing out on the porn video and the expression on her face. As the girls on the video began rubbing their pussies together more vigorously, I suddenly heard a familiar buzzing sound coming from the background.

Was she fucking herself with one of my vibrators while she watched the video?

I switched back to the security camera view, but all I could see was Jenny's left leg shaking while her free arm pumped something between her legs. Suddenly overcome with desire, I rushed over to my suitcase and pulled out the one vibrator I'd had the foresight to pack for the trip–my trusty Lelo G-spot stimulator. I thrust the gently curved rod into my snatch and turned the vibration setting up high as I flipped back to the screen monitoring app.

I could hear Jenny moaning along with the two girls on the video as her oversize melons began to tremble from the rising pleasure emanating within her. When the girls suddenly locked their hips, pulling each other tightly toward one another screaming in unison, Jenny's mouth gaped apart, and she uttered a deep guttural groan. With her body jerking forward and back in rhythmic contractions, I grabbed my long dildo with two hands and clamped down on it as I came hard along with Jenny.

It must have taken a full minute for both of us to stop spasming and cumming from the erotic scene we'd both witnessed. I smiled at the irony of getting off watching Jenny while she watched the girls on the video. My mind reeled with all the possibilities for engagement between the two of us when I returned home. Suddenly I realized Jenny was no longer just an innocent high school student, but a fully developed woman, ready to experiment with all the different ways of satisfying her sexual curiosity.

Fortunately for me, Jenny was far from finished quenching her desire for the evening. I saw her right hand move back to the cursor, and she tapped on the progress bar to return to the middle of the video. As it began replaying, she slid the slider slowly to the right until it reached the part where the two girls began pulling their bodies together in preparation for their mutual orgasm.

Jenny peered down, and I heard a deeper kind of throbbing sound emanating from between her legs. As the girls in the video began moaning more loudly, she moved both of her hands between her legs, pounding her pussy with hard jerking motions. I couldn't be sure which vibrator she was using, but the sight of her fucking herself while watching the two girls soon had me thrusting my Lelo vibrator back inside my own pussy. As the girls moved closer to their moment of climax, Jenny's face scrunched up into a painful grimace.

She seemed to be waiting for them to cum once again before she opened the taps. When they finally did, her orgasm was even stronger as she wailed in unison with the girls, jerking her arms forcefully against her body and her compressed tits as she quivered in the office chair. I screamed along with her, feeling my juices spraying out the sides of my pulsating pussy all over my wet thighs and ass.

After Jenny recovered from her second powerful orgasm, she closed the porn site and flipped the laptop cover closed. No longer being able to see her directly, I switched over to the hall cam view, watching her pull up her jeans as she raised herself from the chair. Then she turned around and exited the office, walking toward the stairs. In her right hand, I could see the familiar outline of my purple Rabbit vibrator with its distinctive protruding ears.

I smiled as I watched her head back upstairs to return the vibrator to my nightstand.

That's it, baby, I said. *Take your time trying out each of my special toys. Neither of us is going anywhere for the next two weeks.*

5

———

Jenny went to sleep soon after watching the lesbian video, and I decided to go for a relaxing swim in the lagoon to wind down. Between the day's snorkeling activity, a little too much sun, and multiple orgasms watching Jenny on constant replay, I slept like a baby that night. When I woke the following morning, she was back at the kitchen table doing her homework, so I went for another long breakfast at the hotel restaurant.

Since Jenny seemed to be preoccupied with her studies, I decided to make the best use of my time by taking a sailing tour of the island. Wearing a long-sleeved linen shirt, capri pants, and plenty of sunscreen, I wasn't taking any chances at getting more sunburned. With Jenny becoming increasingly bold with her sexual escapades back home, I wanted to make sure I could enjoy watching her without any distractions.

I was surprised how large the island was, taking us more than six hours to circumnavigate the atoll in our sleek, forty-foot catamaran. Formed by an extinct volcano, lush green hillsides rose steeply above the water to over two thousand feet above sea level. I marveled at how clear the water was as I gazed at the endless variety of colorful fish through the sturdy nets joining the two hulls. But by the time we'd finished our mid-day picnic on a secluded beach, I was ready to get out of the sun and back to the relative tranquility of my private cabin.

When the sailboat returned to the hotel, it was already early evening Chicago time, and I was eager to see what mischief Jenny had gotten into while I was away. After I got back to my bungalow, I turned on my phone and saw her taking a swim in the backyard pool wearing a skimpy cream-colored bikini. Looking like a young Ursula Andress from the famous beach scene in the James Bond movie *Dr. No*, she looked even *more* mouth-watering partially covered up.

But this time she wasn't alone. She'd invited a young friend over, and as the two girls splashed each other's faces in the pool, my pussy twitched at the sight of the two scantily clad teens. When they got out of the pool, they moved over to the hot tub, where Jenny encouraged her friend to try out the special seat she'd used the previous day. I could see the look of surprise on her girlfriend's face when she felt the gush of the underwater jet flowing between her legs, but she didn't seem interested in staying there long enough to get properly aroused.

Whether she felt self-conscious stimulating herself in front of her girlfriend or Jenny had warned her that I could be monitoring the property, I wasn't sure. But either way, I enjoyed watching the girls' pretty faces as the swirling water flowed over the tops of their bikini-clad bodies. Just to be safe, I kept the camera zoomed out and the audio turned off for fear of signaling that I was watching them. But they seemed to be enjoying themselves, chatting and giggling as they sipped what looked like two wine coolers.

Thank you, Jenny's girlfriend, I said, *for bringing the alcohol and Jenny's swimsuit.* I hoped it would be just the right combination for loosening the two girls up and taking this spring break adventure to the next level.

After twenty minutes or so of lounging in the tub, the two girls scurried out of the tank and dried themselves off in the kitchen, then headed upstairs to get changed. I followed their movement with the inside cameras, and when they got to my bedroom, I turned on the upstairs audio feed so I could hear what they were saying.

Jenny peeled off her swimsuit then flipped open my nightstand drawer and pointed inside.

"Guess what I discovered last night while I was in Mrs. Jackson's bed?" she said.

Jenny's friend peered into the drawer, then looked up at Jenny with wide eyes.

"Holy shit!" she said. "Are those what I think they are?"

"I can assure you they absolutely are," Jenny smiled.

"But they all look so *different*," her friend said. "I've only seen those gross penis-shaped vibrators. How do these things even *work*?"

Jenny peeled off her swimsuit and jumped on the bed, patting the mattress beside her.

"Why don't you come join me and find out? Some of these devices are really incredible. Don't tell me you've never tried one before."

"Nothing like *that*, that's for sure," her friend said, hesitating.

Jenny reached into the drawer and pulled out the tiny Pocket Rocket vibrator.

"Come on, Niki," she said. "It's just us girls. No one's ever going to know if we have a little extra fun on our sleepover."

"What if Mrs. Jackson's watching on her home security cam?"

Jenny peered down the hallway toward my camera at the top of the stairs, and I quickly turned it so it was facing the other way.

"There's only one camera on each floor, and it can't see in here anyway," Jenny said. "Take your swimsuit off and join me on the bed. We deserve a little break from all our studying."

I heard the sound of clothes dropping to the floor followed by a bed squeaking as her friend joined her on the bed. Then I slowly swiped my finger across the screen, turning the camera back in their direction. Niki was more petite than Jenny, with a typically slender high-school figure. She looked to be about average height and build, but with firm, perky breasts and athletic, toned legs. She sat leaning back against the headboard, with her arms crossed over her chest and her legs extended close together in front of her.

Jenny twisted the base of the Pocket Rocket then handed it to her friend, who ran her fingers over the buzzing end.

"Pretty cool, right?" Jenny said, smiling at Niki, glancing between her legs. "Don't be so bashful. Give it a try."

Niki angled her knees slightly apart and placed the nubby end of the vibrator at the top of her slit, then she suddenly jumped.

"I *know*, right?" Jenny said. "That little thing packs quite a punch, doesn't it?"

"Mmm," Niki nodded, spreading her legs a little further apart.

"You can adjust the intensity of the vibrations by turning the cap on the base of the unit. "I like to ramp it up the more turned on I get."

"How many of these things have you *tried* so far?" Niki said, squirming her hips on the mattress.

"Almost all of them. This is nothing compared to some of the *dual-purpose* vibrators."

"Dual purpose?" Niki said, pinching her eyebrows.

"Most of the other ones stimulate you on the inside and the outside at the same time. You haven't experienced a proper orgasm until you've tried one of these things."

"Why did you give me this *little* one to start with then?" Niki panted, obviously beginning to feel the effects of the targeted stimulation on her clit.

"I didn't want to scare you away too fast," Jenny smiled. "Are you ready to step it up?"

"Definitely," Niki grunted.

"Reach in and take out that pink one that looks like a curled-up snake. I think you're going to like the way it moves inside you."

Niki peered into the drawer and shook her head.

"There's two pink objects that look kind of similar," she said. "Which one?"

"Both," Jenny smiled. "We *both* might be able to get in on the action with this one."

Niki pulled the two objects out of the drawer then Jenny took the smaller piece out of her hand.

"What exactly am I supposed to do with this thing?" Niki said, examining the U-shaped We-Vibe device.

"You slide the fat end inside you with the thinner end pointing up. Then press it all the way up until the connecting part is resting against your opening."

"What are you going to do with the *other* attachment?" Niki said.

"You'll see," Jenny said, flashing her a devilish smile.

Up to this point, I'd just been following the playful banter of the two friends as they tried out the tamer device. But when Niki spread her legs further apart and inserted the thick end of the We-Vibe into her slit, I tore off my pants and reached over for my Lelo vibrator resting on the nightstand. Then I watched Niki press the device deep into her hole until the narrower end rested near the base of her mound.

"This feels kind of weird," Niki said, shaking her head. "How do I turn it on?"

"Leave that up to *me*," Jenny smirked, grasping the remote-control unit and tapping one of the buttons.

"You mean you can–*oh!*" Niki grunted, feeling the internal arm of the We-Vibe unit pulsing against the inside of her pussy.

"Damn straight, girl," Jenny said. "I *told* you Mrs. Jackson has an interesting collection of toys. Let me take the driver's seat while you sit back and enjoy the scenery."

"Mmm," Niki purred, glancing at Jenny's voluptuous tits. "You know I've always fantasized about being with you this way. You have the most amazing body..."

Jenny suddenly leaned over and placed her mouth over one of Niki's tits, sucking her pink teats.

"Oh God, Jenny," Niki panted. "That feels so good..."

"You have *no* idea," Jenny said, flicking her finger over the control knob, activating the clitoral stimulator.

"*Uhnn*," Niki grunted, rolling her hips on the bed as Jenny nibbled her tits and neck. "Fuck me Jenny. Make me come with your hot tongue."

"All in due course, baby," Jenny purred. "I just want you to enjoy this little toy a little longer until you warmed up."

"Oh, I'm getting *warmed up*, alright," Niki groaned, running her fingers through Jenny's hair. "I'm going to cum soon if you keep that up."

"You mean *this*?" Jenny said, flipping the control switch, raising the intensity of the two vibrating arms.

"*Yes!*" Niki panted, thrashing her hips as Jenny suckled on her nubs.

"Oh my God," Niki hissed. "I'm going to come, Jenny. Suck my tits while I cum!"

Suddenly, Niki grabbed the back of Jenny's head with two hands, pulling her face hard against her chest, spreading her legs as far apart as they could go. I zoomed in, watching the vibrator buzzing against her pussy as she slowly lifted her hips off the bed.

"Uhnn!" she groaned, as her orgasm took over her body. "*Oh God, oh God, oh God!*"

Jenny pulled back and peered up at her friend, watching the look of ecstasy wash over her face as she quivered over the bed. When Niki finally dropped her hips back down onto the mattress, Jenny turned the vibrator off and straddled her hips, kissing her passionately.

"*Fuck*, that was hot," she said, nibbling Niki's ear. "I knew you'd enjoy these things."

"Not nearly as much as I like *you*," Niki said, grabbing Jenny's ass and pulling her closer as she pressed her tits against Jenny's breasts. "Can we put away the toys now and just concentrate on touching each other?"

"I thought you'd never ask," Jenny smiled, grinding her pussy against Niki's bare mound.

"I love the feeling of your body up against me," Niki panted. "I want to feel you fucking me *straight up* this time. I'm so wet right now."

"I can tell," Jenny said, sliding her body down Niki's abdomen, pressing her thighs apart until her chest rested against Niki's vulva.

"Rub your tits against me, Jenny," Niki pleaded, squirming her hips against Jenny's mounds.

Jenny raised herself up a few inches and grasped one of her globes with two hands, rubbing it playfully up and down Niki's slit.

Up to this point I'd just been rubbing my Lelo vibrator gently against my opening as I absent-mindedly watched the two girls interact. But when I saw Jenny tit-fucking her friend with her voluptuous breasts, I plunged the G-spot stimulator deep into my pussy, rolling it around as I moaned along with Niki.

"*Fuck*," she groaned. "That feels *way* better than a plastic vibrator. You're so warm and wet."

"You know what *also* feels warmer and wetter than a vibrator?" Jenny said, pushing Niki's knees up toward her chest, then lowering her hips over her friend's splayed pussy. As she placed her ass over Niki's twitching vulva, their pussies touched, and they groaned loudly.

"Jesus," Niki gasped. "Where did you learn to do this? Have you been holding out on me?"

"I've been studying a bit more than just math and chemistry since I've been here," Jenny purred, rolling her hips over Niki's upturned cunny.

"*Holy fuck!*" Niki groaned, feeling Jenny's clit pressing against her own. "This is the hottest thing I've ever done. I never even imagined—"

Jenny leaned forward, engulfing Niki's mouth with her own, pressing her tits against the other girl while the two of them ground their pussies together. I could hear the sexy slurping noises of their wet vulvas sliding over one another as their pink folds spread open for my camera. As they picked up the pace of their rocking motion, they moaned into each other's mouths and Niki wrapped her arms around Jenny's back, digging her fingernails into her skin.

Moments later, they both began squealing as their hips trembled in unison. I zoomed in as far as the camera would go, and just as Niki let out a high-pitched scream, Jenny began squirting all over her friend's perineum as Niki's rosebud puckered in and out. In all my years of watching lesbian trib videos, I'd never seen anything so sexy and raw. As I lay exhausted, drenched in my own pool of cum, I reached over and patted the sheet beside me.

If only you were here with me, I thought, imagining Jenny's body merging with my *own* instead of her friend's. *This trip to paradise isn't be complete without you.*

6

Niki went home the following day and for the rest of my vacation I watched old clips of Jenny playing with my toys. She'd occasionally take out a new one and pleasure herself on my bed or while watching lesbian videos, but I soon longed to be next to her, touching her directly. As I neared the end of my trip, I feared I'd lose her forever once the break was over, so I rescheduled my return flight and came home a day early.

When I got to the front door, I didn't feel comfortable barging in on her unannounced, so I tapped the doorbell. She came to the door wrapped in a large bath towel, and her eyes widened as she paused in the doorway.

"Mrs. Jackson!" she said. "I wasn't expecting you until tomorrow. Is everything okay?"

"Yes," I said, feeling Oscar rubbing himself against the bottom of my leg. "I was just feeling a bit sorry for you having to look after this big house all by yourself. I figured you could use an extra day getting ready to return to school."

"I've been studying hard," Jenny said, "so you needn't have worried. But come in out of the cold–it's your house after all."

"I didn't want to just barge in unannounced. I hope I didn't interrupt you in the middle of anything..."

"Actually, I was just getting ready to take another dip in your pool. It's been such a pleasure enjoying the heated water during the cool evenings."

I smiled, peering at Jenny's hourglass figure in the towel.

"And the hot tub too, I hope. It's a singular pleasure soaking in the stimulating bath when it's cold outside."

"Absolutely," Jenny nodded. "Your place is like a virtual playground for a starved teenager like me."

"Tell you what," I said. "Why don't I drop off my stuff in the bedroom and join you there in a few minutes? I could use another dip in the warm water to ease my transition back to the Chicago weather."

"Sure," Jenny said, noticing my erect nipples in my linen blouse from the chill outside. "Should I get changed?"

"It's starting to get dark, so the neighbors shouldn't be able to spy on us. I don't know about you, but I always enjoy soaking in the hot tub in the raw. It's just us girls, after all."

"I agree," Jenny smiled. "I'll meet you there in a few minutes."

I rushed upstairs and tore off my clothes, then threw on a robe and headed downstairs. When I opened the door to the veranda, Jenny had already submerged herself in the tub, and she peered up at me with dripping hair.

"You certainly look like you've made yourself at home," I smiled, dropping my robe and stepping into the swirling water a few feet away from her.

"It's been kind of fun, actually," she said. "I almost don't want to go back home. I could get used to hanging around here a little longer."

My heart skipped a beat, wondering if I should ask her to stay another night.

"Did you have any trouble operating any of the equipment?" I said, making a veiled reference to my sex toy collection. "Has everything been okay with the pool, the car, and other devices?"

"Yes," Jenny smiled. "Good on all fronts. Were you able to check in periodically to make sure I wasn't burning your house down?"

"Once in a while," I said. "I didn't want to interfere with your privacy too much. Mostly just to check that you were safe and well stocked up."

"I've been able to keep everything replenished pretty well," Jenny nodded. "Thanks to the use of your car. Thanks again for letting me have the use it."

"My pleasure," I said. "Have you been able to get out and see many of your friends while I was away?"

"Not too much," Jenny said. "I had a friend come over for a sleepover one night to help break up the monotony."

"Did you show her around and avail yourselves of all the amenities?" I said, resisting the temptation to let her know just how much I knew she'd enjoyed that sleepover.

"Yes," Jenny blinked. "We went for a swim, had a relaxing hot tub–"

"Did you discover the special *nozzle*?" I smiled.

"You mean–"

"The one that sprays in a particularly delightful place."

"It was hard *not* to," Jenny blushed. "Once you find the right spot, you don't exactly want to move."

"And your *friend*? Did she discover it too?"

"Yes, but I think she was a bit self-conscious about trying it in my presence. I think that's something meant to be enjoyed more by yourself..."

"I don't know about *that*," I said, shifting my body over in front of the spigot. "I kind of missed this while I was away. Do you mind–?"

"Not at all," Jenny smiled. "After all, it's just us girls, right?"

"Right," I said, spreading my legs apart and shifting my weight forward to direct the spray onto my buzzing clit. "Mmm, yes–this is one luxury they didn't have at my expensive resort in Bora Bora."

"It must have been fun though," Jenny said, watching the expression on my face as I squirmed under the water. "There must have been lots of other exciting things to do there."

"I guess so," I said, catching my breath. "Snorkeling, sailing, swimming in the lagoon. It gets pretty old though when you're by yourself. I found myself checking in with you just to keep myself company."

"I hope you didn't catch me skinny dipping in your pool."

"I did indeed," I panted. "And in the hot tub. It looked like you were enjoying yourself as much as I am right now."

"I thought *maybe* you were watching me," Jenny said. "I caught the cameras pointed in my direction a few times."

"Did you *like* being watched?" I said.

"Sometimes," Jenny said. "It was kind of *stimulating* to be honest, knowing you were catching me occasionally without any clothes on."

"Oh yes," I groaned. "I caught you more than once."

"Did you enjoy watching me as much as I liked the idea of you watching me?" Jenny said, lifting an eyebrow.

"You have no idea," I panted. "Almost as much as I am right now."

"Mmm," Jenny said, dipping her hands below the surface of the water and shifting her weight on the seat opposite me. "I wish I could have spied on *you* as much as you were with me. You know, I always kind of had a thing for you, even when I was little. I always thought you were the most beautiful woman I'd ever seen."

"Oh my God, Jenny," I said, getting even more turned on knowing she found me attractive. "You've blossomed into the most beautiful, sexy young adult. *You're* the one I've had a crush on since you came over to my place."

"Oh Mrs. Jackson," Jenny panted, her cheeks beginning to flush.

"I think it's time you started calling me Jade," I smiled. "Seeing as how we're both stimulating ourselves under the water while watching each other."

"Jade," Jenny purred. "You have no idea how often I've fantasized about you."

"I must have come a hundred times thinking about you while I was away," I said. "I've wanted to feel your body against mine practically from the moment I left."

"Yes," Jenny moaned. "You're going to make me cum watching you."

"Yes, baby," I hissed. "Let it go. I'm almost there too."

"Uhnn," Jenny groaned, spreading her mouth wide open as she looked at me with glazed eyes.

Suddenly, I felt a bolt of electricity running through me as my orgasm washed over me. While we jerked and moaned together in simultaneous climax under the swirling water, we couldn't take our eyes off each other.

"Oh my God," Jenny panted after we both calmed down. "That was *so* hot."

"Let's get the hell out of here and go upstairs where we can do this *properly*," I said. "I need to feel a *warm body* next to me, not just an artificial water jet."

"I was thinking exactly the same thing," Jenny smiled.

The two of us scampered out of the hot tub and ran upstairs, giggling like two girls. When we got to the bed, I didn't even bother to pull down the covers, pulling her onto the mattress with me and entangling our legs together. It was electrifying feeling her naked body rubbing against mine, and for the longest time I was content to rub our slippery bodies together while we kissed passionately. The feeling of Jenny's big tits pressing against mine was sublime, and I was in no hurry to get down to more serious business.

But after a while, I felt Jenny's hands roaming lower on my body, and when her hand slipped into the cleft under my ass, I pulled back and looked at her.

"Jenny," I panted. "You have no idea how much I've wanted to feel your touch on my body.

"And yours on mine," Jenny grinned.

When she slipped two fingers into my hole, I squeezed her tits with two hands, pinching her large teats with my fingers.

"Uhnn," I groaned, feeling my juices spreading all over her hand. "I want to fuck you so bad."

"Yes please," Jenny said.

I pulled her hand out of my pussy, then pushed her down onto the bed and straddled her crotch with my thighs on either side of her hips.

"Does this position look familiar?" I said.

Jenny's eyes widened as she peered up at me with a look of shock.

"*No way!* You weren't watching me and my girlfriend when we were in your bedroom?!"

"I hope you don't mind," I nodded. "You did leave the door open just enough for my camera to zoom in from down the hallway."

"I was kind of hoping you were," Jenny smiled. "Did you see us playing with your toys too?"

"Absolutely," I grinned. "Your girlfriend is almost as hot as you are."

"Maybe the three of us can try this sometime," Jenny said. "I think she's become attracted to girls as much as I have since I've been here."

"Maybe another time," I said. "Right now, I just want to look at your magnificent body while I fuck you with my pussy."

"Yes, Jade," Jenny purred. "Fuck me with your pussy. I want to feel you cumming against me this time."

I rolled Jenny onto her side, pulling her right leg up onto my chest, then I tilted my hips forward until our pussies touched.

"Oh God," Jenny gasped. "Your pussy feels so hot."

"As hot as your *girlfriend's*?"

"It's *different* with you," she said. "I've never–"

"Been on the bottom before?" I smiled.

"Not like this," she said. "I *like* being fucked by you."

As I mashed my pussy into hers, I heard the familiar sloshing sound of our wet vulvas sucking and caressing each other's lips. I grabbed her tits with my two hands and squeezed them as hard as I could, feeling my ass slide over her slick thigh as we rocked our hips together.

"Jade," Jenny growled, peering at me with wild eyes. "I'm going to cum. Oh God, I'm going to cum all over your hot pussy."

Suddenly, I felt her hips shaking underneath me as a sexy flush rolled over her face.

"Yes, Jenny," I panted. "You're so beautiful. I'm going to cum with you, baby. Oh *fuck*–"

I pulled Jenny's upturned leg hard against my chest, feeling my pussy beginning to pulse in powerful contractions. Unable to hold it any longer, I gushed all over her slit as we wailed in delirious union. After what seemed like an eternity shaking and looking into each other's eyes while we enjoyed a long climax together, I collapsed onto the bed beside her and stroked her pretty face with the back of my hand.

"That was incredible," Jenny panted. "I don't think I've cum that hard in my whole life."

"Not even with my *Rabbit* vibrator or that funny finger-shaped sex toy?"

"Those were pretty good, I have to admit," she smiled. "But nothing like feeling your body next to mine." She looked between our legs at the huge wet spot that had formed on top of the comforter. "Plus, you've got a *special* power that none of those other devices have. That was the most stimulating shower I've had in a long time."

"There's more where that came from," I said, grinning like a Cheshire Cat. "Are you ready to try this again in a more equally yoked position?"

"Yes, but how would that work exactly?" Jenny asked. "Doesn't one of us kind of have to take the lead role when we're connected that way?"

I reached over and swung open my nightstand drawer, pulling out the long double-sided pink dildo.

"Not if something *else* is connecting us together," I smiled. "Have you had a chance to try *this* one yet?"

"I was kind of saving that one for you," Jenny said. "I figured you'd be able to show me how to use it properly."

"You got that right, girl," I smirked. "Now get up on all fours while I fuck you from behind with this thing."

"I like the sound of that," Jenny purred.

As I pressed one end of the dildo into my sopping hole and pressed my ass backwards towards hers, I tilted my head down and peered between my legs at her swinging tits.

This was one holiday I'd never soon forget, I thought to myself.

MORE EROTICA THEMED BUNDLES BY VICTORIA RUSH:

Threesomes

THE LESBIAN COLLECTION

VICTORIA RUSH

2 + 1 = a hundred ways to have fun...

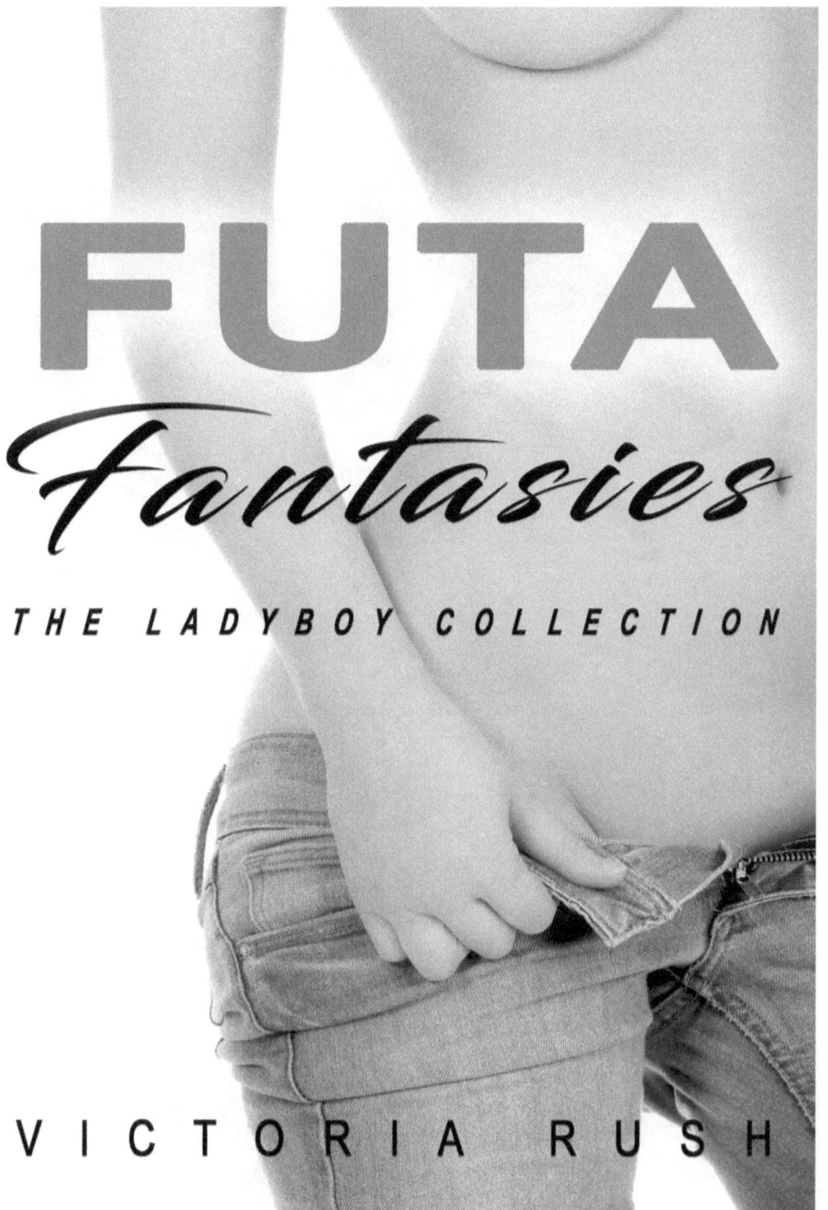

FUTA

Fantasies

THE LADYBOY COLLECTION

VICTORIA RUSH

Some girls have a little more to work with than others...

First
Time
A LESBIAN ANTHOLOGY
VICTORIA RUSH
It's never as good as the first time...

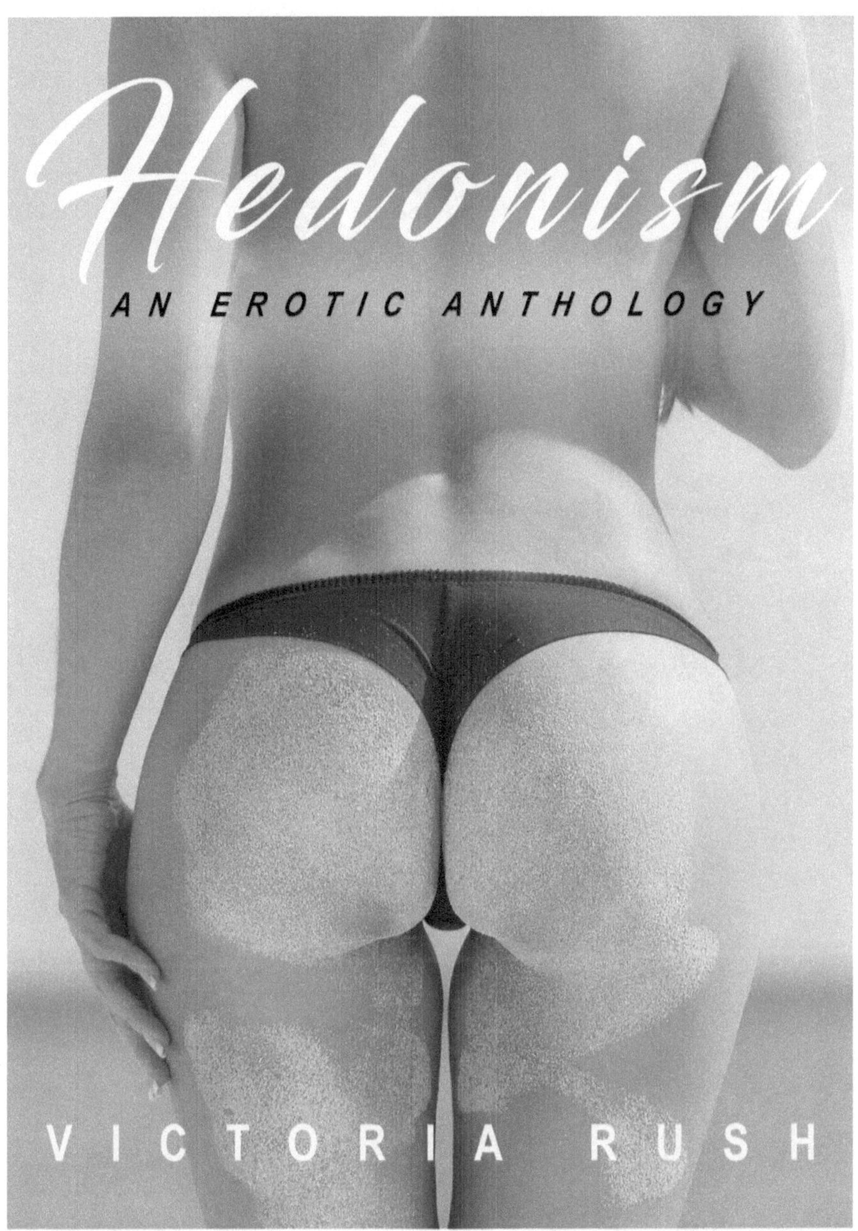

Sometimes all you need to spark up your love life is a little change of scenery...

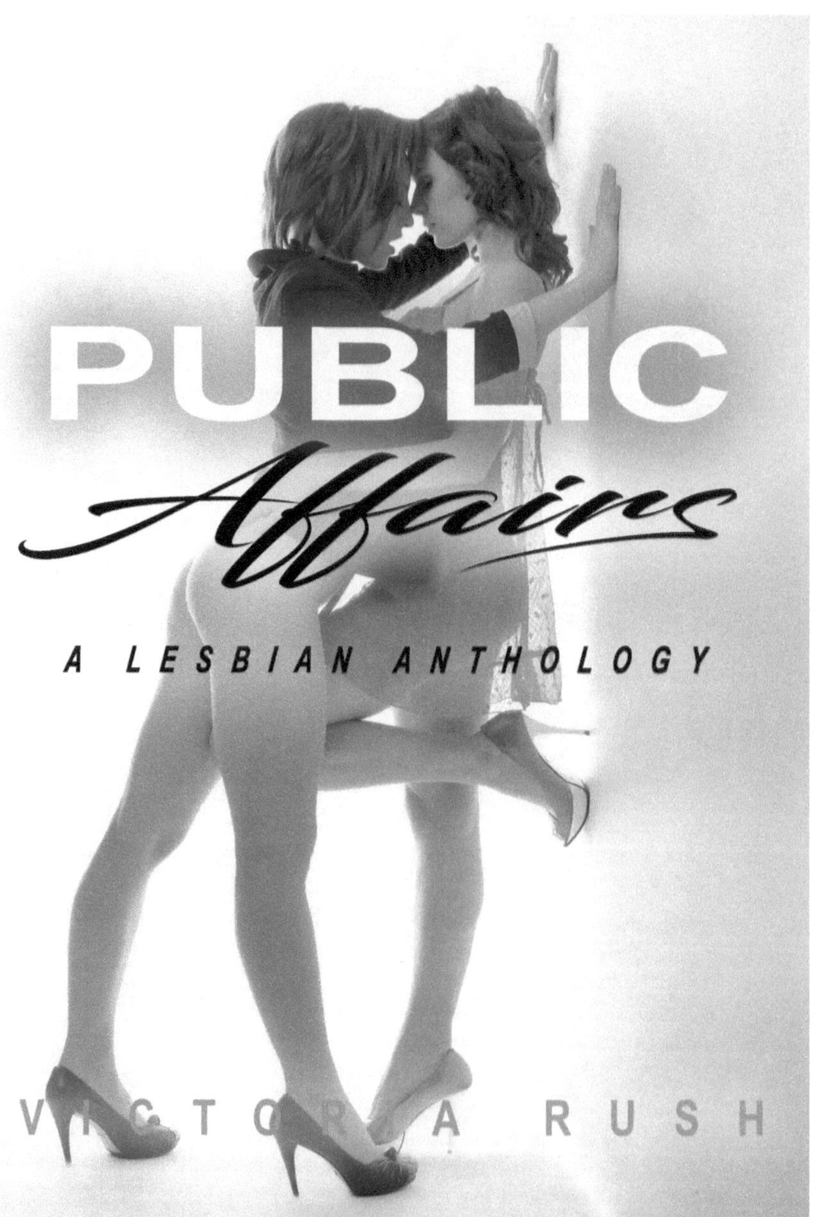

Sometimes the biggest turn-on is knowing you might get caught...